A DAUGHTER'S COURAGE

LIZ HARRIS

Boldwood

First published in 2020 as *The Dark Horizon*. This edition published in Great Britain in 2026 by Boldwood Books Ltd.

Cover Design by JD Smith Design Ltd.

Cover Images: Shutterstock

A CIP catalogue record for this book is available from the British Library.

Paperback ISBN 978-1-80703-083-4

Large Print ISBN 978-1-80703-085-8

Hardback ISBN 978-1-80703-082-7

Trade Paperback ISBN 978-1-80703-084-1

Ebook ISBN 978-1-80703-086-5

Kindle ISBN 978-1-80703-087-2

Audio CD ISBN 978-1-80703-077-3

MP3 CD ISBN 978-1-80703-078-0

Digital audio download ISBN 978-1-80703-079-7

This book is printed on certified sustainable paper. Boldwood Books is dedicated to putting sustainability at the heart of our business. For more information please visit https://www.boldwoodbooks.com/about-us/sustainability/

Boldwood Books Ltd, 23 Bowerdean Street, London, SW6 3TN

www.boldwoodbooks.com

1

OXFORDSHIRE

December 1919

Their heads bent low against the blistering cold from a chill December wind, the mourners stood in the small graveyard behind the grey stone church, the veiled women clad in crêpe of the deepest black and the men in cashmere. Their faces white, they stared down at the hand-crafted coffin that lay at the bottom of the steep-sided grave, the final resting place of Arthur Joseph Linford, aged seventy-one, founder of Linford & Sons, one of the fastest growing building companies in the south of England.

We have entrusted our brother, Arthur Joseph, to God's mercy, and we now commit his body to the ground, the vicar intoned.

Standing slightly apart from the other mourners, Joseph Linford stared at his father's coffin, his face impassive. Then he raised his eyes and looked across the open grave at his son, Robert, and at Robert's wife, Lily. Her face shrouded in a short black chiffon veil, her hand was tucked into her husband's arm.

Joseph scowled.

His gaze moved to his brother, Charles, who was standing

next to Lily. Charles's wife, Sarah, stood on his other side, a clear gap between them. That was another rum marriage, Joseph thought.

Glancing sideways, he looked beyond his wife and daughter to the youngest of the three brothers, Thomas, who was at the far end of the grave.

Obviously in a degree of discomfort caused by his artificial leg, Thomas was leaning heavily on his stick, supported by his wife, Alice.

Joseph's eyes rested a moment on Alice, and he felt the same amazement he always felt when he saw her. It was very easy to see why Thomas had married her, but for the life of him he couldn't understand what she saw in him. It was true that she'd married above her station, but Thomas would not be an easy man to live with, and a woman as good-looking as Alice could surely have done equally well for herself with someone more amenable.

Turning away from them, he looked back across the grave at Robert, and a wave of intense disappointment surged through him.

Followed by anger.

How could Robert, his only son, have been so taken in by a pretty face that he'd blinded himself to the woman's lack of background and education – and then, even worse, how could he have gone and married her? It beggared belief.

He'd been absolutely horrified when Robert had told him that he'd fallen in love with Lily Brown, a Land Girl on the farm that neighboured Chorton House, the family's weekend retreat in Oxfordshire. The minute he'd seen the girl, he'd known how wrong she was for his son, and in the months that had followed, he'd repeatedly told Robert that at eighteen, he was far too young to know his own mind regarding women, and he'd regularly urged him to walk away from her.

But had Robert listened to him and taken his advice?

No.

And a year and a half later, he'd been even more horrified when Robert had told him that Lily was expecting a child and had asked for his consent to their marriage.

He'd refused at first, of course.

A generous pension would be settled on the woman if she agreed to leave the area, he'd told Robert, one that would take account of the child. Or if Robert really couldn't bear to give her up, she could be installed in a small house thereabouts and Robert could discreetly call upon her whenever he wanted until the day came, as Joseph was firmly convinced it would, when Robert opened his eyes, and saw her for the vacuous woman she was. Then he could simply stop visiting her, and focus solely on the life to which he'd been born.

There'd been no reason to wreck his life by marrying her.

But Robert had been adamant. He'd dug in his heels and said that if he had to, he'd wait until he was twenty-one and no longer needed his father's consent, and would marry Lily the day after his birthday.

In his stubborn refusal to listen to reason, Robert had no doubt been emboldened by the support of his grandfather. Joseph's father had not only taken Lily to live with him in his Hampstead house when the farmer evicted her from the farm, but had said that he would engage a live-in nurse for the two weeks prior to the baby's birth, and for one month after. And as if that wasn't bad enough, he'd promised to hire a nanny after that!

The late Arthur Joseph Linford couldn't have made things easier for Robert.

In the end, Joseph had had to agree to them marrying, and

immediately after the wedding, Robert had moved in with Lily and his grandfather. Six months later, James had been born.

No one in the family had attended Robert's wedding, apart from Robert's grandfather and his younger sister, Nellie. The eldest of his three children, Dorothy, probably would have done, but she'd been living in Germany at the time, and still was.

At the thought of Dorothy, his frown deepened.

He'd have to write to Germany, of course, to let her know of her grandfather's death, but that would be the first and last letter he sent her. As far as he was concerned – and his wife and the others were behind him on this – the moment that Dorothy married a German, she'd ceased to be part of the Linford family.

An image of his daughter filled his mind, her dark brown eyes intelligent and laughing, and he felt an acute pang of loss. Why oh why had Dorothy been so weak!

Surreptitiously wiping his eyes, he glanced again at the coffin.

What on earth had his father been thinking of, helping Robert to destroy his life in such a way?

Everyone knew that Robert would one day take over the running of Linford & Sons, and that he'd do it well. Young as he was, he showed all the signs of not only being able to run a successful construction company, but also of having the imagination to take it to even greater heights. Marrying Lily Brown had been blatantly at odds with the interests of the company, and it was astounding that his father, the founder of the company, a man known for never making irrational decisions, had acted so wildly out of character.

A sudden blast of cold air buffeted the stark hedgerows surrounding the hilltop graveyard. A straggle of dead leaves skittered across the hard ground and settled in dank heaps at the feet of the age-worn gravestones. Joseph shivered, and tucked the collar of his coat more tightly around his neck.

Yes, Robert had made an error of judgement, but he didn't deserve to be weighted down for the rest of his life by the consequences of a youthful infatuation, and both as Robert's father, and as chairman of Linford & Sons, it was surely incumbent upon him to take whatever measures might be necessary to prevent that from happening.

His gaze returned to Lily's veiled face, and his eyes narrowed.

Mistakes could be corrected, and this mistake was not going to be an exception. For Robert's sake, and for the sake of Robert's baby son, James, he'd get that woman out of their lives as soon as he could, and he didn't really care how he did it.

2

HAMPSTEAD

Two days later

Robert stood in the middle of the polished parquet floor and stared around the front reception room in disbelief. Never in his wildest dreams had he imagined that his grandfather's Hampstead house would one day be his.

And nor had the rest of his family, judging by their expressions as his grandfather's will had been read out. Stunned surprise had fast given way to disappointment, and finally to resignation.

His own shocked amazement had been followed by numbness. And the need for a stiff drink.

'Lily,' he shouted. Pulling off his black silk tie, he walked across to the mahogany drinks cabinet. 'Where are you?'

He threw the tie over the back of the nearest chair, undid the collar of his starched white shirt, and then picked up one of the decanters from its silver salver and was pouring a large whisky into a cut-glass tumbler as Lily hurried into the room.

'I was with James,' she said, removing her black hat and veil.

'I was telling him we'd got a home. I'm not sure he understood, though,' she added with a giggle.

He turned to her, decanter in hand. 'He'd be pretty smart if he did at under six months,' he said. 'I've just poured a drink. D'you want one, too?'

'Not now, thanks. I'd hate it to go to my head. I want to enjoy every single minute of feeling relieved. Just think, on the way to the solicitor's, we were panicking that we were about to be thrown out of our home. And with a baby, too. And knowing your father wouldn't help us. But look at us now!'

With a loud sigh of happiness, she looked around the room, her gaze taking in the large mirror above the black cast-iron fireplace, the gilt-framed oil paintings hanging from the picture-rail that skirted the upper part of the dark-green walls, and the mahogany-framed three-piece suite upholstered in plush pink velvet.

'For all this to be yours, Robert,' she said, her brow creasing in wonder. 'It doesn't seem possible.'

'To be honest, I feel completely overwhelmed, too. It's like a huge weight's been lifted.' He put down the glass and held out his hand to her. 'Come on, let's go and look at our garden.'

Holding Lily's hand, he led the way through the front hall to the rear reception room and across to the tall sash windows.

Hand in hand with Lily, he stood in front of one of the windows and stared out at the garden. In the thin morning sunlight, the naked arms of the skeletal elms at the far end of the garden shone a silvery-gold, and the sparse winter grass that stretched from the house to the trees was sheened with a gleaming green. Raising his eyes, he looked above the belt of trees to the houses and gardens that lay in the hazy grey distance, and further still, to the vastness of Hampstead Heath.

And he felt a huge wave of gratitude to his grandfather.

'When Grandfather gave me his Model T, I thought he was being unbelievably generous,' he said, a lump in his throat. 'But to be left all this—' He gestured around him. 'And the money to run it, too – it doesn't seem right somehow. We're so lucky, Lily.'

He released her hand and put his arm around her shoulders.

'You deserve it, Robert – you were always very good to your grandfather. He used to tell me how much time you spent with him after your grandmother died. Giving you the house will've been his way of thanking you.'

'Maybe. But Father grew up here, and so did my uncles. They really should've had a share of what used to be their home. And the other grandchildren, too. But I've been given the lot.'

'But your uncles have got their own houses, and Louisa and Christopher obviously live with your Uncle Charles and Aunt Sarah. They're still very young. Like Nellie lives with your parents. We had nowhere to go.' She pulled his arm more tightly around her shoulder. 'But there could be another reason, too. Your grandfather had been really lonely before we moved in, and he might've wanted to show you how glad he'd been of the company.'

He stared down at her in surprise. 'Lonely? But he saw Father regularly, and Uncle Thomas, too. He was always going to Kentish Town, walking around the yard, looking in at the office and giving advice. And he'd often have a coffee with Uncle Thomas while he was there.'

'But he didn't feel at home at the yard like he used to, did he? Him and me talked a lot when it was just us in the house. He was easy to talk to, not like the rest of your family. He told me your father had made so many changes to the company that he hardly recognised it any longer. And although everyone at the yard was very nice to him, he could tell they were secretly longing for him to leave so they could get back to their work. He went there out of habit and for something to do.'

Robert tightened his arm around Lily. 'I didn't realise that. None of us did. But you did, Lily.' He bent down and kissed the top of her head. 'Perhaps by giving us the house, he was thanking you for being a good friend to him. He knew the awful things Father said about you, and that he'd tried to stop us marrying, but because he'll have got to know you, he'll have seen why I love you so much. He'll have known it wasn't the infatuation Father said it was, and maybe he just wanted us to have the best possible start to our marriage.'

She slid her arm around his back and gazed up at him. 'Whatever the reason he did it, I know we're going to be so happy here, Robert. I can tell. What a house for James to grow up in!'

'Yes, it is. But I'm still worried about the family. They were genuinely hurt and upset. You saw them at the solicitor's – only Uncle Thomas bothered to say goodbye. We need to fix that.'

'But how? They all hate me.'

'It won't be easy, I admit. All I can think is that this is the house where the family used to get together in London – everyone came here once a month for Sunday lunch. Perhaps we should try to keep that going. Have a monthly lunch, and perhaps a walk afterwards, like we used to do. We could start in a couple of weeks. If we do that, things might eventually get back to normal. After all, they can't truly think I persuaded Grandfather to leave me the house. I know that Father would never believe that.'

Lily took a step back and stared at him in alarm. 'The thought of your father here is really scary, Robert. He frightens me. Every time he looks at me, his eyes go all funny. I'll always be the gold-digging older woman who trapped his precious son. And now the others probably think that, too, if they didn't before. They may not think you worked on your grandfather, but I'm sure they think *I* did. I do want to help you make things right with your family, but I'd rather wait a bit longer before we invite them.'

He shook his head. 'There isn't a single person who could make Grandfather do something he didn't want to do, and they all know that. You don't get to build a company like Linford & Sons if you're the sort of person who can be pushed into acting against your will. Asking them to lunch is the right thing to do, and we must do so soon.' He pulled her closer to him again. 'But you're not to worry about it, Lily. Mrs Bailey knows what has to be done when there're guests. All you'll have to do is approve the menu. It won't be difficult, I promise you.'

She was quiet for a moment or two, her head resting against his shoulder. 'You used to say over and over again that you'd never forgive your father for the way he behaved towards us,' she said at last, her voice shaking, 'and for the horrible things he said about me. You always said he'd have no place in our lives when we were married.'

He gave an awkward laugh. 'That was in the heat of the moment. Father was only doing what he thought best for me. He was mistaken about what that was, but it was done with the right motives. I want us to be close again. And also, we work together. He'd never consciously allow anything to interfere with company business, but all the same, any awkwardness between us could make things difficult. And it's important he gets to know James, and that James gets to know him. One day, James will run the company.'

'I see.'

He hugged her. 'And I want him to get to know you, too. Once he's spent time with you, he'll see how wonderful you are, and he'll change towards you. All the family will come to love you.

Not as much as I do – that wouldn't be possible – but they're going to really like you.'

She gave a nervous laugh. 'I know this is going to sound very silly to you, Robert, but I always panic when I'm with your family. They've been to proper schools, met lots of different people, and always know what to wear and what to say wherever they go. But I don't. I never know what to talk to them about. I can milk cows, plough fields, mend fences, do just about any job on a farm, but that would hardly interest them. And I can tell them how to make a dress, but they'll never need to know that.'

He put both of his arms around her. 'Don't do yourself down, Lily. There's a lot going on under that beautiful surface. You're strong – you've had to be, given your life. And the skills you've listed show how well you pick up things. There's nothing you can't do if you want to do it. I love that about you. And they will, too, when they've got to know you.' He tilted her face towards his, and kissed her hard on her lips.

She nestled against his chest.

'And don't forget, there's James,' he went on. 'You could always talk about him. And here's a further suggestion – you've hardly been anywhere in London other than Hampstead, so you could start exploring the rest of the city. I'm sure you'd find that interesting, and then you could tell them what you'd seen. Mother or Nellie might go with you if you asked.'

She glanced up at him and pulled a face. 'I wouldn't do that! Just the idea of being alone with them for a whole day is absolutely terrifying!'

'I don't see why,' he said, with a touch of irritation. 'But if you don't like that idea, why don't you ask Aunt Sarah what she does while Uncle Charles is at the bank? And also ask my mother. Father works all hours. Ask Nellie, too – she's not that much younger than you. If you do what they do, you'll be able to join in with their conversation.'

She took a deep breath. 'You're right. I shall do everything you said. I love you, Robert, and I'm not going to let you down. And I want your family to know that I appreciate how lucky we've been.' She smiled up at him, and settled back against his chest.

Above her head, he smiled broadly. 'That's terrific, Lily. Thank you. I want to get things right with them all as soon as possible – nothing's more important than family.' He stopped abruptly, and pulled back. 'God, I'm sorry! That was thoughtless of me. It's not your fault that you've never known what it's like to be part of a loving family. But you will, and then you'll feel about them as I do.'

She reached up and kissed his cheek. 'All right, then. I promise to make a real effort to get on with them, and that means Joseph, too.'

He hugged her tightly 'Thanks, Lily. It's a really exciting time at work at the moment, and Father and I need to be back on good terms if we're going to take advantage of the opportunities.'

'What's so exciting?'

He laughed. 'I doubt you'd find it exciting.'

'I might. I'm not stupid, you know, just because your family thinks I am.'

'Well, then, there are signs that the market's changing, and not every builder's spotted that. *We* have, though – or rather, Father has – and a number of the houses we'll be building in the future will be for people to buy, rather than rent.'

'But you've got to be rich to buy a house!'

'Not any longer. Building societies are expanding and taking on new members all the time, so more people are now able to borrow the money to buy their own house. And a lot of those people want to live outside the city in order to have more space.

Up till now, the need to get into work has made that difficult, but now that they're improving the roads and extending the underground, it's becoming possible. Father saw what was happening, and for some time now, we've been using the money we made from our wartime contracts to buy up building land around London, especially next to the main roads into the city, and that's where we're going to be building those houses.'

She gazed at him in wonder. 'I don't know how you know so much.'

'I don't, but Father does. Believe me, he'll be as keen as I am to put the past behind us. But he's a proud man, and he won't make the first move; that's up to us. We'll invite the family to lunch very soon.' He paused. 'I'd really like your support for this, Lily – genuinely, not just pretending.'

'You've got it,' she said quickly.

'And talking of roads,' he went on, cheerfully, 'it's given me yet another idea – you could start driving again. You used to drive tractors on the farm, so it's just a matter of practising. I seldom need the car during the week, so you could take the car and go and see friends, or do whatever you want.'

'There's plenty of time to think about that,' she said, tucking her arm into his, and sidling closer to him. 'You know, you've not been up to see James since we got back. Why don't we go up and see him? He'll be wondering where you are.'

'At his age? What an amazing child!'

'Believe me, he is.' She slid her free arm across his chest. 'And when we've said hello to him,' she went on, 'Annie could take him out in the pram, and we could have a rest before lunch.' She glanced up at him, a smile hovering on her lips.

He grabbed her hand. 'What are we waiting for? But we'll reverse the order – bed first, and then James.'

Laughing, they ran to the stairs.

3

The mournful hoot of an owl broke into the silence of the night, as it had been doing at regular intervals since she and Robert had gone to bed.

Robert had fallen asleep almost at once, worn out by the excitement of the day and by the plans he'd been making since learning that the house was his. As she'd lain next to him, she'd closed her eyes and waited for sleep. But sleep had eluded her, kept at bay by the anxiety that had been growing within her since their return that morning – the anxiety that she'd end up letting Robert down by not being able to be the sort of wife he wanted, the sort of wife a man in his position should have.

The owl hooted again.

Abandoning all hope of sleep, she slipped out of the bed, wrapped her housecoat tightly around her against the chill night air and padded with slippered feet down the stairs and into the back reception room. She crossed through a shaft of pale moonlight to the sofa that faced the hearth, kicked off her slippers and sat down. Curling her feet beneath her, she gazed at the residue of pale grey ashes in the mottled cast-iron grate.

There'd been a time not so long ago when she'd been the one who'd had to deal with the dregs of the previous night. It had been her job to come down at first light while the rest of the house still slept, open the shutters, rake out and re-lay the fires, blacken and polish the fireplaces, and generally clean up the mess made by her employers the night before.

And every single one of those mornings, as cold dawn had broken and she'd forced herself out of her bed, she'd longed to be a different person in a different life.

Which she now was.

For someone who'd never known her father – at some point in the first few months after her birth, her father had walked out of the cramped, run-down dwelling where she and her mother lived, and had never returned – she'd come a long way.

'He's a bad 'un,' her less-than-useless mother used to say of her father, and she'd reach for a bottle. 'Believe me, gal, we're better off without him.'

Increasingly left to fend for herself as her mother idled her hours away in the local pub, when she was old enough she got into the habit of scouring the countryside for anything she could eat. And she started running along the dirt track that criss-crossed the fields to the small town nearby and asking the shop owners if they'd give her some food in return for a job.

She hardly saw her mother, and when she did, her mother was usually too drunk to bother with her. Occasionally, she'd wondered how her mother had the money for drink, until a girl who worked behind the bar at the local pub told her that her mother ensured a regular supply of drink by dishing out favours to men round the back.

And Robert's father had actually thought she, Lily, was that sort of woman, too.

Well, she wasn't, but that was thanks in part to the amazing good luck she'd had.

Her first stroke of luck had come when she'd been seven or eight.

Loitering outside the baker shop in the town one day, hoping the baker would give her the broken biscuits he couldn't sell, she saw an elderly woman a short distance from her trip on a piece of rough ground.

'Can I help you, ma'am?' she asked, rushing forward.

'Thank'ee, dear,' the woman said, as Lily took her arm and helped her to her feet.

'I'll carry your basket,' Lily said, and picked up the basket from the ground.

Together they walked slowly back to the woman's cottage, which was on the other side of the town. When they reached the cottage, the woman insisted that Lily go in with her.

'What're them dresses for?' Lily asked, when she'd finished devouring the boiled ham put in front of her by the grateful woman. 'Them dresses there,' she said, pointing to two dresses hanging from hooks on the wall.

'I'm a seamstress, my dear,' the woman told her. 'I make dresses and shirts for people hereabouts, and darn their clothes. It brings in a few pennies and gives me something to do. I live on my own, you see, since my daughter wed a farmer and went to live on the farm.'

The following morning, Lily went back to the woman and asked if she needed someone to carry her shopping that day.

'You've come at the right time,' the seamstress said, her face creasing into a smile. 'See that cake.' She indicated a cake on a plate in the centre of the rough wooden table that stood in the middle of the small room. 'I made it in case you called again. Sit yourself down, my dear, and I'll give you a slice. If you like cake, that is.'

'Oh, I do, ma'am,' Lily said, hastily sitting down as a slice of cake, still warm from the oven, was put in front of her. 'Thank you, ma'am.'

'Why don't you call me Auntie Muriel, my dear?'

That had been the start of their friendship.

Every day, as soon as Lily had straightened her bed, she'd run to the town to see Auntie Muriel. As soon as she arrived, she'd be given water with which to wash herself, and something hot to eat. After that, she'd help with the cleaning and preparations for lunch, and then she'd sit and watch Auntie Muriel sew, and listen to her talk about her daughter. For the first time, she learned what a mother's love could be, and she envied the daughter, and swore to herself that one day she, too, would be a really good mother.

On the day that her mother fell into the swollen river, drunk, and drowned, Lily, nine years old, was sitting in Auntie Muriel's cottage, learning how to darn a sock. She never returned to her hovel again.

As time went on, the seamstress's hands became stiff and gnarled. Increasingly, Lily took over her darning and sewing commissions, until the day came, four years later, when Auntie Muriel realised that she couldn't continue to work any longer and would have to take up her daughter's repeated offer that she go and live with her.

'Let me come with you, Auntie Muriel. Please. I'll be ever so good. I'll make all their clothes and do all the cleaning and things,' Lily begged, tears streaming down her cheeks.

Weeping profusely, Auntie Muriel put her arms around Lily and hugged her tightly. 'It hurts me to say this, but I can't take'ee with me, lass. I wish I could. My daughter says the family can't afford another mouth to feed, and she thinks it'd be a fearful responsibility, having a thirteen-year-old girl with all them farmhands around. But I'll not go anywhere till I know ee've got a place to live.'

Soon after that, one of the families that Auntie Muriel had worked for heard about Lily's plight and sent word that they were in need of a housemaid. So, after a tearful goodbye to the seamstress, who was as distraught as Lily, Lily had gone into service.

Meeting Auntie Muriel had been her first stroke of luck, Lily thought, wrapping her housecoat tightly around her knees as she stared at the few small chunks of unburned coal that lay among the debris in the grate. Going to work for that particular family was her second stroke of luck, though it was some years before she'd realised that.

There was one daughter in the family, and she was close in age to Lily. The daughter liked Lily and wanted her as a friend, but her mother had forbidden her to make friends with a servant. Once or twice, however, the mother had yielded to her daughter's pleas and allowed Lily to sit in the room while her daughter was being taught by her governess.

After the third lesson that Lily had watched, during which the daughter tried hard to impress Lily with how clever she was, the governess had told the mother that her daughter's application was infinitely greater when Lily was present.

'Although I don't like the idea,' the mother had told her daughter icily, 'I shall allow Lily to sit with you during your lessons. But only if you've completed your morning chores, Lily,' she'd added, turning to Lily. 'Is that clear?'

'Yes, ma'am. Thank you, ma'am.' And Lily had given a little curtsy.

She wasn't particularly interested in learning to read and write, nor was she particularly keen on the daughter, but she hated the work of a domestic servant, and had swiftly realised that sitting in on the lessons gave her a break in the day she wouldn't otherwise have had.

That Lily knew so little soon began to irritate the daughter, and she told Lily that she'd teach her to read and write. Lily would never be as clever as she was, the daughter informed her, but at least they'd be able to work together on the tasks set by her governess.

To the daughter's ill-disguised annoyance, Lily picked up everything very quickly, and before long, to Lily's surprise as well, she'd mastered the basics of reading and writing and was able to keep up with the daughter.

And then, three years after she'd started as a housemaid, the country went to war and everything changed.

The family let the governess go, and the daughter, who'd started regularly visiting her cousins who lived nearby, no longer wanted to spend as much time with Lily, who was very much prettier than she was.

To Lily's misery, there was no longer any relief from her tasks as a housemaid for people who were increasingly bad-tempered, and forever complaining about the lack of available men to work in the fields, with so many away fighting, and about the subsequent shortage of food, which was made worse by the German naval blockades.

The door to her escape from daily drudgery opened two long years after the start of the war. It was her third stroke of luck.

She'd been in the hall one day, polishing the wooden newel at the foot of the stairs, when she'd heard the family anxiously discussing the failure of the harvest that year.

'With only three weeks of food reserves in the country, there's a real risk of famine,' the father said.

'Cecilia is as worried as we are, but she did have something of interest to say when I called on her earlier today,' the mother said.

'That's hard to believe! It's unusual for that woman to have anything of interest to say,' the father snapped, his tone grumpy. 'It's beyond me why you want her as a friend.'

'Be that as it may, she told me that there's now a Women's Land Army. Women are going to be taking the place of the men who're fighting. Can you believe that! Strange idea that it is, it could actually ease the food situation.'

'A pipe dream,' the father had said, his voice dismissive. 'No woman could ever do what a man can do. Farm work is men's work.'

To Lily's annoyance, she'd dropped her tin of beeswax polish at that moment, and they'd fallen silent.

Her curiosity piqued, the next time she'd been alone with the daughter, she'd asked her about the Land Army, but the daughter said she knew nothing and promptly changed the subject.

'Of course, they won't say nothing,' the milkman had told her when he delivered the milk the following day. 'They don't want you to leave them and go and work on the land, do they? You mark my words, missy, lots of young women like you are doin' just that right now, and they're gettin' four times what they got as a maid.' And he'd agreed that on her next day off, he'd take her into town on his cart so that she could go to the post office and find out how to apply.

It was as she'd filled in the application form, that she'd realised how lucky she'd been to have learned to read and write.

A couple of weeks later, the milkman had come to her rescue again when he took her for her interview at the local recruitment office. They'd given her a free medical, and then questioned her about what she could do and why she wanted to join the Land Army.

'To help farmers,' she'd said, and she'd chosen to join the agricultural section, rather than foraging or timber-cutting.

As she was already nineteen, she was told that she could immediately go to one of the practice farms set up for those who were inexperienced in farm work. After four weeks there, she'd be given an efficiency test and if she passed, they'd find her work on a farm. Her initial contract would be for twelve months, and she'd have a free railway warrant so that she could get to wherever she had to go.

She'd promptly quit her job as a servant and become a Land Girl.

A year and a half later, the war had ended, but by then she'd met Robert. And that had been the greatest stroke of luck in her life.

4

Looking back, Lily realised that she'd loved Robert since the moment she first saw him, but had been too frightened to let herself face the way she felt for someone so much her better, so far out of her reach.

She'd been sitting on the metal plough in the middle of a partially ploughed field, desperately shaking the reins as she tried to make the stubborn horses set off down the field again. She'd just been starting to abandon all hope of ever getting them going, and was filling with embarrassment at the thought of having to go back to the farm for help, when she heard the sound of laughter coming from behind her.

She turned and looked behind her. A boy was standing just inside the hedge at the back of the field, and even at that distance, she could see that he was highly amused by her struggle. He started to walk towards her. She swiftly turned back to the field ahead, and again rattled the reins up and down.

She was still stuck in the middle of the field when he reached her.

'D'you need a hand?' he asked.

She'd been about to decline, but before she'd uttered the words, she glanced down. The clearest blue eyes she'd ever seen were looking up at her. Her swift gaze took in a tall, very good-looking young man with dark hair and broad shoulders, who couldn't have been more than a year or so younger than she. He was staring up at her with undisguised appreciation. Her heart had given a sudden leap, and her refusal had dried in her throat.

'Hang on to the reins,' he said, and he went up to the nearest horse, took hold of the bridle and urged the animal forward. One hoof followed the other, and they began to move.

'Shove over,' he said, coming back to her. She slid across to the far side of the wooden seat, and he climbed up beside her. Grasping the reins, his hands next to hers, he shook them slightly.

'I don't believe it!' she exclaimed as the horses continued to move steadily forward.

'Seeing is believing,' he said, and he turned to her with a grin. A lone dimple appeared in his cheek.

He really is gorgeous, she thought, and she smiled.

She was still smiling as together they finished ploughing the rest of the field.

That had been the first of the many fields they'd ploughed together.

In the following weeks, they'd jointly cleared thistles from fields, hoed mangolds from the ground, dug ditches, milked cows. Whatever the farmer had asked her to do, if Robert was staying at Chorton, he'd do it with her.

And he was staying at Chorton more frequently than ever before.

To her great joy, he didn't seem to mind that she was a couple of years older than he, with very little education, with a life that owed far more to the kindness of others than to her family, and before long, they were deeply in love and talking about marrying, both of them longing to be able to give full vent to the passion that was becoming more and more insistent with each meeting.

'I love you, Lily Brown,' Robert said one afternoon as they lay in each other's arms, both of them breathing heavily, her bodice in disarray. 'It's killing me, having to stop like this when I want you so much. I desperately want to go to sleep beside you at night, and wake up next to you in the morning. I'm going to tell Father about us. I want the whole family to know how much I love you, and I want us to marry as soon as possible.'

She bit her lower lip. 'I want that, too, Robert. I love you so much that it hurts. But d'you think he'll agree? He's so important, and you are, too. And I'm nothing.'

He turned and gazed into her eyes. 'You're not nothing, Lily – you're everything,' he said quietly. 'You're the most beautiful person ever, and as soon as Father meets you, he'll see that. He's coming to Chorton with me next weekend, and that's when we'll ask for his consent. He wants me to be happy, and as you make me happy, I know he'll agree.'

'I do hope you're right,' she said anxiously.

The following weekend, as they stood hand in hand in front of Joseph, Robert told him of his love for Lily, the most wonderful woman in the world. Seeing the look in Joseph's eyes, he started faltering as he neared the moment when he intended to ask for his father's consent. Steeling himself, he forced himself to finish the sentence, and waited.

Joseph exploded in fury.

He shouted abuse at Lily and screamed at her to get out. Terrified, she wanted to run, but Robert gripped her hand and held her at his side. His father then turned on Robert, and furiously accused him of being a reckless idiot, an innocent puppy who'd been preyed upon by a scheming woman from God knows where. Women like that were good for one thing only, he thundered, and that one thing wasn't marriage.

She gasped aloud. A wave of shame and embarrassment swept through her.

She glanced quickly at Robert. His face showed how angry he was.

Spinning round, he headed for the door, pulling her after him, and made across the garden towards the farm, apologising over and over again for his father's appalling rudeness. When they reached the door to her room, he kissed her with frantic intensity, assured her that they would indeed marry, and then went back to Chorton House, where he went straight to his room and slammed the door shut.

'We might not be able to meet quite so frequently in the future,' he told her the following day, having slipped across to her room before leaving for London. 'Father's certain to try to keep me in London as much as possible. But you can be sure I'll come to Chorton whenever I can. I love you, Lily, and I want to marry you. Nothing can ever alter that. Father will see that in the end, and he'll give in.'

She gazed up at him, tears filling her eyes. 'I'll miss you every minute you're not here, Robert. I love you so much. And I know I shouldn't say it, 'cos ladies shouldn't, but I can't wait to be able to do with you what people do when they're married. Just thinking of it keeps me awake at night.'

'Oh, Lily!' He flung his arms around her and kissed her with passion.

'I think it'd be better if we meet without people knowing,' she said, her voice muffled by his jersey. 'If your father knew we were still seeing each other after all what he said, he might not let you come here again, and if he did that, I'd die.'

He nodded. 'You're right. We'll need a place where no one

ever goes. Where we can be together. Oh, Lily,' he said, tightening his arms around her, their bodies pressing hard against each other, 'I can't wait for us to be married, either.'

It hadn't taken her long to find a loft in an outlying barn that was seldom in use, and after that, whenever Robert came to Chorton, he went straight to the loft and waited for her to be able to join him. Those snatched moments in each other's arms were all they lived for.

And then, in the spring after they'd met, his face deathly pale, Robert had told her that his father had given him a project that would keep him in London for the whole of the following month. He wouldn't be able to come to Chorton at all during that time, not so much as once.

They stared at each other, utterly distraught at the idea of being apart for so long.

'On the Friday evening when I can come back to Chorton again, I'll go straight to the loft and wait for you,' he promised her, hugging her close to him. 'Come as soon as you can – we mustn't waste a single minute of our first weekend together after what's going to feel like an eternity. I shall miss you so much.'

'And I'll miss you, too,' she said, sobbing into his shoulder. 'I'll think of you every minute of every day. I love you so much, Robert.'

In the evenings after he'd gone, when her day's work was over, she'd go to the loft and sit there by herself, weeping as she remembered the heady sensation of lying in his arms, her head against his chest, his body pressed against hers; remembering how they used to touch each other for any excuse or for none. And she relived the moments when they'd giggled together as they made their plans for the future.

She just couldn't bear to lose him.

But in no time at all, the likelihood of that happening was preying heavily on her mind.

Robert's father would be doing his best to turn Robert against her, she was sure. He'd be introducing Robert to the kind of girl who'd make the sort of wife he'd want Robert to have. She'd come from the right background, have money, be able to talk about lots of different things, and definitely be very attractive. Attractive enough to make Robert forget her.

But his father wouldn't be obvious about it. He was too clever for that. He'd be cunning in the way he went about things, and whatever Robert might have intended, there was a real chance that he'd fall for one of a succession of beautiful women he just happened to meet, who had so much to offer him.

Her fear of having to face life without him firmly took root, and grew daily.

By the end of the interminable month apart, she'd mentally prepared herself for the fact that he'd want to end things between them, and she'd hurried to the loft as soon as she'd finished her work on the Friday evening, knowing he'd be there as he'd said he would, and wanting the worst to be over as soon as possible.

As she reached the top of the wooden steps, she saw him. He was lying on a bed of hay, his hands clasped behind his head, staring up at the rafters. Her heart overflowed with love, and a lump came to her throat, fearful of what she was about to hear.

Standing on the top rung, her heart pounding, she waited for him to realise she was there.

When he finally did so, he jumped up and stared at her.

The faced each other, and their eyes locked.

Then she stepped off the ladder and walked across to him, trying to quell her trembling. She reached him, took hold of the brim of her felt cloche hat, pulled it off, threw it to the floor, and faced him in trepidation, her heart racing.

But at the look in his eyes, at the heat in his gaze, the trepidation melted away, dissolving in an all-consuming wave of joy mingled with relief.

He still loved her!

'Robert,' she screamed in sheer delight. 'You're back!' And she threw her arms around him. Their lips met in an explosion of mutual passion that shook them both to the core. Pulling apart, they stared at each other, drawing their breath in ragged gasps.

Robert grinned at her, lay back down, and tapped the wooden planks next to him.

Laughing, she dragged off her knee-high boots as fast as she could, lay down beside him and snuggled up close. She slid her hand across his chest. 'I love you, I love you, I love you. I've missed you so much.'

He put his arms around her and pulled her to him. 'And I've missed you, too. God, how I've missed you! You wouldn't believe how much.' He rolled on to his side, raised himself slightly on his elbow, and stared into her face. 'You're so beautiful, Lily. You're even more beautiful than I remembered, and that's saying something. I don't ever want to be separated from you again.'

Lowering his head, he brought his mouth down on hers, lightly at first, and then much harder. She wound her hand behind his head and her lips opened beneath his. Instinctively, she arched towards him, pressing her body up against his.

She felt him shudder, and heard his breathing quicken. His chest rose and fell at a furious pace.

With visible difficulty, he pulled himself away.

Rolling again on to his back, his arm still around her shoulders, he lay without moving for a moment or two, giving his breathing a chance to slow. Then his free hand strayed to her breast as it had started doing in recent months. Lightly, his fingers traced the swell beneath the thin cotton bodice, hesitant, waiting for the moment when she moved his hand away.

She felt the pressure of his hand increase. She knew she should push his hand aside, but she couldn't. Instead of doing what she'd always done in the past, she lay motionless, burning beneath his touch, rendered helpless to stop him by her overwhelming yearning for him.

He paused. Then he ran his fingertips around each of the buttons that ran down the front of her bodice. Returning to the top button, he undid it, and again paused.

Still she didn't move.

'You'll have to tell me when to stop,' he said, his voice thick. 'I'm not in any state to tell myself.'

She turned her head and gazed into eyes that were dark with want. 'You're the one who's beautiful, Robert,' she whispered, a tremor in her voice. 'I love you so much. I know I should tell you to stop right now, but I can't. Every night and every day for the past month, I've thought of you. And you're here now. Please don't think badly of me – but I love you so much that I don't want to stop. Not now.' She placed her hand on top of his, and gently moulded his fingers around her breast. 'I know it'd be wrong of us...' Her voice trailed off.

The only sound was their heavy breathing.

'Lily, Lily,' he said, his voice a croak. He cleared his throat.

For a long moment, each stared at the other, heat burning deep in their eyes, their bodies aching with want.

The air crackled between them.

Then in a sweeping movement, he swung himself on top of her, and pulled open her bodice.

* * *

During the weeks that followed, Joseph, clearly aware that Robert was still seeing Lily whenever he could, but equally aware that he couldn't prevent him from visiting Chorton, was clearly hoping that the affair would burn itself out with the passage of time, and he still flatly refused to agree to them marrying.

It was infatuation, he repeatedly told Robert, not real love. He was at an impressionable age, and when he was a little older, and saw things with more experienced eyes, he was certain to want a different sort of life from the life into which Lily would imprison him.

But Joseph hoped in vain.

The more he verbally attacked her in conversations with Robert, the more Robert's passion for Lily poured forth. At every possible opportunity, in every secluded place they could find, they'd fling off their clothes and come together in the blazing heat of the moment. She'd never in her life been happier, and she was sure that Robert hadn't been, either. And at last she truly believed there was nothing his father could say or do that could destroy the love that Robert had for her.

A month before the war ended, she looked down at her stomach, saw that it was very slightly rounded, and knew for certain the reason for her tender nipples and early-morning nausea. Later that afternoon, with a degree of anxiety about how he'd respond to her news, she haltingly told Robert that she was expecting a child.

To her huge relief, he'd exploded with joy. Lifting her off her feet, he swung her around on the spot.

In great happiness and excitement, he'd immediately rushed off to his father, told him of Lily's condition, and asked for his father's immediate consent to their marriage.

In that moment, the hope that had been building in Joseph that, with all the signs suggesting that the war might be drawing to a close, whereupon the fighting men would return to their jobs, and Lily would almost certainly have to leave the farm and move away in search of work, drained away.

He held out a little longer, but realised eventually that this was a battle he wasn't going to win. The final straw had been when he found out that Robert's grandfather had invited Lily to live in his house, and he'd then given his consent.

* * *

Yes, she'd been very lucky, she thought. She had a darling little son, and lived in a beautiful house with a man she adored, who amazingly seemed to feel the same way about her. He had given her a life that was way beyond anything she could've dreamed of. All the unpleasant things that she used to do when in service were now being done for her by someone else, and she'd never be forced into the sort of dreary job that her background would have limited her to.

She uncurled her legs, stood up, manoeuvred her feet into her slippers and made for the door.

If she had to put a smile on her face and try to convey a warmth for Robert's family, a group of people with whom she was sure she'd never feel at ease, it was a small price to pay for what she had, and for the pleasure it would give Robert.

And as for Joseph, she'd do her best to overcome her fear of him. After all, what harm could he really do to her?

5

Lying awake in their bed, Robert heard Lily creep quietly back up the stairs.

Although his eyes had been closed, he'd been awake when she'd got out of bed some time earlier. She'd clearly been trying not to disturb him, so he'd lain motionless. He'd heard her go past the water closet next to their room and go downstairs. For a moment, he'd wondered whether to follow her, but had decided not to – she obviously wanted some time on her own. And to be honest, he, too, wasn't in the mood for a conversation in the middle of the night. He'd said more than enough that morning as it was.

Perhaps too much, in fact.

He'd certainly felt guilty about it ever since.

Lily had done her best to appear cheerful throughout the rest of the day, but he'd seen the anxiety beneath her every glance, and heard her voice tremble as she'd talked about what they could serve at their first family lunch. And her face had been pale as she'd promised to start driving again, and to find things of interest to do in the day.

And that was his fault.

He'd pressured her into agreeing to host a lunch, and to get out of the house more, when she clearly didn't feel ready to do either of those things. He'd been insensitive and inconsiderate. Loving her in the way he did, he should've been more conscious of her very different upbringing, and never have caused her to feel such panic.

The trouble was, when he left school and started working for the company, he'd never for one moment imagined that before he was even twenty, he'd be a husband and father, and he was still finding his way. If he *had* had a glimpse of such a future, he'd have been horrified. He'd been happy enough at school, where he'd been an average pupil, and slightly above average in sport and anything practical, but since he'd been old enough to understand that one day he'd be in charge of Linford & Sons, running the company had been the only thing he'd seen in his dreams.

Until he met Lily.

He hadn't expected to fall in love so young, and so soon after starting to work for the company, but he hadn't been able to help himself. She was absolutely beautiful, and every minute he spent with her was sheer bliss.

He'd forever be grateful to his grandfather that his grandfather's need to go to Chorton had ended up with him meeting Lily.

His grandmother had died not long before he met Lily, and with his father busy with the company's wartime contracts, his older sister, Dorothy, working in a hospital, and his younger sister, Nellie, still at school, he'd been the one who'd kept his grandfather company whenever he went to Chorton House, which his grandfather had wanted to do every weekend. It had been his grandparents' favourite house.

Once there, his grandfather, lost in grief, preferred to spend most of the day on his own, and Robert had found himself with an unexpected degree of freedom.

While such freedom was very welcome, with his father driving him hard in the week, he'd begun to suspect that his grandfather would cope more easily with his loss if they didn't go quite as regularly to a place which held so many memories for him, and he'd decided to suggest that they stop going to Chorton for a while, and do some things together in London at the weekend.

But then he'd met Lily.

The moment he'd climbed up on the plough, turned to her and felt the full force of the striking blue eyes that shone from a stunning face, a face framed by blonde curls that were escaping the confines of her regulation cloche hat, all thoughts of reducing their visits to Chorton vanished. Instead, he'd found himself unable to stay away, and went there every weekend, even when his grandfather chose to stay in London.

The end result was that he had a wife and a child at a very young age, and instead of feeling carefree, he felt the weight of responsibility. While that was understandable, given the circumstances – he loved Lily with all his heart, and there'd never been any question of him not standing by her, and even now, he wouldn't do anything different – yet when he looked back at their conversation that morning, he cringed. He must've sounded like a middle-aged man, not like the nineteen-year-old he was.

And indeed, middle-aged was how he all too often felt.

His father would've said it was his own fault, and that he should have waited longer, and then married the sort of woman cut out to be a Linford wife. His father was known by the family to expect every person who married a Linford to be able to contribute financially to the family business, and Lily clearly wouldn't be able to do that.

It had made matters worse that in the face of his father's instant dislike on the first occasion that he'd met her, which his father had made blatantly obvious, Lily had been too overawed to talk coherently. His father would not have seen her, therefore, as a charming, sociable woman who just might, despite her poverty, be an asset to the company.

Instead, his father's response had been to force him away from Chorton for a month on the pretext of needing help with their latest project. But contrary to what Joseph had hoped, the month in London had shown him the strength of his feeling for Lily.

Throughout the first weekend in London, he'd desperately missed Lily, and had moped around the house, snapping at Nellie and his mother, and at Dorothy, who'd paid them a fleeting visit to tell them she was being temporarily transferred to the hospital in Alexandra Palace, where they were holding a huge number of German internees. Short of nurses, the internment camp had requested another nurse from the Voluntary Aid Detachment, and Dorothy, to her disappointment as she was happy where she was and wanted to stay there, was the VAD nurse who'd been chosen to go.

Finally, his father, fed up with his attitude, had belatedly accepted an invitation to a charity dinner at the local tennis club the following weekend, and had told Robert that he had to go, too.

It was to be a somewhat subdued affair on account of the war, his father had said, but they'd invited all of the local businessmen involved in the war effort at home. He hoped a change of scene would bring some sanity back into the house, he'd added, and only Dorothy was excused from the occasion.

His mother and Nellie had been delighted at having an opportunity to dress up, but Robert hadn't been at all keen on the idea. Reluctantly agreeing to go for the sake of peace and quiet, and to prove to his father that nothing on earth could make him forget Lily, he'd set off in the blackest of moods, knowing he'd never enjoy himself.

But to his amazement, it wasn't as bad as he'd expected.

Within minutes of his arrival, he'd been introduced to Marian Ames, whose father owned Ames Builders' Merchants, which had branches across the whole of the south of England, and he and Marian had immediately fallen into an easy conversation. She was a slim girl, with dark brown hair, blue eyes and a friendly face. It wasn't a beautiful face, but it was a lively, pleasant one.

Before the evening was halfway through, his father had strolled across to say that Marian's father had invited them all to dinner the following Saturday. The food shops being fairly empty, her father hadn't been able to promise an elegant meal, but his cook could do wonders with very little, and he thought it would be nice for the two families to spend some time together, and enjoy a conversation about something other than bricks and cement.

His father had agreed, and that he'd be seeing Marian the following weekend had become inescapable.

He should have been furious with his father for so obviously using Marian to try to make him forget Lily, but she was easy enough to talk to, and he found he couldn't be as angry with his father as he should have been.

But later that night, he'd lain awake in the dark and felt desperately guilty. In his mind, it was as if he'd betrayed Lily by enjoying Marian's company.

Yet there was no reason why he should feel like that, he'd thought, turning on to his side. Just because he liked Marian, it didn't mean he'd fallen out of love with Lily, because he hadn't.

He'd enjoyed meeting someone new, someone with whom he could chat about lots of different things, but that's all it was.

Somehow or other, during his four weeks in London, he had seen a great deal of Marian. She and her parents would come to his house and they'd go for a walk, or have tea, or he and his family would go to dinner at her home, and then play charades. Or both families would go on a picnic together.

The two fathers, hitherto no more than business acquaintances, seemed to have become close friends overnight, and their families with them, he and Marian had observed to each other in great amusement on more than one occasion.

In no time at all, his month in London was drawing to an end, and Marian would be leaving for the south coast to stay with her aunt.

Before the war, the plan had been for her to go to a finishing school in Switzerland for a year, she'd told him as they lingered in Joseph's dining room after their last Sunday lunch together, their families having left them alone.

With her father making a lot of money, she'd added with a degree of embarrassment, he'd got the finishing school idea into his head, and although she wasn't at all keen on going, he wouldn't listen to her. He believed it was something she ought to do, given he could afford it, and that was that. It would set her up, he'd repeated whenever she'd raised the subject, though for what, he hadn't been able to explain.

But the war had made travel in Europe impossible, and the plan had had to be postponed.

Knowing that she wouldn't yet be going abroad, her aunt had asked her to go and stay with her on the south coast, saying she'd enjoy Marian's company. Henry Ames had accepted the invitation on behalf of his daughter, and she'd be leaving London in two weeks' time, which was the week after Robert's month in London would have come to an end. Because this was now a long-standing arrangement, she was obliged to go. And if the war ended before too long, she'd probably have to take up her place at the finishing school, she'd added in thinly veiled misery.

A weighty silence had hung between them.

Had there been no Lily, he probably would have asked if he could write to her, and perhaps visit her from time to time, and had he done so, he'd known instinctively that her answer would've been yes.

But there *was* a Lily.

And the weeks with Marian had shown him that although he enjoyed Marian's company enormously, and despite her suitability, as his father would have put it, what he felt for Marian didn't come anywhere near what he felt for Lily, and he knew that it never would. His feelings towards Marian were of liking and friendship, but he'd never, at any time, come near to feeling so much as a fraction of the aching that he daily felt for Lily.

Later that afternoon, he and Marian had said an awkward goodbye, both of them saying how much they hoped to meet again when Marian returned to London.

Shortly after she'd left, he'd completed the London project conjured up for him by his father, and was told that he could start going to Chorton again. He'd promptly arranged to go to Chorton at the end of the week.

For the rest of that week he'd been in a turmoil, knowing how close he was to seeing Lily again.

By the time he reached Chorton, he was in a state of heightened anticipation. He'd swiftly unpacked, made straight for the old barn as he'd promised Lily he would, climbed the stairs to the loft, and waited for Lily.

He hadn't had long to wait.

In no time at all, she was standing at the top of the steps looking heart-stoppingly beautiful. God, how he'd wanted her!

And after a month apart, she'd clearly felt the same.

They'd come together and hadn't been able to stop themselves, and what followed had lifted him to the heights of ecstasy.

She had shown him the strength of her love for him, and he'd shown her the strength of his love for her. And in that moment of utter bliss as they lay there, their arms around each other, their passion spent, he'd known that he could never, ever feel about anyone the way he felt about Lily – she was, and always would be, the love of his life.

Outside the bedroom, the stairs creaked.

His back to the door, he heard her enter quietly and shut the door. A moment later, the bed beside him sank a little, and then settled. He turned to face her, took her hand and kissed it, and she nestled close to him. His last thought before drifting into sleep was to dismiss Lily's belief that his father would never accept her. Of course, he would. Of that Robert was sure.

* * *

Cold dawn was breaking in Primrose Hill.

Joseph lay in his bed, his eyes wide open. From the time that he'd come up the stairs, turned off the light, climbed into the bed next to Maud's, hoping for sleep, his eyes had been open. Stubborn sleep had refused to give him any respite from his anxiety about Robert, and he'd lain there worrying, wondering how on earth he could free Robert from the situation he'd got himself into.

He was absolutely certain that Robert would come to regret his marriage – a regret that could ultimately destroy Robert's life. But he also knew that Robert, with the pride of youth, would never confide in him and ask for his help. And much of the blame for that lay at his feet, he recognised.

From the moment he'd set eyes on Lily's pretty, but empty face, he'd felt hostility. She was after a comfortable life, he was sure, and in Robert could see a way of getting it, and he'd never attempted to hide his feelings. And when she'd trapped Robert into marriage, which he was sure had been a deliberate act, his hatred of her plumbed a new depth.

Because he loved Robert, although Robert would never believe it, he wanted the best for him, and despite his disappointment in Robert's marriage, at the time of his father's death, he'd been wondering how to help his son without him knowing. So when Robert was left the Hampstead house, not only had it been a great surprise, but also a huge relief.

Maud and the others had instantly assumed he'd be angry that Dorothy and Nellie had been passed over, not to mention Charles's children, Louisa and Christopher, but they were mistaken – he hadn't in the least bit minded.

Dorothy, who'd shamed the family by marrying a German, was somewhere in Germany – he'd written to her about her grandfather's death, but wouldn't be writing again. Nellie was a girl, so she'd get married, hopefully to someone considerably wealthier than Walter Shawcross, with whom she was currently infatuated, and she would go to live with her husband in a suitable home. As for Louisa and Christopher, they would be well provided for by their parents. Sarah was wealthy in her own right. So, no, he was delighted that Robert had somewhere to live that hadn't involved some subtle intervention on his part.

Over dinner, when he and Maud were still digesting the news about the house, he'd mentioned his concerns about Robert's happiness. He should put it out of his mind, she'd told him – a trifle impatiently, he'd thought. His open antagonism towards

Lily right from the start had ensured that Robert would stick to her like a limpet, and now they must all accept the inevitable consequences of that, and stop dwelling on what might've been.

Maud, he'd realised at that instant, was never going to be a willing ally in whatever plan he devised to save Robert from years of misery and regret.

And Charles was unlikely to be much use, either.

There was nothing wrong with Charles, but he wasn't a risk-taker. He was a sound enough man, but totally impractical, and with a stultifying over-abundance of caution, along with a complete lack of imagination and any real drive. Both he and his father had been greatly relieved when Charles, at the end of his years of schooling, had turned down a polite invitation to join the family firm, and had drifted into banking, where he'd stayed.

Since the day that Charles had first introduced Sarah to the family, he'd asked himself frequently what a competent, ambitious woman like Sarah had seen in his far-from-ambitious brother, and he'd actually thought on several occasions recently that he'd seen the same question in Sarah's eyes.

Charles would take the same line as Maud, he was sure. He would say that whether or not they liked it, Lily was now officially part of their family, and there was nothing anyone could do to change that.

Well, he didn't like it.

And there *would* be something that someone could do to change it. And that someone was him. He just had to come up with a plan. And he would.

6

KNIGHTSBRIDGE

February 1920

Joseph settled heavily into one of the leather armchairs in the library in Charles's house, loosened a couple of waistcoat buttons, and took a pipe from one of the pockets in his jacket and a tin of Three Nuns tobacco from another. Charles's cook always served a pretty good lunch, he thought as he put both the tin and the pipe on the mahogany side table next to him, and the sole they'd been given that day had been no exception.

Sitting back, he closed his eyes and wondered how best to introduce the subject of Lily. He hadn't yet got the remotest idea what to do about her, but he was pretty sure that whatever plan he came up with, he'd need Charles's help to execute it. Charles would instinctively recoil in horror, of course, from the idea of taking any form of action against his nephew's wife, so he'd have to be approached in such a way that he couldn't say no.

The armchair across from him creaked and he opened his eyes to see that Charles had sat down. Straightening up, he smiled at his brother.

'Has your cook ever been known to deliver a sub-standard meal?' he asked, shifting his position to make himself more comfortable. 'She certainly hasn't whenever I've visited.'

'She wouldn't dare! Sarah would be out in the kitchen in a trice, scolding her and telling her where she'd gone wrong.'

Both laughed.

'But seriously,' Charles went on, 'I really *am* afraid that Sarah might say something one day that causes Mrs Morris to up sticks and leave. With more and more women now thinking they can do better for themselves than go into service, it could be well-nigh impossible to replace her if she left.'

'I shouldn't worry too much on the score. Sarah's too clever to let that happen. She knows the situation as well as anyone else, and I can't see her wanting to don an apron and start peeling potatoes, can you?' Joseph paused, picked up his pipe and tobacco tin, opened the tin and took out a wad of tobacco. 'Out of interest,' he asked with studied casualness as he pushed the tobacco firmly into the bowl of his pipe, 'did Sarah say anything about last Sunday's lunch at Robert's?'

'Not really. She can't imagine what he sees in such an unsophisticated woman – apart from the obvious, of course. But as far as she's concerned, they're married now, they've got a child, and we're just going to have to put up with her. At least, unlike Robert, we don't have to live with her.'

'That's pretty much what Maud said.'

Charles smiled. 'But knowing you, Joseph, what you really want to know is what Sarah thinks about Robert getting the house that we'd always understood would one day belong to you, me and Thomas. That's what you're actually asking, isn't it?'

Joseph sighed inwardly. That hadn't been the path he'd wanted to go down. Sarah obviously wouldn't have been concerned by his father's action. With her large private income, neither she, Charles, nor their children, would ever be in want of anything.

He swallowed his irritation at being diverted from the subject he was trying to pursue, and said to Charles with forced cheerfulness, 'How well you know me, Charles. I'm hoping she's taken it in her stride – she's a sensible woman with a good brain. It's a shame she's not a man,' he added drily. 'She'd have been an asset to the company.'

'God forbid, don't let her hear you say that!' Charles exclaimed, holding his hands in the air in feigned horror. 'With women now able to be solicitors and barristers, and even enter Parliament, Sarah would have no compunction at all in joining the firm. A week later she'd oust you and take over the management of the company. In less than a month, you'd find yourself locked away in a dusty back room.'

'You'd be amazed at how appealing that sounds,' Joseph said with a smile. 'What with unemployment and restlessness on the rise among factory and shipyard workers, not to mention the coal miners, and with the terrible inflation we've got, and the increases in income tax that are cutting into our earnings and profits, being relieved of all responsibility for others has a most attractive ring.'

'Take it from me, there's nothing appealing in being bossed around by Sarah.' Charles sat back and stretched out his legs. 'But to go back to the Hampstead house. We knew he'd cut off Dorothy for marrying the Hun, but I think Sarah was quite upset to see Robert favoured in such a way over Nellie. She's very fond of Nellie, you know.'

Joseph nodded. He and Maud had often remarked that Nellie and Sarah were more like sisters than aunt and niece, and when Maud had announced after lunch her intention of sitting quietly in the reception room, he hadn't been in the least bit surprised that Nellie and Sarah had gone off to the shops together.

And as the two of them had set off, arm in arm, he'd observed to Charles that he fervently hoped that Sarah had sufficient energy after such a lunch to keep Nellie in check. Prices were going up, and the Knightsbridge shops weren't cheap at the best of times.

'Her energy's limitless, alas,' Charles said gloomily. 'There's never a minute when she's not behind me, urging me on. I don't mind telling you, it can be quite exhausting.'

'That may be, but you appear to be thriving on it,' Joseph said brightly, feeling that he ought to say something positive, despite Charles looking as spiritless as ever.

Charles snorted. 'If I do, it's because I know I'll have a few hours' peace while the girls are out. I expect they'll be gone for a while, particularly as they don't have Louisa in tow. Although Lou's only ten, she and Sarah invariably rub each other up the wrong way, especially over clothes. And as there's never a time when she doesn't need something new, that happens a lot. Christopher promises to be much easier than his sister, which is a great relief.'

Joseph nodded. 'Don't tell me about girls! Nellie seems to buy a new outfit every other minute. My wallet's looking forward to the day she marries and becomes a drain on someone else.'

He cleared his throat, about to move the conversation on to the topic of Lily and Robert.

'While we're on the subject of Nellie and marriage,' Charles continued, leaning across to the side table to pick up his pipe, 'what d'you think of Walter? I obviously like him or I wouldn't have brought him to Chorton with me that day, but I sense you've never really taken to him.' He paused to blow into the stem of his pipe.

Joseph groaned inwardly. If they were ever going to talk about Lily, they'd have to get on to the subject very soon.

'It's not that,' he said quickly. 'He seems a nice enough lad. It's just that I'd like Nellie to set her sights higher than an articled pupil. Regarding the future—'

'But he won't be articled forever, will he?' Charles cut in. 'He's a bright lad and he'll make an excellent solicitor. As for his family, if this is about money, as I suspect it is, they may not be rich, but they're not exactly destitute. I believe the yearly premium for getting articles is now somewhere between three hundred and five hundred guineas, and they're obviously managing to pay that each year. True, that isn't sufficient for Walter to be able to put money into the business in the way that our mother and both of our wives did, but personally, I think Nellie could do a lot worse. It's up to you, though – it's *your* consent she'll need, not mine.'

'Well, I certainly hope he doesn't ask for it. He's not what I would've chosen for her.'

But he wouldn't be voicing his disapproval to Nellie, he vowed to himself, not after what had happened with Robert. He'd learned his lesson the hard way. His open hostility had probably pushed Robert closer to Lily.

And anyway, there was no need for him to worry about Nellie – she wasn't even eighteen yet, and wouldn't be until June, he thought, shifting in his seat. At her young age she was more than likely to change her mind about Walter. Women were known to be fickle.

'The world's a different place – the war did that,' Charles was saying, a note of warning in his voice. 'Young people have minds of their own these days.'

Joseph shrugged impatiently. 'That may be, but one thing that hasn't changed, and never will, I'm sure, is that children from families of any standing need to ally themselves with suitable partners. With new opportunities in construction opening up daily, we need to be in a position to take advantage of them. Being women, our daughters can't work for the company, but they benefit from it, and the least they should do is contribute to it in the only way they can.'

'You old romantic, Joseph,' Charles murmured.

They looked at each other, and then both laughed.

'Fair enough,' Joseph said, smiling. 'I won't put it to Nellie quite like that. And it'd be pointless to do so, anyway – she'd only throw Alice back at me, even though it's irrelevant, given the circumstances.'

'And she'd be right. Alice may not have had a penny to her name, but nevertheless, she's a real asset. Given Thomas's war injuries, marrying a nurse is the one sensible thing he's done since the foolhardy moment he signed on the line and went off to fight.'

'I take your point,' Joseph said. He glanced surreptitiously at his watch, and cleared his throat. 'Talking of wives, what are your thoughts about Lily these days?'

'None really,' Charles remarked in mild surprise. 'She's obviously completely unsuitable for Robert. I'm sure she makes the bedroom side of things enviably pleasant, but other than that, it's hard to see what they've got in common. Apart from their son, of course.'

'And that keeps me awake at night, Charles. To be honest, I now wish I'd handled things very differently.'

'Well, we all warned you. You should've taken our advice and invited her to Chorton as often as possible, getting as many of the family there as you could. Robert would have soon seen her deficiencies. But it's too late now – there's not a thing you can do.'

Joseph drew deeply on his pipe, took it from his mouth and studied its bowl. 'Not necessarily,' he said at last.

Charles frowned. 'What does that mean?'

'Just what it sounds. Robert will come to regret being tied to Lily, if he hasn't already done so. It was a youthful infatuation that would never have ended in marriage if she hadn't become pregnant. I'm sure the pregnancy was deliberate on her part.'

Charles stared at him in concern. 'I agree with everything you say. But much as you might want to alter the situation, there's nothing you really *can* do, is there?'

'Maybe, maybe not. But as you all seem to think my resistance pushed him into the marriage, which I now acknowledge could well be true, it's up to me to get him out of the mess he's in.'

Charles leaned forward, rested his elbows on his knees and stared intently at Joseph. 'I've got a really bad feeling about this, Joseph. They're married, and they've got a child. I think you should let it go.'

'I would if I thought he'd always be content with his choice.'

Charles straightened up and laughed in derision. 'And how many people are always content, as you put it? A little dissatisfaction on Robert's part is hardly a reason to interfere.'

'It'll end up more than that, I'm sure. Robert will come to feel imprisoned, and be really miserable. He's got his whole his life ahead of him, Charles. Who'd want their son to be unhappy throughout his adult life?'

'And what about James?' Charles asked, with a gesture of despair. 'Lily is James's mother as well as Robert's wife.'

'Believe me, I'm thinking of James as much as I'm thinking of Robert. If a marriage is bad, it affects a child. I don't want my grandson living in an unhappy home.'

'But as I say, what can you do about it?'

'I don't yet know, but as soon as I do, I'll tell you.'

'You aren't thinking of divorce, are you? Apart from the expense, one or other would have to prove adultery, but neither would want to be seen as adulterous, particularly Lily. She'd become a social outcast, and James would automatically be given to Robert. She'd never agree to that.'

Joseph gave a wave of dismissal. 'I know all that. I've looked into divorce and ruled it out. Apart from anything, it'd be Robert who'd have to petition for divorce, and he'd refuse to do so. And the same goes for legal separation, which would've been much less satisfactory, anyway.'

'Well, I'm glad we're agreed on that,' Charles said, sitting back with a theatrical sigh of relief.

'Divorce was never a serious consideration. It could harm Robert's chances of making a good second marriage, and nothing must jeopardise that. But apart from that, he's got too nice a nature to put the mother of his child through everything a divorce entails. I know his limitations.'

Charles raised his eyebrows. 'You see kindness and a nice nature as limitations?'

Joseph smiled. 'Perhaps I could've put it better. But there's another reason why divorce is ruled out – it wouldn't guarantee that we never saw Lily again. She's just the sort of woman to turn up in a year or two, resentful and out to make trouble. No, it's got to be something more final than that.'

'I don't know,' Charles said, shaking his head. 'Playing around with other people's lives is risky. Robert's a smart lad, and I'm sure he'll make a go of his marriage. If I were you, I'd accept the situation and leave it there.'

'You're probably right.' Joseph paused. 'But if I *do* come up with something, can I count on you for help?'

Charles hesitated. He brushed an imaginary piece of fluff from his sleeve.

'After all,' Joseph went on, tapping the pipe into the ashtray on the table next to him, his eyes on Charles, 'you and I are closer than a great many brothers, what with the firm's money being entrusted to your bank. And we're talking about a far from insignificant sum, for which the bank has thanked you in different ways over the years.'

'And you know how grateful I am,' Charles said quietly.

'And I also know that it goes against the grain for you to take chances, Charles, but I'd like to think you'd overcome any initial reserve and help me if I asked.' He paused, and again tapped his pipe against the ashtray. 'If you like, you could look upon it as a way of thanking me for Linford & Son's continued support for your bank.'

'I see,' Charles said slowly. 'In that case, of course I'll help.'

Joseph gave him a broad smile. 'Good man. But let's forget about all that for the moment. Didn't you say something about a wonderful port?'

7

KENTISH TOWN

March 1920

When Arthur Joseph Linford had purchased the builders' yard in 1875, he'd known what he was doing. Kentish Town, although not far from central London, wasn't considered a desirable residential area, so he was able to get a lot of ground for a very reasonable price. It meant that the yard had plenty of room for their carts, and there were many labourers in the vicinity looking for work.

Furthermore, in addition to the simple, but quite large, brick storage building on the far side of the yard, there was also a brick house with a grey slate roof on the opposite side, the front door of which opened on to the pavement, and at the side of which there was a small garden.

He was very excited at having found business premises which also offered on-site accommodation.

As Arthur and his young wife had walked hand in hand through the three small rooms on either side of the narrow entrance hall, and had then climbed the steep central staircase to the landing and seen the four small bedrooms, he'd realised instantly that there were sufficient rooms in the house for two company offices downstairs, and an adequate living space for him and Bertha during the week.

He'd ask his men to check the drainage, and the arrangements for the disposal of the waste in the ash pit in the corner of the garden at the side of the house, he'd told her as they finished exploring the upstairs bedrooms and stood on the landing, looking around. And he'd get them to install running tap water in the kitchen and a hot-water boiler. They'd leave the outside privy where it was, but he'd build an indoor water closet leading off the landing, and he'd fit out the two attic rooms for a housekeeper. The house already had gas lighting, and a cellar in which to store coal for the boiler and fires, so on the whole there was very little they'd need to do to it.

As they'd started walking slowly back down the stairs, he'd seen a degree of uncertainty on Bertha's face, as if she wasn't quite sure why he was suggesting such changes to the house, but was beginning to have the glimmer of an idea, and sincerely hoped she was wrong.

For the first time, it occurred to him to question how she might react to his plan, and he'd felt a sudden nervousness. Halfway down the staircase, he'd taken a deep breath, and had told her that he thought they should live there during the week.

She'd stopped, and turned to him in less-than-pleased surprise.

'Here!' she'd exclaimed.

Although her father had put a large sum of money at his disposal on their marriage, he'd said, his voice shaking slightly, and he could certainly use some of it to get them a better house in London, the most sensible thing to do at that present time would be to put all of the money into the company. If they did that, they'd be in the position to take maximum advantage of the growing demand for houses from the increasing population.

At the moment, poorer people had no choice but to continue renting the back-to-back terraced housing that Linford & Sons and others had been building for many years, he'd told her, his words tumbling over themselves, but he was convinced that the days of such houses were numbered, especially in the south.

The politicians kept on trying to get clauses into Acts, banning such housing, he'd said, gripping her hand over-tightly in his nervousness. So far, they'd always been forced to drop the clauses in the face of strong opposition from industrial towns, which claimed that if it weren't for low-cost houses like back-to-backs, house prices would go up, and therefore so would the rent. But one day the banning clauses would get through, he said, and Linford & Sons needed to be ready for that day.

'I see,' she'd murmured.

And the demand wasn't just for houses in town, he'd continued as they started walking down the stairs again. There were signs that workmen and people with a little money were starting to want properties that weren't as cramped – they wanted more space, with a garden, that was possibly on the edge of the town rather than in the middle. With the railways expanding as they were, especially in the north and north-east of London, people could now rent a house slightly out of the town and still get into work.

If they used all of the money her father had given them, he'd urged her, they'd be able to build a large number of houses like that, and that's what he wanted to do. They could get themselves a bigger house in a more attractive part of London later on.

And they had Chorton House, after all, their gift from her father at the time of their marriage, he'd added when she didn't say anything. So they could escape to Oxfordshire at weekends.

But to live in Chorton during the week would be impossible – it was much too far from the yard. By living in Kentish Town, in the house which came with the premises, they wouldn't need to eat into their capital.

Did she agree, he'd asked anxiously.

She'd given a loud sigh, and looked at him ruefully. It wasn't how she'd imagined them beginning their married life, she'd told him, but she trusted him to know what was best for them, and she agreed.

Hugging her hard, he'd assured her that they wouldn't be in Kentish Town for any longer than necessary, and by the time she was pregnant with Thomas eight years later, he'd been able to make good his promise, and they'd moved into a large house in Hampstead, close both to Hampstead Village and to the Heath.

With his business thriving, and with no further need for living space in the Kentish Town house, he'd turned three of the downstairs rooms into the sort of offices befitting a company of the reputation and size of Linford & Sons.

And that's how things had remained at Kentish Town until Thomas came home from the war, missing his right leg and three fingers on his right hand.

Alice stood in the open doorway to Thomas's office, watching him. He'd moved his wheelchair across to the sash window, as he often did, and was sitting there motionless, staring towards the straggle of plane trees on the opposite side of the road, which partially blocked from sight the line of run-down shops behind them.

'It's typical April weather even though it's only March,' she said, going further into the room. 'Although I sheltered from the rain, I still got quite wet.'

'So, it's lucky me, is it, that I can't go out walking, and have to stay home?'

'You know I didn't mean that,' she said, opening her umbrella and standing it in the corner of the room to dry. 'And you know perfectly well you could go out for a walk if you wore your prosthesis, and you also know that if you didn't want to wear it, I'd be happy to wheel you wherever you wanted to go.'

He didn't move, but continued to look straight ahead.

'Is there anything I can get you?' she asked, unbuttoning her raincoat.

'A proper right leg and a good hand.'

She hesitated, took off her coat and hung it over one of the high-backed wooden chairs at the table, and then dragged the other chair across the floor, and sat down next to him.

He glanced at her sideways and scowled. 'By the look on your face, this is a pull-yourself-together talk. Don't bother, Alice – you'd be wasting your time. I've heard it all before.' He turned back to the view.

She angled her chair to see his face. 'I know that, and I wasn't going to waste my time, as you put it – when you're in your self-pitying mood, there's no getting you out of it. No, I was going to tell you that I bumped into Joseph. He was going into the yard as I was walking past, so we stopped and chatted for a moment.'

'Since he seldom talks about anything other than the company, that must have been riveting.'

She smiled. 'You're right, it *was* about the firm. He was full of the new North London development, and what excellent progress they'd made in a very little time.' She hesitated. 'He's taking Charles to see it on Friday, and also Robert and Lily, and then they're going back to Primrose Hill for lunch. He asked if we'd like to go, too. He said he'd pick us up. He was in a hurry this morning, but he said he'd drop in tomorrow and ask you himself.' She paused. 'I'd quite like to see it, so shall we go?'

'You can if you want, but I'm not.'

She leaned closer and smiled encouragingly. 'I think we *should* go, Thomas. You need to get out more, and it'd be nice for you to go somewhere with your brothers.'

'You mean, so they can feel good about themselves, being seen taking a cripple out!'

She straightened up. 'That's not the reason Joseph wants you to join them, and you know it. He thought you'd be interested in seeing the new building. After all, you've done a lot of work on it behind the scenes, and will be doing plenty more. That's all it is.'

'Don't be so naïve, Alice – it's not about me, it's about them. They think that taking me out for a walk will help them stop feeling guilty about not fighting. About being asleep in their warm beds when we were risking our lives night and day, drowning in mud – filthy, stinking, oozing sort of mud that sucks you in – or trying to survive in cramped, dirty front-line trenches, dodging rats as big as cats, being shelled on from every direction. They were safe at home while I was losing my best friend, who'd been a part of me for most of my life. Can you imagine what it was like to see David die in front of my eyes? One minute he was scrambling up the slope next to me, and the next he'd been blown to smithereens and there was virtually nothing left of him – just a helmet. And where were my brothers during all of this? Ah, yes, safe at home, making money out of the war.'

She groaned inwardly.

She'd lost count of the number of times she'd heard the same thing from Thomas, and the number of times she'd told him he was being unfair on his brothers. The work they'd done at home while Thomas was fighting had been essential for the war effort – building airstrips and repairing airfields, and doing clearance and other building work. And with so many bankers away fighting, Charles had been needed at the bank. But Thomas didn't want to hear it.

'They've no reason to feel guilty, and I'm sure they don't,' she settled for. 'They're just desperately upset you were hurt, and want to do whatever they can to help.'

'You're wrong. They feel guilty that they didn't have the guts to face the horror of war – all that gas, the relentless machine-gun fire, feeling one's skin being torn off on barbed-wire defences – and so they should.'

'No, they shouldn't,' she said quietly. 'It was your choice to fight – no one forced you to. In fact, it was just the opposite. Both Joseph and Charles have told me how they begged you to stay at home and help with the contracted work, but you refused point-blank. You and David were going to fight, and that was that. So, you can't really blame them for what happened to you.'

'I can do as I like.' He swung his wheelchair round and faced her. 'But you go, if you want.'

'Sitting here all day, every day, Thomas, feeling sorry for yourself, is the very worst thing you could do. If you practised using your left hand, like I keep suggesting, you'd soon be able to use it almost as well as you did your right, and you wouldn't feel as helpless. You need to get out, and going with Joseph on Friday would be a start.' She hesitated, leaned forward and took hold of his good hand. 'Promise me you'll tell Joseph we'll go with him. Please, Thomas.'

He pulled his hand away. 'I promise,' he said, his face sullen. 'There, satisfied?'

'Yes, I am.' She stood up and moved the wooden chair back to its position by the table. 'I'll make us some tea,' she said with a smile.

'Alice!' she heard him call as she reached the door. Her hand on the door handle, she paused and turned towards him.

'I'm sorry,' he said. 'I hardly slept last night. I kept on having those nightmares again, and waking up sweating, with my heart thumping all over the place. And feeling scared all over again. But you must know it as I woke you up. But you also know I love you, don't you, even though I can be really horrible at times? I can hear myself and I hate myself, but I can't seem to stop.'

'I *do* understand, Thomas,' she reassured him. 'It's probably not much help to tell you that attacks of anxiety are normal after everything you've been through, but they are, and that's the truth. They *will* pass, though.'

'I certainly hope so, for your sake as much as for mine. And you can thank Joseph and tell him we'll go with him on Friday.'

She smiled at him, and nodded. 'I'll get us that tea and perhaps we'll drink it in the sitting-room. You should have a change from the office whenever you can, even if it's only going into the next room.' And she went out into the hall.

Closing the door behind her, she leaned back against the wood in relief.

Thank goodness she hadn't mentioned that she'd seen Charles, too, that morning, she thought, Thomas being in the mood he was in. But at least she'd be going somewhere other than the shops on the Friday when they went out with Joseph, and she'd have Lily to talk to. She looked forward to that. She'd hadn't seen that much of Lily so far, but when she had, she'd sensed that Lily could use a friend.

And she knew that *she* certainly could.

Living with Thomas was far from easy.

8

THE FOLLOWING FRIDAY

With Robert at his side, and Alice, Thomas and Charles behind him, Joseph led the way across the site of the development under way in the north of London, and came to a stop in the middle of the wide expanse of muddy ground. All around them were half-built roofless brick structures and tarpaulins. He beamed at the small group and then, with apologies to Robert, who already knew what he was about to tell the others, he began to explain the changes in company policy.

Linford & Sons would continue selling to potential landlords, he assured them, and also with being landlords themselves – the rental division would carry on administering that side of things – but their emphasis was now going to be on affordable houses for sale, which they were building in pairs, rather than in lines. He then suggested that they take a look at one or two of the new houses under construction, to see the internal layout.

'Mind you don't slip in the mud,' he called after them, as Charles led the way to the nearest two houses, followed by Alice and Thomas.

'I take it Lily didn't want to come, after all?' Joseph said, turning back to Robert.

'You're wrong about that – she did. But James has got a nasty cold and she didn't want to leave him.'

Joseph raised his eyebrows. 'You no longer have a nanny?'

'Of course, we do. But when a child's not well, it wants its mother.'

'If you want to think that, so be it.'

Robert glared at his father. 'If you're trying to make me angry with Lily, it's not working. She's hardly at fault for being a good mother.'

Joseph shrugged, and both turned towards the others, who'd started to make their way back to them, Charles walking alongside Thomas, slowing his pace to match his brother's, and Alice trailing behind them.

'So, what d'you think?' Joseph asked when they reached him.

'I can't say they look much different from the rows of identical houses you used to build on the smaller plots you bought from farmers,' Charles said. 'At a glance, the interior seems pretty much the same. And you're still using local bricks, and presumably ordering the decorative detail from catalogues. That's *your* area, isn't it, Thomas?'

'I do other things, too,' Thomas snapped.

'The internal layout's not quite the same,' Joseph corrected. 'Most of the houses have three bedrooms upstairs and an internal bathroom. There's obviously no longer a need for servants' quarters.'

'I noticed that. Also the lack of outside privies. That's progress indeed,' Charles said.

'These days everyone wants a plumbed-in kitchen and an internal water closet, and we're giving them that. We're making sure that we rigidly follow the new regulations about drainage and sewage, though, and that there's separate clean running water for drinking.'

'How clever of you, Joseph, to know what people want like that,' Alice ventured, her eyes full of admiration.

Joseph smiled warmly at her. 'You get a feel for it, Alice, and it's my job to know. But it's a team effort. Thomas does his bit, and Robert, too.' He turned to Charles. 'This'll interest you, Charles, being a money man – another thing we're doing is significantly altering the way we work so as to cut our costs. We've no choice. Most of our wartime contracts have come to an end, and we've wasted a valuable opportunity for getting an input of money.'

He glared pointedly at Robert.

'Could you be trying to say something, Father?' Robert asked, his voice soothing.

Joseph scowled, and turned back to Charles. 'We're employing fewer men, and instead of buying equipment, we're hiring it when we need it. And we're reducing our fixed overheads by having only a small staff, who can deal with just about everything.'

Charles stared at him in surprise. 'But even if some of your contracts *have* finished, if there's a leap in demand as you say there is, need you cut back quite so drastically?'

'Oh, there's definitely a demand. There's been a housing shortage since before the war. A third of all households have too little space, and far too many are having to share with another family. The cuts are because the capital outlay for building houses for sale is far greater than building houses for rent. It means we have to free up as much capital as we can in order to profit from the situation.'

Charles nodded. 'I can see that.'

No one knew what the future held, Joseph continued, his voice doom-laden. The central government, convinced that private builders would be unable to provide sufficient quality housing at economic rents, had started to subsidise local-authority building, and local authorities could prove to be formidable competitors.

'Without extra funds coming in, we've no choice but to cut costs,' he finished, and frowned again at Robert.

'And the high demand for houses to buy is the only reason we're building such houses, is it, Father, despite the extra costs involved?' Robert asked mildly.

Joseph grunted.

Robert grinned at his father and turned to Alice. 'Father conveniently forgot to mention that rents are still pegged at their pre-war level, Alice,' he told her. 'They were frozen during the war in an emergency Act of Parliament at a time when there was rapid inflation and a shortage of housing, and the Act hasn't yet been repealed. It means that rents are uneconomic in the face of the spiralling costs of building materials and labour, so there's now no incentive to build low-cost housing for rent.' He looked in amusement at his father. 'As much as anything, that's behind our need to make savings, wouldn't you say, Father?'

'He's got you there, Joseph,' Charles said with a smile.

Joseph laughed, and clapped Robert on the shoulder. 'Point taken.'

'What about lawyers and accountants?' Charles asked. 'Will you still retain them?'

Joseph shook his head. ''Fraid not. We'll hire them locally when we need them.'

'I've got to take my hat off to you, Joseph,' Charles said in approval. 'You're always streaks ahead of everyone else. No wonder the company's thriving, despite the country being so unsettled. If you're a fraction as canny as your father, Robert, Linford & Sons has got a golden future.'

Joseph nodded his thanks to Charles. 'Well, I think that's about it,' he said. 'Thomas has probably stood for long enough, so I suggest we call it a day and get back to Primrose Hill. Maud's arranged a lunch for us all. I assume you're joining us, Charles?'

'If I may, I will, thanks,' Charles said. 'And I'll drop Thomas and Alice back in Kentish Town afterwards – it's more or less on my way home.'

'Fine. It'll save me going out again.'

'I don't think so.' Thomas turned to Joseph. 'You brought us, Joseph, so you can take us back after lunch. If it's not too much trouble, that is.'

Alice glanced quickly at Thomas, and then at Charles, and went red.

Ouch, Robert thought.

'Of course, it isn't,' Joseph said quickly. 'Anything that gives me more time with your charming wife is more than welcome. We don't see enough of you both as it is.' He paused. 'You know, Alice,' he added, 'I was thinking that it might benefit you and Thomas if you learned to drive. If you want, we can free up a company vehicle for you. You see more women drivers these days, so why not you, too? I know that driving isn't something that really interests a woman, and they'll obviously never be as good as a man, but with Thomas's limited mobility, it might be worth thinking about.'

'I'd be happy to help you learn,' Charles said. 'You only have to ask.'

'Alice and I are fine as we are,' Thomas retorted sharply. 'She doesn't want to drive. So, thank you for the suggestion, but no, thank you. Right, Joseph. As you said a moment ago, I've stood for long enough. I'm ready to go.'

* * *

Sitting at the table, waiting for their dinner to be served, Lily stared across at Robert and wondered what he'd been thinking about since he returned from the trip with Joseph. He'd hardly said anything since he'd got back, and for all the attention he was paying her now, she might just as well have stayed in the nursery with James and eaten her dinner up there.

'Poor little James has been snuffling all day,' she said at last, in an attempt to get a conversation going.

'I'm sure he enjoyed having you with him, then.' He stopped running a finger around the rim of his glass and glanced at her across the table. 'You know, Lily,' he went on, 'you mustn't worry about leaving him with Annie. It's her job. I'm not criticising you, but I would've liked you to have been with *me* today. You'd have learned something about the company's plans, and Father would've have thought you were interested, and that would have pleased him.' He gave her a wry smile. 'James being ill wasn't an excuse to avoid Father, was it?'

She gave an awkward laugh. 'Just a weeny bit, if I'm honest. I *was* worried about James, but I was probably even more worried about being with your father all day. He really doesn't like me.'

He stared at her in despair. 'He won't if you don't give him a chance to get to know you.'

The door opened and Mrs Bailey came in. Neither spoke while she set down the main course of poached salmon, boiled potatoes, peas and carrots.

'It's tinned peaches for afterwards,' she said as she was leaving the room. 'With custard. It's only powdered, but it's better than nothing.'

The door clicked shut behind Mrs Bailey. Lily got up, ran across to Robert and hugged him tightly. 'I promise I'll come next time, Robert, even if James has got a really terrible cold. And even if it'll be just you, me and your frightening father.' She bent down and kissed the top of his head.

He turned to her and put his hand on the side of her face to stop her moving back. Slowly, he ran his fingers down her cheek. 'I love you so much, Lily. It's why I want you with me for every possible minute of the day. You don't know how much I wish at times that it was just you and me, and that we could shut out the rest of the world.'

For a long moment, each stared into the eyes of the other. Then Lily lowered her head and their lips met.

She drew back, smiled at him and returned to her seat. Picking up her knife and fork, she started to eat, and he did the same.

'So, are you going to tell me what happened today, Robert?' she asked as they'd sat in silence for several minutes.

'Nothing.'

'I don't believe you. You've not been your usual self since you got back, and I can tell that something's bothering you. And don't say it's to do with me not going today, because it's not.'

He hesitated. 'You're right – I *have* had something on my mind since I got home, and you're right again that it's nothing to do with anything you've done or not done. But happen is the wrong word. Nothing actually happened. It's just that there was something a little strange, and I haven't been able to stop thinking about it.'

'Strange in what way?'

Robert put down his knife and fork, and sat back.

'Well, it was two things, actually. Uncle Charles suggested running Alice and Uncle Thomas back to Kentish Town after lunch so Father wouldn't have to go out again, but Uncle Thomas wouldn't have it. He insisted that Father took them home. He was quite sharp about it, in fact.'

'But you're always saying your Uncle Thomas is permanently angry with everyone. He was probably just being awkward for the sake of it.'

'I might've thought that, too, if it hadn't been for what was said a minute or two afterwards.'

And he told her about Joseph's suggestion that Alice learn to drive, and that Charles's offer of help was rudely refused.

'It would be so much easier for everyone if Alice could drive,' he added.

'And you don't think it was just Thomas being awkward again?'

He shook his head. 'Thinking about it, no, I don't.'

'But why would he be like that?'

'I'm not sure, but whenever we're all together, Uncle Charles is always really friendly towards Alice. Like the rest of us, he feels sorry for her, having to bear the brunt of Uncle Thomas's frequent bad moods. I'm wondering if Uncle Thomas sees such kindness as a criticism of the way he behaves towards Alice.'

She thought for a moment. 'You could be right. Your uncle *is* nice to her – he's nicer to her than he is to me.'

He picked up his knife and fork. 'I'm sure that'll change. Anyway, that's all it was. Eat up and then we'll go and sit in the back room. Mrs Bailey's lit the fire as it's been rather dank today.'

* * *

Sitting close together on the sofa in the rear reception room after dinner, they stared at the log fire blazing in the hearth, their faces gleaming in the red-gold glow thrown out by the burning embers.

'What can you hear?' she asked after a few minutes.

'Nothing,' he said in surprise.

'Nor can I. Mrs Bailey is obviously in her room, probably fast asleep. Annie will definitely be asleep by now – James was a lot of work today as he was a little off colour – and James is certainly asleep or we'd hear him. We're the only ones awake.'

'I see,' he said with a half-smile. 'And where are you going from there?'

'You wanted it to be just you and me at times. Well, it is now.' She glanced up at him from beneath long dark eyelashes. 'D'you remember how in the days before James, we used to go swimming or run through the fields, as free as you like, not wearing a stitch of clothing? And then we'd lie down and do what we were both longing to do. D'you remember that?'

He nodded. 'It feels a long time ago.'

'No one's awake but us. We could feel that same freedom again.'

'What are you saying?'

She stood up, took his hand, and pulled him to his feet. Then she took a step back and faced him.

Very slowly, she undid the buttons that ran down the front of her dress. She let the dress fall to the floor, and kicked it aside. One by one, she removed her undergarments until she stood before him naked, her skin golden in the light of the fire.

She heard him draw in his breath.

'It's your turn now, Robert,' she said, and she went up to him, slid her fingers under the shoulders of his jacket, and began to ease his jacket down over his arms. Then she dropped the jacket to the floor, and raised her hands to his shirt.

9

KNIGHTSBRIDGE

April 1920

Sarah smoothed down the skirt of her olive-green chemise, and stared at herself in the full-length mirror.

She felt a stab of guilt at how much she'd spent on herself, but the outfit would be ideal for her afternoon tea with Nellie. Nellie always credited her with being her fashion inspiration, and she didn't want to let herself down. But while Nellie's imitation of her style was highly flattering, privately she thought that Nellie ought to dress more like the seventeen-year-old she was.

She turned sideways to inspect her profile, pushed a few stray stands of dark brown hair into the chignon beneath the hat, and smiled at the thought of the pleasant afternoon ahead. Although Nellie had been circumspect, she had a pretty good idea what they'd be discussing over tea.

When Nellie had contacted her saying that they were surely due for another tea together, and adding that she was frantic for help, she was pretty sure that it would be something to do with Walter. She knew that Nellie was desperate for Joseph's consent to her marrying Walter, and she probably wanted advice about how to persuade him.

She'd have to do some thinking on the way to meet her niece, she thought, and she picked up her purple felt bag, and went out.

* * *

'I love that dress,' Nellie said, taking a sip of her tea. 'I've been admiring it ever since you got here. I'm so jealous.'

Sarah felt an inward glow of satisfaction. 'I'm glad you like it. It's new. I bought it after my latest row with Charles.'

Nellie giggled. 'Oh, dear. What was it about this time? Although I think I can guess.'

'And I'm sure you'd be right. Yes – there's another opportunity for promotion. But will he apply? No. He's happy to carry on doing what he's been doing since time began, even though it's long stopped being a challenge. It's so frustrating.' She paused, and gave Nellie a guilty smile. 'But I shouldn't really be talking to you like that about your uncle.'

Nellie shrugged. 'That's all right. When you've finished going on about Uncle Charles, I'm going to have a moan about his brother.'

'Well, I won't say I'm exactly surprised,' Sarah said in amusement, and she reached for a small sandwich. 'What's your father done this time?'

'It's what he *hasn't* done!'

'Let me guess, it's about Walter, isn't it?'

'You're right, as always. I absolutely do not want to have to wait until I'm twenty-one to marry him. We love each other and want to get married as soon as possible. But Father's insisting that I find someone with enough money to compensate for Robert marrying penniless Lily, and he won't attempt to get to know

Walter. Whenever I bring Walter home, Father disappears into his study. And when we're at dinner and he can't avoid being in the same room, he hardly speaks to him. It's as if he cares more about the business than my happiness.'

Sarah shook her head. 'I'm afraid that sounds just like Joseph. You'd think he'd have learned his lesson with Robert. His resistance pushed Robert into Lily's arms, and she cleverly made sure he stayed there.'

'I've never known what Robert saw in her. She's pretty, but she's not the only pretty woman around. And she so dull, talking incessantly about James. Someone else's baby's hardly an interesting topic. Nor are family outings. When they came over a couple of days ago, she went on and on about going to Leigh-on-Sea last weekend. And having ice cream. And Robert buying her a bottle of Gardenia perfume, which is her favourite. It was so tedious.'

'I expect there's something more to her that Robert's seen, but we haven't yet. I'm sure we soon will.' Sarah paused and looked up at Nellie. 'Talking of babies, I don't know if your father's told you, but Dorothy's expecting. Joseph wrote to her when your grandfather died, and she wrote back saying she was having a baby in the spring. I don't know exactly when. I was quite surprised that Joseph passed on the news, since it's clear he'll never forgive her for marrying a German, and I don't blame him.'

'I *did* know. Father told me she'd written, but said he wasn't going to reply. As far as he's concerned, she's no longer his daughter. But I don't feel like that – she's my sister and always will be. And I'm surprised at how much I miss her, even though I hardly saw her after she started nursing. I think Father's being too harsh – it's not Dotty's fault she fell in love with a German. No one can help who they fall in love with. It must be awful to be cut off from everyone like that. I told Father I wanted to write to her, but he wouldn't give me her address. I'll find it, though, and then I'll write.'

'You're right that you can't help who you fall in love with, but you *can* help who you marry. No matter how much it hurt, she should never have married a German. Just think how Thomas must feel! It was a German bomb that took off his leg. And the terrible time he had in the trenches. But to go back to your favourite subject,' she said, finishing the sandwich and taking a fairy cake from the tiered china cake-stand on the table, 'namely Walter. I thoroughly approve of him and I'll be happy to help. What d'you want me to do?'

Nellie gave an exaggerated sigh. 'I wish I knew! All I know is, I want to be able to announce my engagement on my eighteenth birthday, and that means at the end of June. Father said he'd get the family together at Chorton for my birthday weekend, and I want to tell everyone then.'

Sarah sat back in her chair and stared across the table at Nellie. 'I don't know about June – that's a tad optimistic. June's only two months away. But I do have an idea about how to break through your father's resistance to Walter. You'd have to be prepared to take this slowly, though.'

Nellie's eyes shone with excitement. 'What is it?'

'I remembered something Charles told me when he came back from visiting the new development. Apparently, Joseph's cutting back on the company's overheads so as to increase their ready capital. One of the ways they'll do that will be by employing local lawyers as they're needed, rather than indefinitely retaining a firm.'

'Walter's really smart. They should use him.'

'Exactly. Charles has always said how sharp he is. But apart from the obvious exceptions of Dorothy's husband and Alice, Linford spouses have always put money into the company, and

Joseph can't see beyond that. I'm sure that Walter's relative lack of money is the only thing your father has against him. But if Joseph could be made to see that Walter's brain and legal expertise could be very valuable to the company, it might just sway his attitude.'

'Walter knows masses about the law.'

'He doesn't need to know masses about the law – he needs to know masses about the law relating to property and buildings. Walter's in a commercial practice, so the cases he deals with there won't involve Property Law. But if he were to keep himself abreast of any relevant changes in the property world, and with property cases before the courts, he'd have something to discuss with your father whenever they met. You know your father – he never tires of talking about anything relating to the company. I'm pretty sure it wouldn't be long before he saw the benefit of having a son-in-law who could help him with the legal side of things.'

'That's it! You're brilliant, Aunt Sarah!'

'Now don't get too excited! Walter's already very busy, and I don't imagine he'll be able to do much before June. But there's sufficient time for him to make a start, assuming he agrees, and even before your birthday weekend, there may be the odd occasion when he could introduce a conversation about something likely to trigger Joseph's interest. An unusual case, for example, that he'd been reading about – property-related, obviously. It'd be a start. If he can do that a few times, I'm sure it would pave the way to being accepted.'

Nellie beamed at Sarah. 'That's so inspired. Walter is bound to agree.'

'Then, on that happy note, shall we throw caution to the winds and each have another cake?'

10

HAMPSTEAD

May 1920

Lily steered the large black pram on to the gravelled path that led from East Heath Road on to Hampstead Heath, and walked in a line parallel with the pond at the bottom of the short grassy slope, making sure that she didn't catch up with Sarah and Maud, who were some way ahead of her, and who had Louisa, Christopher and Nellie at their heels.

The dreaded Sunday lunches weren't getting any easier, whatever Robert might want to pretend, she thought, scowling at their backs.

Glancing behind her, she saw that Joseph was fast approaching, closely followed by Robert and Charles. She turned back quickly to face the path and pushed the pram forward as rapidly as she could.

'Anyone would think you were trying to get away from me.' Joseph's voice came from just behind her shoulder.

She groaned inwardly.

Stopping, she turned to him, and gave an awkward laugh. 'Of

course, I wasn't. I was miles away. I was thinking how lucky we were to live close to such a large open space. James loves it here.' And she began to push the pram again.

'It's why my father chose the house,' he said. 'It somewhat made up for not being able to live at Chorton during the week. And I was thinking along the same lines when I bought the place in Primrose Hill.'

'I like your house,' she said, and desperately searched for something else to say.

To her great relief, Robert moved forward and started walking on the other side of the pram from Joseph.

Joseph dropped back to join Charles.

'I heard you mentioning Chorton just now, Joseph, and I was wondering if Thomas and Alice will be joining us there on Nellie's birthday weekend. D'you know if they are?' Charles asked.

'I haven't heard a word from them, but you can be sure that they *will* come. It's one thing to turn down Robert's invitation to lunch, but quite another to miss Nellie's birthday. I've made it clear they've got to come. She'd be really upset if they didn't.'

'D'you want Sarah and me to pick them up?'

'No need. Maud and I will take them.'

'James might be walking by the time of Nellie's party,' Lily said over her shoulder to Joseph and Charles. 'After all, he'll be almost a year old, and he's so close now.' Both smiled politely. She turned back to the path and glanced at Robert. 'When he starts walking, Robert, we'll have to watch him really closely as he'll be into everything. And especially when we come to the Heath. He loves the ducks, and I can just see him leaping into the water to join them.' She laughed, leaned over the pram and squeezed James's hand.

'I was pleased to see you making an effort with Walter today,'

Charles said to Joseph. 'I thought you'd like him if you gave him a chance.'

'Like's a bit strong, but I'll concede he alerted me to something of interest. Apparently, there are proposals for a Law of Property Act – they're planning to update the law. It's a few years off, Walter reckons, but when it comes, it's bound to address conveyancing, and there'll be a section on mortgages. Both will affect Linford & Sons, so it'll be useful to have advance notice of what's planned. To give Walter his due, he explained it in a way that was easy to grasp.'

'Sounds utterly absorbing.'

Joseph smiled at him. 'Amazingly, it *was*. Walter's going to keep his ear to the ground and let me know how things are developing. You're right, he's a bright lad. And a hard worker. He's got an afternoon and evening's work ahead of him, he told me when he took off after lunch. He's clearly not afraid of knuckling down to what has to be done.'

'Good for Walter. Aha, we seem to be stopping,' Charles remarked, as Lily and Robert came to a halt ahead of them, halfway along the track.

Lily was staring towards a group of children who'd gathered at the water's edge. They were calling loudly to a family of ducks visible among the reeds on the far side of the pond, and furiously waving pieces of bread in the air.

She turned and smiled broadly at Robert. Her smile widened to embrace Joseph and Charles. 'Just look at those children!' she exclaimed. 'Don't they look sweet! I'm going to let James watch them feed the ducks.' And she angled the pram so that James was facing the pond.

Shrugging slightly, Robert glanced apologetically at his father and uncle.

The ducks left the reeds and started swimming strongly

towards the children, ever-widening ripples fanning out in their wake.

'Aren't they adorable, Robert?' she said, as the children began frantically throwing their pieces of bread towards the ducks.

Some of the larger chunks hit the ducks, and they promptly scattered in fear and sped back to the safety of the reeds.

Loud wails filled the air as the children ran back up the slope to their mothers in tears.

'Hm. They're not quite so adorable now,' Robert said. 'Time to go, I think. Father and Uncle Charles will be getting restless. And the others are so far ahead that they're out of sight. It's been nice having a break from the incessant discussion about what to wear for Nellie's birthday, but I suppose we ought to try and catch them up now.'

He put his hand on the pram and turned it firmly to face the way ahead.

'I do hope we'll soon find that James is to have a brother or sister, don't you?' Joseph heard Lily say as she resumed pushing the pram along the path.

Joseph bent down at once and pretended to be tying his shoelace. Charles stood hovering next to him. When he was sure Robert and Lily were out of earshot, Joseph stood up, and he and Charles resumed walking.

'Did you hear that, Charles? She's not yet expecting again, but she's obviously hoping it'll happen soon.'

'That's not really surprising, is it? She's clearly keen on babies, and at one, James won't be a baby for much longer.'

Joseph glared at the ground. 'It hadn't occurred to me they'd want another child.'

'I don't know why not. Nor why you're so bothered about it.'

'If Lily's expecting, it'll complicate things. I need to get rid of her before that happens.'

Charles stopped abruptly, and stared at Joseph in dismay. 'Surely, you've abandoned that idea! I know you don't like her, but I assumed you'd got used to her by now. And she and Robert appear to be getting on all right.'

'If I thought that was so, I'd accept the situation. But I don't think it is. He's making the best that he can of his mistake, but it's no more than that. If I don't do something soon, he'll end up a very unhappy man, and he doesn't deserve that.'

'You need to stop thinking like that and leave him to make his own decisions.'

'Well, I'm not going to. Lily Brown's an unscrupulous woman, who took advantage of Robert's decency, knowing he'd always do the so-called honourable thing. He was trapped by her, but I'm going to free him.'

Charles started walking again. 'I really don't think you should interfere in their lives, Joseph, but I've said I'll help if I can, and I will. When you come up with a plan, let me know what you want me to do, and I'll do it. But I do hope you change your mind. Think seriously about what you'll be doing not just to Robert and Lily, but also to James.'

'Don't think I haven't considered James – he's my grandson, dammit! While he obviously recognises Lily, he's much too young to know the difference between a mother and a nanny. I doubt that his attachment to Lily is any stronger than his bond with Annie, and as Annie will be here to look after him when Lily has gone, he won't notice Lily's absence. Believe me, if I thought either Robert or James would suffer in the long run, I'd leave well alone.'

Charles glanced across at him. 'I can see you're convinced that what you're planning is right, Joseph, but I'm afraid I can't agree with you. I think it's very wrong.'

Joseph shrugged. 'Then we'll have to disagree, won't we?'

* * *

The last light of day was slowly failing.

Robert stood in the garden, listening to Lily's voice, which was floating out of the open bedroom window, carrying to him her words to James as she helped Annie get him ready for bed.

He couldn't wait for Lily to come back downstairs and be with him. They ought to be having a quiet drink together before Mrs Bailey served the light supper he'd asked for, rather than him having to stand alone in the garden, waiting for her to finish with James. He'd told her more than once that putting James to bed was Annie's job, and she should leave it to Annie, but he knew Lily loved spending the last few minutes of James's day with him, and he hadn't the heart to ask her more firmly not to do so.

The strains of Lily singing 'Twinkle, Twinkle, Little Star' drifted down to the garden.

Come on, Lily, he thought.

He could understand that deprived of maternal affection as a child, Lily was determined that James would feel a mother's love, but at the same time, *he* needed her, too. And now she was talking about having another child! If that happened, he could find himself spending even less time with her, he thought in despair.

On the other hand, it would benefit James to have a brother or sister. If he remained an only child, it was likely Lily would spoil and over-indulge him, and James could become a deeply unpleasant child, disliked by the family and when he was older, also by the people who worked for them.

It was surprising, in fact, that he hadn't already got her pregnant again.

No matter how tired he was at the end of a hard day's work, he had only to lie alongside Lily to feel alive again. He still wanted her every bit as much as he'd wanted her the day he first saw her, if not more, now that he knew the bliss she could give him. The truth was, he couldn't have enough of her. And nor, as he regularly found with a sense of wonder, could she of him.

A memory forced itself into his mind of his father, during one of their many rows about Lily, warning him that the time would come when he'd deeply regret having a wife from so different a background.

His father had been so wrong.

He loved Lily with all his heart. Yes, it would be nice if she had a few interests outside the house, but there was plenty of time for her to develop those when James was a little older. She was a truly lovely person, warm and caring, and that was all that really mattered. The things that made a good Linford wife in the eyes of the others, weren't the things that would make a good wife for him. For him, Lily was absolutely everything he wanted and would ever need.

He glanced at his watch. Perhaps they'd skip supper and go straight to bed.

* * *

Lounging in the plush velvet armchair in the corner of their bedroom, a half-empty glass of whisky in his hand, Joseph idly watched his wife getting ready for bed.

A slender, sophisticated figure in an ivory silk nightdress, she was sitting in front of the mirror on her dressing-table, systematically applying cream to her face. On one side of the dressing-table stood a cluster of bottles and perfume atomisers, and on the other, her ivory-bonded leather jewellery box, into which she'd just placed the necklace she'd worn that evening.

His eyes settled on the jewellery box. They narrowed thoughtfully, and he straightened up.

'Why d'you always wear the same few pieces of jewellery, Maud?' he asked. 'You've been given some lovely things over the years, but I never see you wearing them.'

She paused in the middle of applying cream to her chin. 'Since when did you start to notice what I was wearing?' she asked, amusement in her voice. 'Or have any opinion about it?'

'Since just now when I watched you take off that necklace. I can't remember when I last saw you wearing anything else. Take your emeralds, for example. Your mother didn't give them to you for them to be locked in a bank vault for eternity – she'll have expected you to wear them.'

For a moment, Maud stared at his reflected image, and then broke into a smile. 'This is so unlike you, Joseph, that I'm wondering what's on your mind. If my birthday wasn't three months away, I'd be convinced you were testing me for gift ideas! Is that what this is about?'

He laughed. 'Sorry to disappoint you, Maud, but it's actually Nellie's birthday I've been pondering.'

She turned sharply on her stool to face him. 'Surely you're not thinking of getting her an expensive piece of jewellery! Not for her eighteenth. By all means, when she comes of age, but not now. She's already much too indulged as it is.'

'Wrong again, I'm afraid. No, it's just that when we were at Robert's for lunch, I heard you tell Sarah you were thinking of wearing your green velvet dress for Nellie's party, and it occurred to me that your emerald necklace would go well with it.'

'All right, I'll wear the emeralds, if you want. I'm not sure that I won't look like a glittering leprechaun, but if that's what you want. I'll ask Charles to get the necklace from the bank vault and bring it to Chorton with him. With your sudden interest in decorative accessories, Joseph,' she added, her voice taking on a teasing note, 'you could always make further economies in the business by pushing Thomas out of the way and directing your attention to the household interiors of all future developments.'

He finished his whisky and grinned at her. 'I appreciate your unusual interest in company matters, Maud dear, and the uncharacteristic thrift in your train of thought, but if I were you, I'd keep that suggestion from Thomas – he's angry enough with the family as it is.'

11

THE BEGINNING OF JUNE 1920

Wreathed in the musky fumes of his tobacco smoke, Joseph settled more comfortably in his favourite armchair by the marble fireplace in the dark oak-panelled library of the Club. Drawing deeply on his pipe, he waited for Charles to join him. With the sense of calm that prevailed in the room, and the soothing low hum of men's voices in the background, this was his favourite place for thinking, and that evening had been no exception.

It might not be the greatest plan ever, he admitted to himself, but given all the possible risks involved, he couldn't see himself being able to come up with anything better. But he couldn't help feeling uneasy. Despite his best efforts, there was always a risk that he might've overlooked something crucial. Unfortunately, though, he wouldn't discover any flaws until his plan was put into action.

He drew on his pipe again, and caught the mingled scents of beeswax and tobacco in the air.

From the moment he'd heard Lily talking to Robert about another baby, he'd known that he had to accelerate things, but he'd been struggling with when and how to go about it. The key people involved would all have to be there, so it must be an occasion when the family was assembled together. And there would have to be a good reason for Maud to remove her jewellery from the vault in the bank and bring it with her.

In the end, there'd been one possibility only – Nellie's birthday weekend in June.

They'd all be at Chorton quite frequently during the summer, possibly with the exception of Alice and Thomas, who were unlikely to go there as often as the others, but he couldn't think of any other occasion on which Maud would take her emeralds with her. Indeed, she'd only agreed to wear them on Nellie's birthday, which should really be no more than a modest family affair, because he'd goaded her into doing so.

It was when he'd seen Maud's jewellery box that he'd had the idea of framing Lily for theft.

If Lily could be caught in possession of the emeralds at a time when everyone else was out on a picnic, a discovery Charles would witness, she could be threatened with exposure as a thief. A conviction for theft would lead to imprisonment. She'd deny everything, of course, but it would be pointed out to her that it would be her word against the word of both a leading builder and a respected banker, and she'd know that she'd never be believed.

He would then give her a stark choice – to leave the house before the others got back and never return, or be seen as a convicted thief by her son and husband.

She'd be told that if she left at once, he'd hold off reporting the theft to the police until she'd had time to get away. However, it would stay on file at the police station, and if she ever returned, it would be used to send her to prison. He would promise her, though, that should she leave, Robert would never be told of the accusation against her – all he would know was that when he got back from the family picnic on the Sunday afternoon, Lily had gone.

He had no doubt at all that Lily would agree to leave, albeit reluctantly.

He knew that what he was planning to do was harsh – cruel even – tearing a mother from her child and banishing her from all that she knew. But he was absolutely convinced that in the long run this was in the interests of both Robert and James, and it was their interests that were paramount. Once he'd got over her disappearance, Robert would be a much more contented man than he could ever have been with Lily, and James would grow up in a happy home.

And it could be argued that it was in Lily's best interests, too.

She didn't seem any more comfortable in the presence of the family than she had in the early days of her marriage, despite the efforts of Nellie and the other wives to include her in their conversation. He'd heard them suggest on several occasions, for example, that they all have lunch together, but she'd always find an excuse to get out of whatever was proposed. And her discomfort whenever she realised that she'd said something clumsy or inappropriate that might embarrass Robert, which was happening with increasing frequency, was painful to see.

It would surely be best for her to have a fresh start in another country.

If she was too far away ever to return to England, she'd have to settle down and make a new life for herself. Being a very attractive woman, she'd soon find herself another husband – someone more suited to her. She'd have more children, and be happier than she ever could have been with Robert. And that was the truth.

Having got that far in his planning, he'd been wondering where to send her when a group of labourers had ventured one day into the building yard looking for casual work. With so many businesses failing, and with factories closing as the markets shrank, there were no proper jobs to be had, the labourers had told him. They'd gone on to say that they weren't expecting an upturn any time soon, so each was trying to raise the five pounds needed to buy a ticket to sail steerage to New York. America, they'd heard, was where they'd find work.

That's what he would do for Lily, he'd decided on the spot – he'd buy her a ticket for New York.

But he'd send her second class – steerage was bound to be overcrowded and cramped, and he wasn't a mean man. And he'd see that she had sufficient funds to provide for herself while she looked for work. If women were needed for clerical work and retailing in England, and they were, there were certain to be similar openings in America, and as she could read and write, she was sure to find a job.

And there was her sewing. She used to be a seamstress, after all. He was confident there'd be a demand for good needlewomen in a place like New York.

For Lily to go to New York was definitely the best solution, he'd felt in satisfaction, for her and for the family.

Nellie's birthday celebration would be on the Saturday evening, so they'd be relaxing on the Sunday. As they often did on their Chorton weekends in summer, they'd have a picnic on the Sunday afternoon. Robert and Lily would have to be separated, of course. Robert would go with the others, but Joseph would need only observe that James seemed to be coming down with a cold for Lily to refuse to leave her son's side, especially as his nanny would have been given the Sunday off and sent back to London.

Lily was bound to be overjoyed at not having to go on the picnic with the others, and Robert was sure to be discreetly relieved that he wouldn't have to pretend not to notice how much Lily was hating being there.

Charles would obviously not go on the picnic, either.

With everyone gone, Joseph would confront Lily about the emeralds. Charles would back him up, and then take Lily to the port in his car. He would see her on to the boat and wait for it to set sail, just to be on the safe side. Charles wouldn't return to Chorton that evening, and Robert would be told that he was out somewhere, still searching for Lily.

He would ensure that before Lily left, she wrote a note that discouraged any suspicion that she might have left unwillingly. The note, plus knowing from her dejected demeanour how much she disliked being surrounded by the family, would be certain to convince them.

It should all work out perfectly.

With the key points in place, all he had to do was make sure that everyone who was still at Chorton that Sunday afternoon went on the picnic by the river – or if it rained, picnicked in the old boathouse in which the children used to play. The only exceptions would be Lily, and Charles and him.

As for what he'd say to Robert and the others about Lily's disappearance when they got back, he hadn't yet worked that out in detail. He'd assure Robert, though, that Lily was certain to return once she'd resolved whatever the problem was, and that the best thing he could do was maintain the same routine as always, so that when she did return, it would all be familiar to her. By the time it became obvious that she wasn't coming back, Robert would be over the worst and would have started to settle into a life without Lily.

And that, he told Charles, when Charles had joined him and they were sipping a glass of excellent claret, was how it was going to be done.

12

HAMPSTEAD

The middle of June 1920

Smiling to herself, Lily rounded Hampstead Underground Station and started walking down the high street. Robert was going to love the dress she'd just bought for Nellie's party. It suited her to perfection, the assistant had said, and the full-length mirror on the fitting-room wall confirmed that the assistant hadn't been lying. But much as she was longing for him to see her in it, she was going to save that until the night of the party. She'd appear with a flourish, and he'd be bowled over. And so would the others, too. She knew they wondered why on earth he'd married her – well, that would show them, in no uncertain terms.

Her smile widened.

And since she was on her own, James being with Annie, and was in the right frame of mind to spend a little more money, she'd go down to Hudson's and get some ideas for James's room. Robert had said she could have it redecorated, and could choose whatever wallpaper she wanted. Or even have it painted, if she preferred. She felt in the mood to look at colours.

She was still smiling when she reached the place on the opposite side of the road from where Perrin's Lane led into the high street. Needing to cross over, she moved to the edge of the pavement, and looked up and down the road, waiting for a gap between the cars and horse-drawn carriages. When it seemed safe, she stepped off the kerb and took a couple of steps on to the roadway, glancing as she did so at the opposite pavement.

She stopped abruptly.

Standing next to the electrician's shop on the right-hand corner of Perrin's Lane was Robert. He had his back to her, but it was unmistakably Robert.

And he wasn't alone. He was talking to a dark-haired woman in what was clearly a relaxed, casual sort of way. She could see the woman's face – she was looking up at Robert and laughing. And she could tell from the movement of Robert's shoulders that he was laughing, too.

Clutching her paper bag to her chest, she stepped back on to the pavement and stared at them both, her smile gone, her heart beating fast.

She might not be as clever as Robert, but she could tell when two people knew each other, and Robert certainly had a connection of some kind with that woman, whoever she was. They'd definitely met before, and more than once. Every gesture he made, every angle of his head, every wave of his hand, told her that. And every glance the woman gave him said the same thing.

What's more, she could tell that Robert liked the woman. And that the feeling was mutual.

She felt cold all over.

Oblivious to the people moving swiftly aside to avoid her, she inched further back on the pavement, until the cold hard glass of a shop window stopped her. Pressing back against the glass, she stood shrouded in the shadow thrown by the shop's awning, and watched them for a moment or two.

Then she spun round, hurried back up the street to Flask Walk, turned right and headed swiftly for the safety of home.

* * *

At the sound of the key in the lock, Lily rushed into the entrance hall, and stood facing the front door.

'I saw you,' she shouted as Robert stepped into the house. 'I saw you outside Skoyles. You was talking to some woman or other. And don't say you wasn't.'

He looked at her in surprise. 'I bumped into a woman I used to know, and we talked for a while. That's all.'

He closed the door behind him, hung his hat on the coat stand by the door, and went into the front reception room.

She followed him.

'You were all friendly and laughing with her,' she accused his back. 'Don't say you wasn't.'

'I've no intention of denying it,' he said, turning to her, a hint of annoyance in his voice. 'What *is* this, Lily? Surely I'm allowed to talk to a friend, aren't I?'

'But you're married to me, so you shouldn't be talking to another woman all friendly-like. It's not right. Whatever you say, you know you shouldn't.'

He stared at her in exaggerated incredulity. 'So because I'm married, I mustn't speak to anyone else – or at least, not to another woman? Not unless it's a dull, humourless conversation? Is that what you're saying?'

'You know what I mean. And you wasn't just speaking to her –

it was how you was speaking to her. Like you really knew her. Not like she was someone you just met.'

'I saw her a few times before we got married, but not in the way I think you mean. Her father's got a chain of builders' merchants, so our families are friends and we did some joint family things together in the past. It was no more than that.'

'I don't believe you.'

He went up to her and took her hand. 'I first met her that time I was in London for several weeks. But I returned to Chorton the minute I could, desperate to see you. You know I did. As for seeing her since then, she's just got back from a year in a finishing school in Switzerland, so I couldn't have seen her till now, even if I'd wanted to. Which I didn't.'

'Did you love her? If you lie, I'll know it.'

He laughed dismissively. 'Of course, I didn't. We got on quite well and I liked her. But I loved *you*.' He tightened his hold on her hand. 'Meeting her didn't change that. If anything, it made me realise how much I loved you. And still do, as you must surely know. I swear to you, Lily, today's the first time I've seen her since then.'

She stood silently for a moment, biting her lip.

'Is she married?' she asked at last.

He shook his head. 'Hardly. I've just told you she was at a finishing school. Someone may be courting her now, of course, but before you ask, I wouldn't know as I'd never bring up anything so personal.'

She stared at him accusingly. 'I bet your father would've liked you to marry her. Her family's obviously got pots of money – you can tell that by her clothes. And if she went to a la-di-da finishing school—' her voice caught in her throat, '—well, that makes her just the sort of person your father would've wanted for his precious son.'

He released her hand. 'That may be, but it never mattered to me what my father wanted,' he said quietly. 'I married *you*, didn't I?'

She stared up at him, her eyes filling with tears.

'I know you did. But I was expecting James, wasn't I? And it's in your nature to do the right thing. You'd never have seen me slung off the farm, with a baby on the way, and left to fend for myself.' A loud sob escaped her. 'If I hadn't got in the family way with James, would you still've married me, Robert?'

He tried to take her hand again, but she pulled it away.

'You're being silly. Of course, I would,' he said. 'I've loved you since the day I met you, Lily. You make my life worth living. Nothing could ever alter that.'

'I don't believe you.'

And she spun round and ran up the stairs to James.

Breathing heavily, she stopped outside the nursery, her hand on the door handle. Fighting back tears, she forced herself not to turn the handle, not to go into James. Not yet.

Sitting with James would calm her, she knew, but it would be wrong of her to let him see her so upset. Babies were good at sensing things, and James would pick up on her distress, and that would unsettle him. She couldn't bear to think of him being miserable, not even for a minute.

Tears started rolling down her cheeks.

Robert was right – she'd been really silly in the things she'd been thinking, in the way she'd accused Robert.

She was so angry with herself – she'd handled everything so badly.

If only she'd talked to him calmly. If that other woman had been Robert's wife and had come upon him with Lily, she would've been all dignified. She would never have lost control and screamed accusations at him.

And she should never have said that she didn't believe that Robert would have married her even if she hadn't been pregnant. Of course, she believed it.

But Robert had looked so happy, and so at ease with that other woman, that she'd panicked. For those few moments today, when she'd seen him enjoying himself in the way that he was, she'd glimpsed him as he used to be with her, laughing and carefree. As he'd been before he had the responsibility for a wife and a child.

And that had hurt, really hurt.

And it had frightened her.

Maybe he, too, would remember the way he'd been in the past, and compare it with the life that had been thrust upon him, and would regret the change. Her words to him that morning might just have hastened that on.

13

LATE JUNE 1920

Built in the mid-nineteenth century, Chorton House stood on a gentle slope, an imposing large stone house with sash windows and a roof of smooth grey slate.

For most of the year, the extensive gardens were home to a host of brightly coloured flowers, while throughout the year, thickets of trees and bushes provided secret hiding places for the children who'd grown up there, and who looked upon Chorton House as their second home.

A dry-stone wall surrounded the house and gardens, and a wide gravelled drive, flanked by an expanse of verdant lawn on either side, led up from wrought-iron gates set into the wall to the main entrance of the house.

From its slightly elevated position, the house looked out across the fields of the neighbouring farm, which lay both to the right of Chorton House and on the other side of the country lane that ran alongside the wall on the southern side of the garden.

Beyond the fields to the south of the house rose a jumble of gables and roofs – thatched roofs and tiled – which signalled the nearby village. And behind the village rolled the hills of Oxfordshire, their lush green slopes punctuated by clusters of dark-green trees and patches of honey-coloured stone that marked out the houses that stood alone.

When Bertha Chorton's builder father had bought the house as a wedding present for his only child, it had been a modest dwelling – four bedrooms, a dining room, a reception room and very basic servants' quarters. As he'd presented the house to Bertha and his son-in-law, Arthur Linford, he'd asked only that the name of Chorton be kept alive in the name of the house. Immensely grateful, both for the house and for the faith in his abilities shown by Bertha's father, who'd made a handsome investment in Arthur's newly formed building company, Arthur had readily agreed.

By the time he was celebrating the tenth anniversary of his marriage to Bertha, Arthur and his father-in-law had considerably increased the size of the house by adding a two-storey wing on either side, constructed from carefully sourced stone that matched the material used for the original building.

The new left wing afforded a much larger dining room and three reception rooms, all of which were heated by open fires. Arthur claimed one of the reception rooms for himself, and that was henceforth referred to as the library. The identical wing on the other side of a central staircase was given over to a large kitchen, scullery and pantry, a boiler room, and a housekeeper's room and servants' quarters, which included a bathroom and water closet.

The staircase led up to the extended first floor, where there was a large landing that led to eight bedrooms, each with a fireplace, and to two bathrooms with an integral water closet. The attic rooms had been converted into bedrooms for the servants.

Arthur and Bertha had lived in London during the week, but

at every weekend, they'd headed straight for Oxfordshire and Chorton House, the place that they truly loved.

To the great sadness of their respective parents, Bertha's first two pregnancies had ended in miscarriages, but on their third wedding anniversary, to everyone's huge delight, the young couple celebrated the arrival of their first child – a son, whom they called Joseph.

Joseph had been joined two years later by Charles, and then Thomas, who arrived four years after Charles.

The weekends and holidays spent at Chorton House had been idyllic for the children. Whatever the weather, there was always something to occupy them, inside the house and out. The garden, which had been tended for years by Mr Spencer, the housekeeper's husband, was a place of endless adventure. And when the weather was unsuitable for going outside, they cocooned themselves inside the house, which was warm and rambling, full as it was with faded rugs that covered the stone flags, large comfortable sofas, a jug of dried flowers on the table in every room, and a fire in every hearth whenever cold weather called for it.

Particularly in the winter, the children would cluster around the solid oak table that stood in the heart of the kitchen, begging the cook to make their favourite biscuits or to let them scrape clean the bowl after she'd spooned the cake mixture into a tin and put it into the oven to cook.

A table that would comfortably seat twelve stood in front of the window in the smallest reception room, and this was where they ate their family meals, rather than in the larger, more formal dining room, which was kept for special occasions.

One such special occasion was the family gathering at Chorton to celebrate Nellie's eighteenth birthday.

* * *

Apart from Walter, who had to visit a client in prison and so couldn't be there until Saturday evening, the family had arrived at various times during the course of the day.

Robert and Lily were among the first. He parked the car in front of the house, got out and went to the back of the car to help Annie out with the baby. Having suggested that Annie take James straight into the house, he went around to the front passenger door, opened it for Lily and stood aside for her to get out.

She didn't move. Her face pale, she stared down at her hands, which were clasped in her lap.

'What *is* this, Lily?' he asked wearily. 'You haven't said a word since we left Hampstead. In fact, you've hardly spoken for several days. You can't still be angry about the other day, surely? If you are, I don't know what else I can say to convince you that you're worrying about nothing.'

She looked up at him. 'I was thinking about the weekend, if you really want to know, and not about you. Or about that woman. I believe what you said about you and her, and I'm sorry I was so nasty about it. I'm thinking how much I'm going to hate the next two days. Thomas is the only one in the family who's ever nice to me.'

'Well, you certainly won't enjoy the weekend if you feel so negative about it before you've even got out of the car!' he said in visible irritation. 'If only you'd make more of an effort to get to know them all, you might surprise yourself by actually liking them. But if you can't, you'll just have to pretend you're enjoying it. After all, it's not for long.'

'I'll do my best,' she said. And she swung her legs round and climbed out of the car.

* * *

That evening, the housekeeper, Mrs Spencer, did them proud with a dining table that groaned beneath watercress salad, platters of cold fillets of bass with horseradish sauce, salmon mousse with cucumber, braised veal, leg of lamb, rhubarb flummery and Bakewell pudding, all set out as a buffet.

Everyone had dressed for the occasion, inspired by Maud, who'd told them well before the weekend that she'd be wearing her emeralds and that she expected everyone else to make an effort, too. When Thomas had voiced his surprise at having to dress formally for what was, after all, only an eighteenth birthday, Maud had dismissed his comment with an airy wave. A birthday was a birthday, she'd said, and after the wartime deprivations, and with the country still being in such a sombre mood, they should make the most of any occasion on which to get out their finery.

Nellie, delighted at her mother's suggestion, had worn a white-beaded, fringed flapper dress, elbow-length white silk gloves, a long coil of pearls around her neck and a narrow, white-beaded band around her head.

'It's a pleasure to see you in something more suitable for your age, not something your Aunt Sarah would wear,' Maud had told her with an approving smile.

Nellie had given her an ironic little curtsy, and had then gone quickly across to the window, where she'd stood watching the drive, clearly waiting for her first glimpse of Walter's car. The moment she'd seen it, she'd dashed to the front door, flung it open and run out to greet him. All but dragging him into the house, she'd issued him with instructions to change quickly and get back down to her as speedily as he could. They'd already missed too much of the time they could've been together, she'd told him as she'd pushed him towards the staircase, and she didn't want to waste another minute.

Maud had looked stunning in a green velvet dress that shimmered the length of her body, which was set off to perfection by her emerald necklace and a single emerald in each ear. Sarah had worn an ankle-length creation of filmy black lace over cream taffeta. Hanging from the dress were clusters of heavy jet hand-sewn beads. Louisa was wearing a miniature version of her mother's dress, but in pink lace over cream taffeta. Even without the beads, Maud thought disapprovingly, it looked far too adult for a ten-year-old child. Six-year-old Christopher was going around looking very pleased with himself in a dark blue velveteen jacket and long trousers.

Urged on by Alice, Thomas looked unusually smart in a classic black dinner jacket with black silk satin lapels. He'd come awkwardly down the stairs, keeping his balance by resting his injured hand on the mahogany banister, and holding his cane in his good hand. When he reached the bottom, he'd opted to sit in the wheelchair, which had been placed by the wall in readiness. At his side, Alice looked beautiful in a white chiffon dress with a tight beaded bodice and a slightly full skirt that fell to the floor.

'Both of you look wonderful,' Maud said, going towards them. 'Thank you, Alice,' she added, smiling warmly at her, and she squeezed Alice's hand.

Robert and Lily had been the last to join the others downstairs.

'I can't wait for this to be over,' Lily said as they'd sat in their bedroom upstairs.

She'd paused in arranging her hair and was sitting motionless in her peignoir in front of the dressing-table, while Robert, wearing a new single-breasted black dinner jacket over a starched white shirt, and straight-legged trousers, sat in the moss green velvet bedroom chair, waiting for her to be ready.

'So you've mentioned several times,' he said, running his hand across his forehead in despair, clearly impatient to go downstairs whence the muffled sounds of those gathering below were increasing in volume.

'You can't know how awful it is, pretending to enjoy yourself, like I have to.'

He got up from the chair, walked across to the door and opened it. 'Enough's enough. I'll wait for you downstairs.' She glanced at him quickly, alarm on her face. 'Don't worry,' he added drily. 'I'll wait for you at the foot of the stairs – you won't have to go in by yourself.' He stepped on to the landing, and turned to her. 'Please, don't be too long, Lily. I can't wait to see you in your new dress. I'm sure you'll look stunning.'

The door clicked shut behind him.

Twenty minutes later, Lily left their room.

When she reached the top of the staircase, she saw Robert at the bottom, leaning casually against the newel post, his eyes on the open door leading to the front reception room. She went down a couple of steps, and paused. At the sound of shoes on the wooden stairs, he glanced up and saw her standing there.

He straightened up at once, moved away from the newel post and stood staring up at her in open admiration.

Slowly and deliberately, she walked down the stairs, a slender figure in a mid-calf scarlet silk dress with a dropped waist. Her blonde hair, coiled on top of her head in defiance of the fashion for cropped styles, was threaded with sparkling beads that matched her dress, and her long scarlet silk gloves were ringed with glittering bands of the same beads.

As she stepped off the bottom step, Robert was enveloped in a haze of gardenia.

'You look beautiful, Lily,' he said quietly, gazing at her with love. 'Absolutely beautiful. Mother need not have bothered with her emeralds because no one will notice them – they will all be looking at you. How you could think for one minute that I'd ever want to be with anyone else is beyond me. You do believe me, don't you?'

She nodded. 'I suppose so. And you look ever so nice, too.'

With a broad smile, he offered her his arm.

And she took it.

* * *

After the buffet, Joseph called for silence and made a short speech in praise of Nellie, and they all toasted her. Then all but Lily and Thomas settled into a game of charades. Thomas had gone straight to a seat at the side of the room as soon as the word charades was mentioned. A moment later, Lily had shaken her head when asked to be part of Nellie's team, and had gone to join him.

'So you don't want to make a fool of yourself, either,' Thomas murmured as they sat together, side by side, their backs to the wall, facing the teams, who were in full swing.

'Oh, I don't think they look foolish,' she said quickly. 'It's just I wouldn't know what the words meant that they've got to act out.'

He nodded. 'There may be a little bit of that in it, but basically, you think the game's ridiculous, and you don't want to be a part of it, any more than I do. Be honest. That's true, isn't?'

She giggled. 'Maybe it is. But don't tell Robert.'

'My lips are sealed.' He shifted his position to face her. 'I suppose we ought not to sit here in silence or we'll look as silly as they do. Last time I asked you, you hadn't yet decided if you liked living in London. What're your thoughts now?'

She opened her mouth to reply.

'The truth, mind you,' he said, 'and not what you think you ought to say.'

'When we spoke last time, you were blunt like that. Are you always that way?'

''Fraid so.' He gave her a rueful grin. 'When I talk to anyone, that is,' he added. 'Usually I don't bother to speak to anyone.'

'Why d'you talk to me, then?'

'Because I like you. There, you see – blunt again. You and me, we're alike in some ways. For a start, we're both outsiders among the close-knit perfection of Linfords, and that makes us kindred spirits.'

'But you're a Linford,' Lily said, 'so you're one of them. Not like me.'

'It's not just being a Linford, it's being the right sort of Linford. Robert's sister, Dorothy, is a Linford, but you won't find more of an outsider than her. So, kindred spirit, how're you finding it living in London?'

'If it was just me, Robert and James, I'd be happy. But it isn't. There's always one Linford or another sticking their nose in where it's not wanted. Your brother's the worst. He hates me. He looks as me like I'm some kind of gold-digging tramp.'

'If I were you, I'd just say yes to everything, and then forget about them and carry on doing exactly what you want to do.'

She giggled. 'You're right! We *are* alike – that's what I planned to do. But when you're married to Robert, it doesn't always work. When I pretend I've forgotten to do something I agreed to do, he just looks sad, and then I feel guilty.'

There was a shriek of laughter from those playing charades, and one of the teams could be heard loudly congratulating themselves. They glanced across at the game.

'What about you?' she went on, when the players had settled into a new round. 'D'you like London?'

'There's a before-the-war answer and one for after the war. Before I joined up, in the absence of any particular ambition, I started working for the company. It was pure tedium, but I had money in my pocket, and if you were young at that time and had the wherewithal, the possibilities in London were endless. I wouldn't have wanted to live anywhere else. And then I went to fight. Having the wherewithal means nothing if you don't have two good legs and two good hands, so it doesn't really matter now where I live.'

'But you've got Alice,' she said, in surprise. 'And who you live with matters. I don't really know her yet, but she seems lovely.'

'And you've got Robert. I *do* really know him, and he *is* lovely.'

'But you haven't got Alice's father shoved in your face from morning till night,' she retorted.

'True. But you've got attributes you could use to push Joseph out of the way, if you set your mind to it. You're a beautiful woman, Lily Linford. Play your cards right and Robert will hear and see only you, and not his father.'

'I don't know,' she said, and she bit her lip. 'Robert's sort of different now.'

'Take it from me, I know what I'm talking about, leg or no leg. He's a man. And you're the sort of woman a man dreams of when he closes his eyes.'

'D'you really think so?'

'Now you're fishing,' he said, and he gave her a slow grin.

'Are you flirting with me?' she asked with a half-smile.

He threw back his head and laughed. 'If the pre-war Thomas had flirted with you, you'd certainly have known it. The post-war Thomas doesn't flirt. Too scary for the ladies. You looked lost and I'm just trying to help.'

Her face broke out into a smile. 'Well, you have done. And I'll take your advice. And I can be blunt, too – apart from Robert and James, you're the only Linford I like.'

* * *

In the break between the next games, Lily rose from her seat and excused herself to Thomas, saying she was just going up to check on James.

He smiled broadly. 'See you tomorrow.'

'I'm only going to check on James.'

'Which means we'll see you tomorrow.'

Laughing, she moved towards the door.

'Lily,' she heard Sarah call after her. Turning, she saw Sarah hurrying across the room to her, followed by Louisa and Christopher, their faces sulky.

'I assume you're going upstairs,' she said. 'Would you be terribly kind and take the children up with you? It's time they were in bed.'

Agreeing, Lily led the way upstairs.

She didn't come back down again.

White with fatigue, Thomas sat where he was, nursing a whisky, and watching Alice join in with the paper games that followed charades, which became wilder and wilder as the evening progressed and more and more bottles of wine were opened.

Tired though he obviously was, he couldn't be persuaded to go upstairs until everyone else was also going to bed.

14

'I can't see myself getting your father on his own at all this weekend,' Walter told Nellie in despair on the Sunday morning. 'After lunch, we've got to go off for the picnic. And knowing Joseph, when we get back, he'll disappear into the library with his whisky and pipe and stay there for the rest of the evening. I can hardly disturb him when it's clear that he wants to be alone. And we're leaving early tomorrow morning.'

Nellie bit her lip. 'What about having a word with him at the picnic?'

Walter laughed. 'I can just see me chasing your father along the river bank, trying to engage him in a discussion about the intricacies of Property Law, interrupted by comments about salmon or trout. Mind you, if I thought it'd win your father around, I'd be happy to spew forth on fishing, although I know nothing about it.'

'And nor does Father so you'd be on safe ground there,' Nellie said cheerfully. 'We've got to come up with a better idea, then.' She thought for a moment. 'There's no alternative, you'll just have to catch him this evening. I'm sure he only goes off to the library because he gets bored with sitting and chatting, and prefers to think about work. But I know he's interested in the property stuff you've been telling him, 'cos he's said so, so he won't mind at all if you interrupt him. Trust me.'

'Be it on your head, then. Although I'm pretty sure he'll want to know what I've lined up to tell him this time.'

* * *

Sunday morning ended with a light al fresco lunch on the terrace at the back of the house, surrounded by the riot of red geraniums that overflowed the tubs bordering the terrace. All around them, the jasmine-scented air was alive with the flutter of insects' wings.

After lunch, they went around to the front of the house to wave goodbye to Thomas and Alice, and to Maud, who was going to drive them back to London in Joseph's car, and wouldn't return that evening.

'You couldn't have asked for a better afternoon for a picnic,' Nellie said as the car disappeared from sight, and they went back inside the house. 'I don't envy them having to miss it. Let's get ready really quickly. Did you hear that, Louisa? No mucking around now.'

'Christopher's the slowcoach, not me,' Louisa said, her voice quivering with indignation. 'Isn't he, Mummy?'

'With the prospect of cake ahead of you,' Sarah said with a smile, 'I'm sure you'll both be equally speedy. When you've changed, you can help Mrs Spencer bring out the baskets – she'll have finished them by then.'

'I'm afraid you'll have to picnic without me,' Charles said when they reached the foot of the staircase. 'I had a highly disturbed night, and it's just hit me how tired I am. My fault entirely – I should've gone more easily on the wine. As soon as you've finished in the bedroom, Sarah, I'll try to get some sleep.'

Sarah frowned in annoyance. 'I told you last night you were overdoing it. It really is too bad of you.'

'Unfortunately, Charles isn't the only one under the weather today,' Joseph cut in. 'I was about to say that I had a headache, and the last thing I need is an afternoon in the sun. In fact, it's no bad thing if I stay here. Mrs Spencer was going to keep an eye on James so that Lily can go off and enjoy the picnic, but Charles and I can keep an ear open for the boy. It means that Mrs Spencer can have her customary afternoon break. I'll take myself off to the quiet of the library, which will restore me no end, I'm sure.'

* * *

There was a light knock on the door of Nellie's room. She opened the door and saw Walter standing there.

'I'll be a couple of minutes longer,' she said.

'It's not that. It's that I've just had a marvellous idea,' he whispered.

'What is it?'

'Your Uncle Charles is planning to go to sleep, so your father will definitely be on his own in the library. When you go down, tell the others that I've got the worst stomach imaginable. You can say I didn't mention it earlier as I thought it had settled down, but I thought wrong and I'm going to have to stay behind. Then, when you're all out of the house, I'll wander into the library on some pretext or other and start a conversation with your father.'

'That's brilliant, Walter!'

He grinned. 'It is, isn't it? I don't for one minute believe he's got a headache – I think he just doesn't want to go on the picnic.

Christopher and Louisa have been getting more and more excited all morning, and on several occasions, I saw him look at them wearily. We've so little time together that I hate not going with you, but I won't have a better opportunity to waylay him than this, and it'll give me a substantial amount of time with him.'

Nellie hugged him. 'That's an excellent idea,' she said gleefully. 'Wait in your room till we've gone, and then go after Father.'

* * *

Half-hidden by the heavy brocade curtains in the front reception room, Joseph watched Robert, Lily, Nellie and Sarah leave the house and go towards the wooden horse-drawn cart. The two horses were pawing the ground in restlessness. Christopher and Louisa, who'd run out ahead of the others, were handing the driver the baskets to load in the back of the cart.

There was a slight sound next to him, and he felt a sudden movement of air. Glancing sideways, he saw that Charles had joined him. 'Well?' he asked.

Charles nodded. 'I've done it. Just in case anything went wrong, and it needed to look as though there'd been a search, I pulled out a couple of drawers and made it seem as if someone had been looking for valuables, and I left Maud's jewellery box open. I also rifled through the drawers in my room, and the room that Alice and Thomas had been in. I thought it'd seem more realistic.'

'Good work.'

'And I've packed a bag with some things for Lily, and one for myself so that I can go straight back to London after her boat has sailed.' He paused. 'Are you sure you don't want to reconsider this, Joseph? It's not too late.'

'Quite sure, thank you – this is the right thing to do.' He took the emeralds from Charles.

'These are people's lives you're playing with.'

'It's two lives that interest me – my son's and my grandson's. I'm going to give Robert's life back to him.'

Charles turned away, his shoulders slumped in defeat. 'So, what's next?'

Joseph looked out of the window. 'What's next is getting Lily back into the house before they set off, which looks as if it'll be quite soon. She mustn't go upstairs to James or she'll see that there's nothing wrong with him. Also, if she goes into her room, she'll see the disarray. She's not so stupid that she wouldn't suspect something.'

'What's the plan, then?'

'I'm going to go out now and get her back in. You wait in the hall and take her straight to the library. Don't let her argue with you. I'll be right behind you. We'll challenge her as soon as we're in the library and get the whole thing over as quickly as possible, just in case the picnic ends sooner than expected.'

'Which could easily happen as there'll only be five of them.'

'True. Fortunately, we don't need to worry about Mrs Spencer – the library's far enough away from her room for her not to hear a thing, even if Lily makes a fuss.'

'And then, presumably I'll take Lily upstairs.'

'That's right. Watch her closely to see that she doesn't try to secrete a message for Robert – I'll have her write a two-word note before she leaves the library, and that's the only note she must leave. All she'll write is "I'm sorry".' He glanced through the window at the cart. 'Right. It's time to set this thing in motion.'

* * *

With a feeling of dread, Lily stood and waited while the driver loaded the last of the baskets and picnic equipment on to the back of the cart. When they were stacked securely, he climbed up on to the front, took hold of the horses' reins and waited for his passengers to climb into the back.

Louisa and Christopher were the first to scramble up behind him. Christopher sat on the bench on one side of the cart and Louisa on the other. Robert helped Sarah and Nellie up, and then turned to help Lily, too. He paused as he heard the sound of feet coming fast across the gravel towards them, his hand still under Lily's elbow.

'You *do* surprise me,' he said when he saw his father hurrying up to them. 'I thought you'd have been an unlovely sight by now, fast asleep in your armchair.'

'I certainly hope that's soon the case,' Joseph said, panting slightly. 'But before I settled down, I wanted to ensure that Lily wasn't worried.'

'Worried about what?' Lily pushed Robert's hand away and took a step forward, her face paling with sudden anxiety.

'There's no cause for alarm,' Joseph told her. 'It's just that when I was upstairs, I heard James coughing so I went in to see him, and thought he was a little flushed. I doubt that it's anything serious – it's probably no more than the start of a cold. But I wanted to assure you that I'll watch him closely, and if there's any reason for concern, I won't hesitate to send for the doctor. So, there's no need for you not to go off and enjoy yourself this afternoon.'

He smiled reassuringly at her, turned and started to go back towards the house.

Her face stricken, she looked up at Robert.

He shrugged. 'If you must,' he said, resignation weighting his voice.

She started to run towards the house.

With a rueful smile at Sarah, Robert climbed into the cart, sat down on the other side of Nellie and told the driver they could set off. The driver shook the reins and the cart creaked forward across the gravel.

Lily had overtaken Joseph and was inside the house before Joseph had even reached the front door.

He paused on the doorstep and watched the cart move slowly down the drive, the gravel splitting and cracking beneath the turning wheels as it made its way to the iron gates and out on to the road. When he heard it pick up speed as the horses broke into a trot, he went inside the house, smiling in satisfaction.

* * *

Standing in the centre of the library, Joseph confronted Lily, the emerald necklace in one of his hands and the matching earrings in the other. Charles stood at his side.

His expression grave, Joseph held out the emeralds for Lily to see. 'These belong to Maud, Lily, but they were found in *your* room. How d'you account for that?'

'What're you talking about? I never touched them.'

'You must've done. They were in your room.'

'And so was Robert. He must've put them there 'cos I certainly didn't.'

'They should've been in my wife's jewellery box, but when I went to give them to Charles to return them to the vault, I found they weren't there. He and I went on a search, and as I say, we found them in your room, in your bag. In *your* bag, not Robert's.'

'You're talking rubbish,' she said, her voice shaking with fear. 'I said I never touched them, and I never did.'

'Indeed? Well, we'll just have to see what the police say.'

'The police?' The blood drained from her face.

'Yes, of course. We're talking about theft. Something punishable by imprisonment.'

'But I didn't take them.' She began to cry. 'You've got to believe me.'

'Oh, but I do, and so does Charles,' Joseph said steadily. 'But the police won't. And nor will anyone else, if this gets out.'

She stared uncomprehendingly at him, and then fearful denial gave way to a sudden understanding. 'You can't... I'll tell them you're lying.' Her words were distorted by tears, and she swallowed hard.

'It'll be your word against ours. And who do you think they'll believe – a successful builder and a banker, or you, a nobody?'

Wiping her eyes with her hands, she took a step back, her chest heaving rapidly. 'Why're you doing this? What've I ever done to you?'

'You trapped my son into marrying you – that's what you did,' Joseph said coldly. 'You're the wrong woman for him, and I think you know that. Look at yourself. You're clearly not happy. I'm doing you a favour.'

'A favour! Telling the police I stole what I didn't! That's a favour, is it? Sending me to prison for what I never did?'

'There *is* an alternative.'

She frowned at him in fright and puzzlement. 'What d'you mean?'

'I'm giving you a choice, Lily. I'm quite prepared to report the theft to the police. And if I do so, by the time that Robert and the others get back, you'll already have been taken to the police station. You'll be arrested and charged, and eventually tried in Court and sent to prison. And everyone will know what you did.

Or you can take the boat ticket I've got you, made out to a Lily Brown.' He patted the pocket of his jacket. 'You'd sail to New York tomorrow, and never return.'

She stared at him, her mouth falling open in panic. 'New York?' she gasped, trying to digest what he'd said. 'And what about James? How will I manage, miles away in a place I don't know, just me an' him?'

'Oh, there's no question of you taking James – James stays here.'

'No!' she screamed. Lurching forward, she pummelled Joseph's chest with her fists. 'You can't have him. He's my son and I love him. And I love Robert, too. You can't do this.'

Charles moved fast. He dragged her from Joseph, and put his hand across her mouth, forcing her screams back into her throat.

Smoothing the creases from the front of his jacket, Joseph moved closer to her. 'It's your choice, Lily,' he said quietly. 'Either your husband and son will always believe you're a common thief – and make no mistake about it, James will be told you're in prison for theft when he's old enough to understand. Or you'll just disappear.'

'Disappear?' she echoed.

'You'll write a note saying you're sorry. You'll leave it in your bedroom for Robert to find, and then you'll go with Charles. He'll drive you to Southampton, and book you into a hotel overnight as your boat sets sail tomorrow morning. And don't think you'll be able to escape – you won't. Charles will wait with you till you've sailed. Your connection with this family will end the minute you leave this house, and we'll never see or hear from you again.'

'I knew you hated me,' she cried, tears streaming down her cheeks. 'I told Robert, but he never believed me. I was right, though, wasn't I? And you can't really love Robert. Not properly, you can't. Or James. They love me and if I get sent to prison or if I disappear, as you put it, they'll be unhappy. If you truly cared about them, you wouldn't make them unhappy.'

'But I don't think Robert *does* love you. He mistook infatuation and lust for love. I'm sure those feelings are long gone, though, and you'll increasingly become an embarrassment to him. If you're truly honest with yourself, Lily, you'll agree that I'm right.'

She gave a noisy gulp.

'I'll give you a sum of money to help you settle in New York,' Joseph went on evenly. 'You're an enterprising young woman, and you've already shown that if you want something, you'll go after it ruthlessly. I haven't the slightest doubt that you'll be able to make a living for yourself in New York, perhaps find another husband, maybe have another child.' He paused. 'Well, what's it to be, then – prison or freedom?'

She shook her head violently. 'I can't. There's got to be another way. I'll learn how to be a better wife to Robert. That's what I'll do. I'll ask Maud. She can teach me, and then I'll do what you both tell me to do. I can change, Joseph. I can learn to do better, and then I won't be an embarrassment. Really, I won't. Just give me a chance, I beg of you. It's my husband and child what you're talking about.' She gave a loud sob. 'And I won't tell Robert what you said. Honest I won't. Please, Joseph, give me a chance. Let me stay with James. Please.'

'As I said,' Joseph repeated, determinedly pushing back the wave of sympathy for her that unexpectedly flooded him, 'you must choose between prison or freedom.'

She gave a loud cry. 'Freedom, of course. What choice have I got?' And she broke down.

'A wise decision, I rather think.' He hesitated. 'There's one other thing you need to know, so I want you to listen carefully. Are you listening, Lily?'

She looked up at him in despair, her face wet, and nodded.

'No one here will be told of the theft – no one except the police, that is. I intend to report it to them, and ask them to keep it on record, but I shall tell them that I don't wish to pursue it or have it made public for family reasons. But if ever, at any time, you show your face to any member of this family again, or to anyone who'd connect you with us, I shall see to it that the police go after you. The theft isn't going to disappear just because *you're* disappearing. It'll stay on their books for ever. Is that completely clear?'

Choking on the words she tried to utter, she nodded again.

He glanced at Charles, who released Lily. Pulling two envelopes from his pocket, he gave them to Charles, and then went across to the top drawer of his bureau. 'Before you go,' he said, holding out the paper and pen, 'I want you to write the words "I'm sorry" on this piece of paper.'

Sobbing loudly, she took the paper and pen, went to the nearest table, wrote the words, and then gave the paper back to him. He glanced at it, put it in his pocket and held out his hand for the pen.

'Let's go upstairs and get your bag, Lily,' Charles said quietly. 'You can look in on James, but you mustn't wake him. Then we'll get off to Southampton.'

She looked up at him, her face pleading.

He shook his head. 'I'm sorry,' he said helplessly, and he took her gently by the arm and led her across to the library door.

'Remember, Lily,' Joseph called after her as she and Charles reached the door. 'If we never see you again, I promise that the only ones in the family who'll know about the theft will be you, Charles and me. Just three people.'

As the door closed behind Charles and Lily, Joseph turned to walk across to the bureau.

'Actually, sir, the number's four.'

Joseph spun round. Walter had risen from the sofa in front of the fireplace, and was standing, his back to the hearth, facing him.

15

'I'm sorry, sir, but I was rather stuck where I was. Earlier on, I assumed you'd go to the library when the others left, so I came along to tell you about a case I thought would interest you. The room was empty when I got here, so I took the liberty of sitting on the sofa to wait for you. I must've dozed off at some point. I woke to the sound of voices, and was about to leap up and tell you I was here, but when I heard what you were saying, I thought I'd better stay put, rather than complicate things.'

Joseph shifted awkwardly, and moved his weight from one foot to the other. 'Well, you obviously heard everything.' He gave a slight cough in embarrassment. 'I'm afraid I don't quite know what to say.'

Walter cleared his throat. 'I wouldn't want to interfere with something that wasn't any of my business, sir, but I wonder if I might make a suggestion or two.'

Joseph shrugged in visible discomfort. 'Obviously, you must say what you want.'

'I'm wondering if it's sufficient for Lily to just disappear, or if you shouldn't do something stronger, something more final than that?'

'I'm not sure what you mean,' Joseph said, embarrassment giving way to surprise, and an element of relief.

'Well, I love Nellie very much, sir, and if she vanished, I wouldn't rest till I'd done everything I could to find her. Whatever you think Robert feels about Lily now, I'm certain he'd do everything in his power to find her. He's that sort of person. If I were him, I'd immediately hire an investigator. In a mere matter of days, any investigator worth his salt would've discovered that a Lily Brown sailed to New York this weekend. Robert would never believe that someone like Lily would willingly leave her own child and go miles away to a place she doesn't know. And nor would anyone else. They'd soon work out that she'd somehow been banished, and I'm afraid it'd come back to you, sir.'

Joseph went white. 'I did wonder. But I hoped that her note, and knowing how unhappy she always seems with us, would convince Robert she'd left of her own volition. But the way you put it, I think you're right – he *would* look for her.' He stared at Walter in mounting alarm. 'What can I do? Have you any ideas, assuming you're willing to help?'

'Of course, I'll help, sir. In my opinion, Robert will need to believe she's dead. It's the only thing that would stop him from searching for her. And since there won't be a body, she'll have to have drowned. It'll be suicide.'

'Drowned?' Joseph echoed, frowning.

'Yes, drowned. The "I'm sorry" note will be interpreted as a suicide note. I can drive Robert's car to the coast, and take with me anything she could've been wearing. She'll have to leave her suitcase here or it'll look suspicious. Charles will need to buy her some things before she sails.'

'That won't be a problem – there'll be time before the boat leaves.'

'I'll leave Robert's car by the beach, and put her cardigan and shoes near the water. It'll look as if she deliberately walked into the sea. Leigh-on-Sea would be the best place to do this as she's been there with Robert. We'll report her disappearance to the police. They'll find the car and her clothes, and draw the obvious conclusion. There's a small station at Leigh, so I can catch a train back to London. That would do it, don't you think?'

'It does sound foolproof,' Joseph said slowly.

'I suggest I set off as soon as Charles has left with Lily, and that he takes *my* car to Southampton. You can tell the others that he and I went off in my car, looking for Lily when we realised she'd gone. That'll account for the whereabouts of the cars. As soon as we've gone, you can remove any trace of a search upstairs and place the note in position.'

Joseph thought for a moment. 'What about the theft? I told her I'd report it to the police.'

Walter smiled. 'I'm assuming you'd no intention of doing so. You wouldn't want to risk an investigation, for the same reason that you wouldn't want Robert to hire a detective.'

'You're right; I wasn't going to report it.'

'And that's something Lily might work out when she's calmed down. In case she does, you'd be wise to have covered yourself, though. It would be prudent to have in existence a sworn statement to back up your claim. You'd say that you'd made a statement, but for the sake of the family, hadn't wanted to publicise the theft, so hadn't contacted the police.'

'But where would the statement be, if not with the police?'

'In the solicitor's where I work. You could come to my office this week and make a sworn statement. I'll get it witnessed and dated, and put in the safe as insurance. It'd be purely a precautionary measure.'

Joseph shook his head in admiration. 'When Charles said you were sharp, Walter, he wasn't mistaken. I'm immensely grateful to you for your advice, and I'm going to take it.'

'I should tell you, sir, that I don't know whether such a statement could be acted upon in law,' Walter added. 'The maximum period of time between a criminal deed and someone being prosecuted for that deed varies. But Lily wouldn't know that.'

'I really don't know how to thank you. I can't tell you how glad I am that you were here today.' Joseph paused. 'And talking of you being here – out of interest, why did you pass on going to the picnic with Nellie this afternoon in favour of coming to talk to me?'

Walter grinned and went slightly red. 'A while ago, Nellie told me that I'd have to make a great effort for you to get to know me better if you were ever going to give us your consent. I've been taking advantage of every opportunity to speak to you, hoping you'll eventually forget that I'm not really what you want for her.'

Joseph laughed. 'That sounds just like Nellie! So that's why you've begun to take such a keen interest in Property Law, is it, even though it's outside your field?'

'It's why I started to look into it, sir, but I've found that it genuinely interests me and when I qualify next year, I'm going to find a practice that specialises in property matters.'

'Good for you. Well, you can tell Nellie that her plan seems to be working. But for now, perhaps you'd better get ready to leave as soon as Charles has gone, which probably won't be long now.'

Walter started to move, and then visibly hesitated.

'What is it?' Joseph asked.

Walter coloured. 'I want you to know that I'd never hold you to ransom about me marrying Nellie, by threatening to use what I heard today. I would never say anything to anyone, whatever you decided. I wouldn't want to win your consent through blackmail.'

'I believe you, Walter. It wouldn't cross my mind that you'd do such a thing. I already know you too well for that.'

'Thank you, sir.'

'Any reservations I had about you and Nellie were based purely upon your ability to contribute to Linford & Sons. It sounds mercenary, I know, but that's how it was. But I've learned something this afternoon. You've shown me that you, like Alice, can make a different kind of contribution to the family, but an equally valuable one. And I'm beginning to think that your intelligence and loyalty is actually worth more than anything financial. Charles has frequently urged me to recognise the value of your attributes, and I've now seen that for myself.'

* * *

Lily leaned over the cot and stared at her sleeping son, her vision blurred. She wiped her eyes the better to see him, the better to capture his image and store it in her mind for ever.

No, not for ever!

Until the day she saw him again.

And she *would* see him again. And she'd see Robert, too.

'I love you, darling James,' she whispered into the milk-scented air that enveloped her baby. 'One day, I'll come back for you and be your mother again. I promise you that from the bottom of my heart. I'm just leaving you for a short time, and that's only because I have to. But I'll never stop loving you, not for one minute, and I shall think of you every single day of my life until I see you again.'

She stretched out her hand to touch him, to feel once more

the creamy softness of his skin, but Charles caught her wrist and gently pulled her back from the cot.

'He's asleep. It's better to leave him be, Lily,' he said. 'We must go now.'

She stood still. 'I can't!'

'I'm afraid we must. Come on.'

Her hands flew to her mouth. Hunching her shoulders, she opened her mouth to scream, but Charles moved swiftly behind her, slid his hand around her head to her mouth, and silenced her.

They stood immobile for a moment, her tears trickling between his fingers and running down the back of his hand and his arm.

'I'm sorry, Lily,' she heard him whisper behind her. 'I really am. But I've no choice, either.'

Her breathing gradually calming, he lessened his pressure on her mouth, and she took a loud gulp of air.

Still holding her firmly with one hand, he bent down over the cot, pulled out James's shawl and pushed it into her arms. 'You can keep that, if you want,' he said. Then he picked up her bag and started to propel her towards the door.

Tightly gripping the shawl, and drawing each breath with difficulty, she started to move towards the door. With every step she took, she looked over her shoulder at James with longing. When they reached the door, Charles paused, and they turned so that she could have a last look at her baby.

Her knees threatening to give way, she wiped her eyes to clear her vision, stared hard at the cot, and gave a loud sob. Then, in a daze of grief-stricken disbelief, she allowed herself to be led down the stairs, held upright by Charles's arms.

Joseph was standing by the front door when they reached the bottom of the staircase, and he opened the door when he saw them. He said a few quiet words to Charles, gave him the key to Walter's car and took Lily's bag from him. Blind with anguish, she didn't notice her bag being tucked behind the front door.

She stepped out on to the doorstep, and stopped. She wiped her hands across her face, smearing her tears across her wet cheeks, and turned to face Joseph, her face deathly pale, her eyes filled with hate.

'I promise you this,' she said, her voice trembling. 'You've not seen the last of me. One day, I'll come back. Just you wait.'

'It'd be better if you didn't, Lily,' he said quietly. 'I'm sure you wouldn't want to end up in prison. You've got an opportunity now to make a new life for yourself, a life which could make you much happier than you've been with us. Take advantage of it.'

And he closed the door in her face.

16

JUST OVER A WEEK LATER

From the growing jubilation, and the way in which people were thronging towards the front of the ship, Lily realised that they must be nearing New York. Standing at the railing at the front of the second-class deck, surrounded by mounting excitement, she stared with unseeing eyes at the wall of morning fog through which they were sailing, and felt more alone than ever before.

And more afraid.

And so very angry with herself.

She'd been so stupid. She'd done everything all wrong from the minute Joseph confronted her. She could see that now. But panic had clouded her thinking.

When Joseph had accused her, it was as if her brain had gone dead.

It had stayed that way for her first few desperate days on the boat. Hour after hour, she'd lain on her narrow bunk, her face buried in the soft white wool of the shawl, trying to smell James in the stitches, trying to catch the scent of his baby powder, of the soap they always washed him with, and perhaps pick up a hint of milk.

But every day, it got harder to find any trace of him. Instead of the sweet scent of James, she began to smell the sweat from her hands, the rancid stink of cooked food, and the fetid odour of damp.

Finally, when she'd no more tears to shed, fragments of her last conversation with Joseph had started to creep into her mind, and she'd begun to relive the events of that Sunday afternoon, tortured and painful though they were. It was then, in a moment of utter anguish, and pain-filled frustration, that she'd realised that if she'd been thinking clearly when Joseph had accused her of theft, she'd still be with her son and her husband.

Anger consumed her at what she'd failed to see. Anger at herself for accepting without question everything Joseph said. Anger at Joseph for his cunning and his cruelty. And anger at Robert for not being there to save her.

Joseph had counted on her being too stunned by his accusation, and too frightened, to stand up to him. And he'd been right.

If she'd been able to think clearly, she'd have realised that Robert would never believe her capable of stealing, and nor would the others. They'd have seen it for what it was – Joseph's attempt to get rid of a woman he hated. And whatever else she thought of them, they weren't the sort of people to let anyone be convicted for a crime they didn't commit.

And all that about the police. That was just to frighten her.

If he *did* report it, and asked them to keep it a secret, they'd probably still have to look for her. And once they did, they'd soon discover she'd gone to New York. No one would think – not the police, not the family – that she'd have abandoned her son and her husband and gone there out of choice. Someone must have sent her, they'd reason. And they'd realise that someone could only be Joseph.

And if he was right about them not looking for her, but

keeping the report so they could charge her if she ever went back, well, she didn't believe that, either. Joseph wouldn't be able to prove anything. But she could prove she'd been sent to New York the day after the picnic, so it'd be clear that Joseph must've bought the ticket before the weekend.

He'd be the one in trouble, not her.

She'd been such a fool to have been so blindly obedient!

If only she'd used the time in Southampton to think it all through. If she'd done so, she'd never have got on the boat – she'd have stood her ground, gone back and faced Joseph. Charles had never seemed happy with Joseph's plan, and he might have turned his back and allowed her to escape. But if he hadn't, all she'd needed to do was wait until the ticket was in her hand, and then break away from Charles and call for help.

She could've used some of the money Joseph had given her to return to Chorton.

But instead, she'd panicked, and she'd spent those first unbearably dreadful days weeping for the son and husband she'd lost, thereby wasting her chance to get back to them.

And what Joseph had said about Robert's feelings for her? They were lies.

She loved Robert deeply, and she knew he loved her with all his heart. Whatever she'd said about that other woman, it had been insecurity speaking, not any real belief that Robert was attracted to someone other than her. She knew with every ounce of her being that Robert loved her as deeply as she loved him.

What would he be thinking now, believing she'd left him out of choice?

If he never learned the truth, it would destroy their marriage, and her grief at not being with Robert, at perhaps never again seeing him, was all but suffocating her.

But even if he did discover what had happened, her marriage would still be over.

She was certain that he'd come and find her. He'd get a detective to look for her. But when Robert begged her to come back, which she was sure he would, Joseph's action, although done without Robert's knowledge, made it impossible for her ever again to mix with the Linfords.

And Robert was a Linford.

No matter how angry he'd be with his father for what he'd done – and she was sure he'd be genuinely furious – he would never cut off ties with his father, whatever he might say in the heat of the moment. He'd shown in the past that when it came to it, he'd always find a reason to forgive Joseph.

She stared rigidly ahead. She must accept that she'd lost Robert, the love of her life, but she couldn't lose James. She was his mother. He belonged with her, and she was going to go back and reclaim him, even though it would mean taking him away from Robert. Robert would obviously beg her to let him keep James, but knowing what his father had put her through, in the end he'd have to agree to let her take her son.

So, with the money Joseph had given her, she could turn around as soon as she reached New York and go back to England. And in her heart, that's what she ached to do.

But she was now forcing herself to listen to her head, and her head was telling her that after buying a ticket back, she wouldn't have enough left to support herself and James, and she'd have to be able to do that if she was going to wipe the Linfords from their lives.

Much as it hurt – and it was tearing her apart – she'd come to accept that it'd be wiser to stay in New York for a while. She'd learned from people on the boat that there was work to be had there, and the best revenge on Joseph would be to return as a successful woman, who had her own money, who was able to raise James with a degree of comfort. And she was going to work from morning till night to make that happen.

She couldn't wait for that day.

And also for the day when she saw Robert again.

Even if their marriage was over, she yearned to see him just one more time, to feel again the warmth in his gaze when he looked at her, to let her eyes absorb every inch of his face, to feel the shiver of anticipation that always ran through her when she stood next to him, inches from the body she loved to touch – the body she'd never touch again.

Tears welled up, but she pushed them back.

And she couldn't wait for the day when she exposed Joseph for the cruel liar he was. Then she'd walk out with James, and they wouldn't dare stop her. And when James was old enough to understand what she'd done and why, he'd be proud of her.

All of a sudden, she heard a voice shout out from the steerage deck below, 'I see the lady!'

A hush descended on the boat, and held for a long moment.

No one spoke, no baby cried, no person coughed. Glancing on either side of her, she saw that every face was staring in the same direction, and was filled with the same sense of wonder. She followed their gaze. A tall statue with an upraised arm was gradually taking shape through the mist.

And then it emerged.

There was a mighty roar.

Feet thundered across the deck below. And from behind her, people surged forward, the weight of their bodies pressing her hard against the railing in their frantic attempt to catch their first sight of America. Crushed against the metal railing, she looked down at the steerage deck and saw a multitude of heads – bare heads, hatted heads, heads covered with kerchiefs and shawls – all facing the stone monument.

A monument that reminded her of how far she was from her husband and son.

All around her, voices swelled in song as the people on her deck started joining in with the singing that rose from the deck below, getting louder and louder, a jumble of words she couldn't understand, filled with an emotion she could hear, but not share.

Putting her hands to her ears to block out the explosion of joy that was rising from the people who thronged the decks, she turned away from the view and struggled back towards the stairs that led down to the cabins, forcing a path through the tide of people who were pressing forward. Finally reaching the steps, she clambered down to her corridor, ran along to her cabin, rushed in, pushed the door shut behind her and leaned back against it, breathing heavily.

She would not cry, she absolutely would not.

Yes, she'd lost Robert for ever, her wonderful Robert, but she would at least see him again. Her separation from James was only temporary, and when he was living with her again, she'd always have a part of Robert beside her.

'Hudson River Pier,' she heard one of the crew yell from the end of the corridor. 'Get your bags and go to the upper deck.' Repeating it over and over again, he walked along the corridor, knocking on each of the cabin doors.

Moments later, the ship juddered to a halt, and the sound of clanking chains was followed by something being affixed to the decks with a thud. All along the corridor, doors opened and closed with a bang, and footsteps headed towards the stairs.

Her heart beating fast in trepidation, she rushed across to her bunk, tucked James's shawl into her bag, put on her hat, picked up the bag, opened her cabin door and joined the stream of passengers, their faces drawn with fatigue, their eyes glistening with emotion.

Reaching the upper deck, she stood in a line with the other second-class passengers who had chosen to disembark at the Hudson River Pier, rather than get off earlier on, and stared down at the lower deck at the steerage passengers, each wearing a name tag with a number written large on it, who were being directed by the ship's officers to leave the boat and assemble in a waiting area on the pier.

'They're going on ferries from here to Ellis Island,' she heard an English passenger in the line behind her say. 'But they've finished with us and we can go straight into the city.'

She felt a stab of relief that Joseph had at least got her a second-class ticket.

Like all the other passengers, she'd been questioned in Southampton, and then given a quick medical examination by the steamship doctor before embarking. But they all had to be questioned and examined a second time. This would take place on Ellis Island for the steerage passengers, but the first- and second-class passengers had been checked by officials when the boat stopped in the quarantine area at the entrance to New York Harbour, and they were now free to leave.

Her turn to disembark arrived.

In a daze, she walked along the gangway, stepped on to American soil, and panicked. Her steps faltered, and she stopped. Beneath her feet, the ground rolled like waves.

Making lots of money had seemed so easy when she'd been on the boat, but now, standing in an unfamiliar place, which was so big and so hot and so noisy, with crowds of people everywhere, she felt very small, and very scared.

She stood for a moment or two in the burgeoning heat, steadying herself. Then someone pushed her from behind, and she found herself standing in a queue that stretched back from a kiosk headed Money Exchange. She felt movement at her back, and saw that others had come to stand in line behind her.

When she reached the front of the queue, she handed over the English money that Joseph had given her, took the American dollars they gave her in exchange and moved across to the nearest patch of grass. Dropping her bag on the grass, she sat down heavily on top of it.

What to do now, she thought in terror, fanning her face with her hand as she looked around. Where could she go?

And how to describe herself if she had to? Who was she now?

She wasn't Lily Linford and never would be again. But she wasn't Lily Brown, either, whatever her boat ticket said. Lily Brown had died on the day she got married.

Nor was she a mother, not at that moment.

Mesmerised, she stared at all the legs walking in front of her, at the children stumbling along between their parents, at infants being pushed in a pram by their mother, at babies as young as James in the arms of their parents, and at wives, laden with bags, gazing with love at their husbands.

A lump filled her throat.

She swallowed hard and stood up. She'd cried enough, and must stop. She was going to have to lock her love for Robert in the past. It would live there forever, but Robert could never be a part of her future. James could, though, and all that mattered now was getting him back. And to make that happen, she needed to find somewhere to live, and then get a job.

The family she'd sat next to on the boat had talked incessantly to each other about their relatives in Delancey Street and Orchard Street. She hadn't spoken to them at all, being too distraught for conversation, but they'd seemed pleasant people, and the streets' names had stuck in her mind, so that seemed a good place to begin.

She brushed the sandy grit from her skirt, picked up her bag and turned towards the city.

With a powerful sense of purpose propelling her feet away from the ocean that separated her from Robert and James, she put first one foot forward, and then another.

17

LOWER EAST SIDE, NEW YORK

July 1920

Standing on the corner of Delancey Street, Lily stared down Orchard Street in bewilderment. Tall red-brick buildings, each one like the next, flanked both sides of the cobbled street, trapping the heat between them, shutting out the light.

Crowds of people jammed into the long narrow street, filling almost every inch of the space as they swarmed across the pavements and on to the road itself: men in black hats and jackets; women in skirts and blouses or dark dresses, invariably with a shawl or kerchief covering their head and a basket hanging from their arm; children standing at their parents' side, or weaving their way between shoppers, or carrying loaves of bread in their arms.

Every so often, she glimpsed men and young boys staggering beneath a weight of garments in their arms or straining to carry enormous black bags or pushing a cart.

And the noise!

Wooden pushcarts lined both sides of the road, piled high

with fruit and vegetables, or with poultry, or fish, eggs, soap, shoes, clothes, ribbons, shawls – far more than she could take in at a glance. Every vendor seemed to be shouting as loudly as possible in an attempt to attract customers, and every solitary pedlar noisily hawked his wares. Customers haggled over prices, raising their voices as they leaned across the pushcarts and fingered the goods. And groups of people, standing between the pushcarts, jabbered excitedly at each other. The occasional words reached her, but she couldn't understand what they meant – no one was talking in English.

Once or twice, a car or horse-drawn trolley turned off Delancey Street, passed in front of her and proceeded with difficulty down the middle of Orchard Street, sending people scurrying to one side or the other, like a boat cutting through the waves.

High above the street-level din, bells clanged, and every so often, a siren screeched or an elevated train could be heard roaring along its track.

And all above and around her, a sickly-sweet smell clung to the heavy warm air.

Her head was spinning.

It was like a long open-air market, but noisier, more crowded, more frenetic than any she'd seen before, and it frightened her. She couldn't stay there. She must find somewhere else, somewhere less daunting. However pleasant those people on the boat had seemed, coming here had been a mistake.

She took a step back.

And she caught the smell of cooked onions and frying fish.

Her mouth watered. She couldn't remember when she'd last had a proper meal. Weighted down by misery on the boat, she hadn't been interested in food, and at each meal, she'd managed no more than a few mouthfuls of whatever was on her plate. But now, with the aroma of cooked food all around her, she realised how hungry she was, and that she needed to eat.

She picked up her bag, took a deep breath and approached the dense crowd of people and pushcarts.

On the fringe of the crowd, she stopped. She couldn't do it.

She couldn't walk into a mass of people she didn't know, people she wouldn't be able to understand, who wouldn't be able to understand her. It was unthinkable. Despite her hunger, she'd just have to wait a bit longer.

She turned around and took a few steps back to Delancey Street. It was much wider than Orchard Street, and not as crowded. There was bound to be a food shop somewhere along there. She'd just have to keep walking.

If only she didn't feel so tired, though, and so lacking in energy.

She swayed slightly.

'Are you lost?' a voice asked from behind her.

Turning, she saw a black-haired girl, a little younger than she was, in a brown dress, and with a grey kerchief tied round her head.

'Do you need help?' the girl asked, her dark brown eyes full of concern.

Lily shook her head. 'I'm going somewhere else. I need a room and a job. And food. But I can't go down there.' She nodded towards Orchard Street. 'There're too many people. And I won't understand them. And the noise. It's so hot.'

Her knees gave way. She dropped her bag. There was a sharp pin-point of red, and then the world went black.

She felt the girl grip her arms, and hold her.

'You're coming home with me,' she heard the girl say, as if from a long way off. 'You can stay with us tonight. We're lucky –

we've got three rooms, so there's space for you. Tomorrow you can think about what to do.'

The fuzziness in her head clearing a little, Lily opened her mouth to protest that she'd be fine, but she felt herself sway again.

'My name's Ruth,' she heard the girl say.

Ruth picked up Lily's bag, put her other arm around Lily's shoulders, and started to help her slowly down Orchard Street. Halfway along, Ruth stopped in front of one of the tall five-storeyed buildings.

'Here we are,' she said, and helped Lily up the steps to the entrance. 'We're on the second floor.' She opened the front door and went in.

Following her, Lily stepped out of the bright sunshine into a dark hall.

A pungent smell of oil and paint hit her, and she leaned against the wall for support.

As her eyes accustomed themselves to the dim light, she saw that they were in a narrow lobby that ended in a fuzzy rectangle of pale light that suggested a semi-glazed door leading to a yard outside. A steep staircase on the right led to the upper floors. Lamps, spaced out along either side of the wall in the hall, threw out weak rings of amber light, most of which was absorbed by the dark-green burlap-lined walls.

A small, framed picture of a cottage in the middle of a field caught Lily's eye. Illuminated by a beam of lamplight, the green field shone with startling brilliance. She took an involuntary step towards it, and as she stared at it, tears of longing for her country sprang to her eyes.

'*Momma* put that up there so everyone in the tenement could enjoy it,' Ruth said, nodding towards the picture. 'We've a similar one in our apartment. It's her dream to have a house like that, with flowers in the garden, and fields around it. And sunlight and fresh air. We brought the pictures from Kishinev with us, and the first thing *Momma* did when we arrived was hang them up. There was no electric light back then so you could hardly see the one down here, but she thought it would make everybody happy, and it did. You see, it's everyone's dream, not just *Momma*'s.'

Lily glanced at Ruth, and saw that she was smiling at the picture.

'It's a lovely dream to have,' she said, feeling she ought to say something.

'Yes, it is, and one day it will happen. But right now, you need food. Come on.' Still carrying Lily's bag, Ruth started to climb the steep wooden stairs.

Gripping the mahogany banister tightly, Lily followed her.

When they reached the first landing, Ruth pointed to the door immediately opposite them. 'The Abelmans live there – they're the other family on our floor. They've got a jewellery business. They share the water closet with us. We don't have to go down to the privy in the yard any more as there's now one on every floor. It's in there.' She indicated a door halfway along the landing. 'And this is where we live.' She stopped in front of a door at the foot of the stairs leading up to the next floor.

'But you said the second floor.'

Ruth looked at her in surprise. 'This *is* the second floor. The first floor's where we came in. Ah, here's *Momma*!' she exclaimed as the door opened. 'She must have heard my voice.'

A woman stood in the open doorway, wearing a black blouse and a long black skirt, with a colourful apron over it. Her face was deeply lined and her dark hair greying. She stared at Lily in open curiosity.

Ruth spoke rapidly to her mother in a language that Lily couldn't understand.

When Ruth finished speaking, her mother wiped her hands on her apron and smiled at Lily. Then she stood aside and gestured for them to go in. Ruth went first, lightly touching a small wooden case that was fixed on the wall to the right of the doorway, and then she waited for Lily to step in after her.

The door clicked shut behind them.

Lily found herself standing in a tiny, rather hot and smoky kitchen. To her right, there was an open doorway, and through it she could see a small dark windowless room. Most of the space seemed to be taken up by beds.

Sweat trickled down her face, and she wiped it away with her hand.

Ruth spoke again to her mother, who nodded, pulled one of the chairs from beneath a round wooden table that stood between the small dark room and the sink, and indicated that Lily should sit.

Gratefully, she did, and she realised then how exhausted she was.

Looking around the room with tired eyes, she saw that pots and pans were hanging from shelves on the wall on the other side of the sink, and there was a water tap on the wall above the sink. Fixed high above the shelves was a unit that looked like a water heater. On the far side of the unit stood a tall, glass-fronted cupboard. Its upper shelves were filled with china, and on the lower shelf, there was a bulky metal urn with a handle on either side and a tap at the bottom.

Steam was coming from a large pot on a round stove in the centre of the kitchen. A pipe for the smoke led up from the stove. Ruth's mother moved across to the pot and began to stir the contents.

A wave of despair shot through Lily, and she could so easily have cried again. Everything about the place reminded her of the cramped little cottage in which she'd lived with her mother, and the modest home she'd shared with Auntie Muriel after that. It was a life she thought she'd escaped for ever.

'You're not to move,' Ruth told her. She put Lily's bag down and went across to the glass-fronted cupboard, opened a drawer and took out some cutlery.

The sudden strident whirr of a machine blasted out in the apartment.

Startled, Lily jumped.

She stared towards the noise, which seemed to have come from the room on the other side of the kitchen. The door to the room was open, and through both the open doorway, and the large glass window in the wall that divided the kitchen from the room beyond, she could see that it was larger than the kitchen, and there were people in it. And there was what looked like a sewing machine under one of the two small windows.

A man was sitting at the machine, his back to her, and another man was standing by a heap of garments piled high on a sofa that took up one wall. Hunched in an armchair opposite the sofa, a girl was bending over a garment that she appeared to be sewing.

Indicating the far room, she frowned questioningly at Ruth, who'd just finished laying the table.

'That's *Abba* and Isaak in the parlour,' Ruth told her. 'Isaak's my older brother. Vera's with them – she works for us. They've an order of pants to finish, and two dozen shirtwaists. And later today, Pavel – he's my younger brother – will be bringing a number of coats for us to sew. They're working hard so we mustn't disturb them – you'll meet them later.'

'I suppose the window in the wall is to give them more light,' Lily said, indicating the window between the two rooms.

It was a tubercular window, Ruth explained. It let light and air into the kitchen and bedroom, and that was good for their health.

Her mother said something to Ruth, and with a final stir to the contents in the pot, started spooning food into a bowl.

Ruth took a large metal saucepan from a hook on the wall, placed it in the sink and turned on the tap. 'While *Momma*'s getting your food, I'll heat some water for you to wash with when you've eaten. And then you must rest.'

Lily started to thank Ruth for her kindness, but Ruth's mother put a plate of chicken stew in front of her, and indicated with signs that she should eat and not talk, and Lily fell hungrily upon her food.

'We're lucky to have a faucet in the kitchen,' Ruth said, turning off the tap. With her mother's help, she heaved the metal pot from the sink to the stove. 'The apartments in the tenement building where Vera lives don't have running water. People have to go down to a communal faucet in the hallway.'

She stoked the coal inside the stove, and went and sat next to Lily.

'What's your name?' she asked.

18

Lily opened her eyes.

Darkness was lifting from the parlour, driven out by the increasing intensity of the early-morning sun, which was pushing its light and heat through the shimmering yellow curtains that veiled the two small windows into the corners of the room.

Lying motionless on the sofa, the crocheted cover she'd been given having slipped to the floor during the night, her eyes adjusted slowly to the muted light. In the silence of the apartment, she could hear with clarity the sound of movement in the street outside.

But there was no sound from the small room beyond the kitchen, where Ruth and her parents were sleeping. She had no idea what time they'd gone to bed as she'd retired as soon as they'd finished using the parlour for their sewing, and she'd fallen asleep the moment her head had hit the pillow.

When Ruth had told her that her parents, who usually slept on the sofa, would sleep that night in the room that Ruth normally shared with her brothers, and her brothers would sleep on the fire escape, her urge to sleep had fought against the feeling that she really ought to refuse Ruth's parents' offer.

To her guilty relief, her weak protest had been emphatically silenced. Isaak and Pavel were delighted to be going outside, Ruth had told her. On hot summer days, they often took their sheets and bedspreads on to the roof or the fire escape and made themselves a sleeping tent. A lot of other tenement kids, as Ruth called the children, did that, too, and it was like one big club out there.

The noise from the street was getting louder, and Lily could now distinguish a number of different voices. Rising from the sofa, she went across to the closest window, feeling the linoleum beneath her bare feet already warm, and moved aside the flimsy curtain.

The tenement roofs on the opposite side of the road were outlined in black against an early morning sky that was streaked with pink and a luminous grey.

On the street itself, the first stallholders to arrive were bumping their pushcarts over the cobbles, clearly heading towards their roadside pitch; horse-drawn wagons clip-clopped along the road, able to move with relative ease in the fairly empty street; vendors were calling to each other in passing, their voices muffled, and intermittently lost in the roar whenever an elevated train thundered past. Immediately below her window, a child was pulling a small wagon filled with loaves and rolls.

She leaned closer to the glass and stared down at the child. He couldn't be older than ten, she thought. She looked further along the street and saw that he wasn't the only young child who was out at so early an hour – there were others, too, scurrying from their tenement homes, obviously anxious to reach their place of work on time.

She drew back.

If she'd brought James with her, he might have ended up one

of those children, out on the street, scavenging for work. And for the first time since she'd left Chorton House, she wondered if perhaps Joseph had been right in refusing to let her take James, despite the intense agony of leaving him.

She'd ended up in New York through her own fear and stupidity.

And now that she'd had a glimpse of the sort of place in which, in all probability, she'd be living if she was going to save any money at all, she could see that James was better off with Robert at the moment. She loved him far too much to want to subject him to the sort of life she was going to have to live for the next few months.

But just as soon as she'd made enough money, she'd go back and reclaim him. She was going to work as hard as she possibly could to make that the day come quickly. She longed so much to see him again.

And Robert, too.

Loneliness ached deep within her, and her eyes filled with tears.

You're not to cry, she told herself fiercely, and she blinked back the tears and turned to face the room.

A pile of clothes lay in a heap on the floor beneath the window that divided the parlour from the kitchen. Vaguely, she remembered the clothes being moved from the sofa the evening before so that she could sleep there.

Very quietly so as not to disturb the family, she moved across to the pile and picked up the garment on top. It was a plain white blouse with long sleeves and a pleated front. Sorting quickly through the rest of the clothes, she found two dozen or so identical blouses, and several identical pairs of men's trousers. Glancing around, she saw another pile of men's trousers on the table next to the mantelpiece. They'd been carefully laid out, as if ready to be taken somewhere else.

She looked back at the garments on the floor, and then down at the blouse in her hand. Ruth had said something the night before about having to finish off some clothes – perhaps it was these.

She took the blouse across to the window, held it up to the light and then turned it inside out. There were numerous threads hanging from the inside seams, and these would have to be clipped with great care so that the blouse wasn't ruined. After that, the blouse would be ready to be worn. That must be what Ruth had meant.

Well, she could easily do that. It was one of the things she'd learned all those years ago from Auntie Muriel, and it was the very least she could do to repay the family for their kindness and hospitality. She dreaded to think what might have happened if she hadn't met Ruth at the very moment when she was most in need of help, but hadn't realised it.

She drew the curtains right back, sat down at the sewing machine, picked up the smallest pair of clippers from the side table, arranged the blouse on her lap and began to work.

* * *

Ruth exchanged glances with her father. He held one of the blouses in his hands, having just examined the seams.

'You finished all those shirtwaists in that short space of time? And the trousers?' Ruth asked, pointing to the pile of clothes that Lily had carefully folded and arranged on the sofa.

'It wasn't difficult,' Lily said. 'I've done this work before, back in England.'

'In England, you work in dress factory?' Alexei Erlikh asked.

Lily shook her head. 'No, I lived with a seamstress. She taught me everything.'

'You can cut material, make whole dress?' Alexei asked.

Lily nodded.

He looked at the blouse again, and then back at her. 'You can make pattern, cut material, make dress? Just you?'

She nodded again, and glanced enquiringly at Ruth.

'Vera is one of the two girls who work for us,' Ruth explained. 'She finishes the clothes we're sent, and I do, too. Like you've done with the blouses. Then she irons them using a damp cloth to make steam. But she cannot do what the other girl, Esther, does. Esther works part of the week, but not every day. She's our baster – she tacks patterns on to fabric. But she cannot do what Vera does.'

'I see.'

Ruth smiled. 'I think this sounds strange to you. *Abba* is surprised that you can do all the tasks yourself, because here in a factory or in the tenements, people do one job only. That way, everyone gets very good and very fast at their one task.'

'That's very different from how I'm used to working.'

'It sounds it. *Abba* is very good cutter, and Isaak, too. But neither can design and make a dress to order. And they aren't finishers. Not many people can do all tasks.'

'I understand.' She glanced curiously at the finished clothes. 'Where do your trousers and blouses come from?'

'From the factories. The large orders go to them as they can fulfil them quickly. They pass them on to us for detailed work, like finishing.'

Ruth's father said something to her.

'We are paid by the piece,' she said. 'The factory is given money for the whole order, and the foreman pays people like us to do particular parts of the garment. We have to accept low rates, as if we don't, someone else will. *Abba* would like me to be a dressmaker, not someone who can only sew seams or finish a garment. I'd be paid more money, you see. Ladies come to a dressmaker, tell them what they want, and the dressmaker designs and cuts the pattern, and then makes up the dress. I'm not skilled for this, and never will be. But you can do this, can't you?'

Lily nodded slowly.

Alexei put his hand on Ruth's arm, and again spoke to her. She replied, and then turned to Lily.

'*Abba* asks if you like to live here and work for him. You said you need somewhere to live and a job, and you will have a home here with us. This is a happy home. You will like my brothers and parents, though I fear *Momma* will never learn English. And we're not far from the public baths in Allen Street so we can go there once a week.'

'But your brothers can't sleep outside indefinitely.'

'When the weather turns cold, they'll come back inside, and we'll put a bed for you in the kitchen. I've slept there before, and it's warm and comfortable. At first, you will be a finisher, but we will tell customers you are a dressmaker, and when you get dress-making work, you will be paid more. So, will you work for us, Lily?'

'I'm going back to England the day I've saved enough money,' Lily said, feeling she should be honest about her plans.

'And one day, we'll leave for a cottage like the cottage that's in *Momma*'s dream. No one stays long in Lower East Side. Everyone moves as soon as they can afford it and once they understand how to live in America. We will, and you will, too, I'm sure. But you'll be able to save a little money by living with us, and when we leave, maybe you'll be able to rent your own room and work only for yourself. This is not impossible, not in America.'

Lily looked at Ruth, and from Ruth to Alexei, who was staring anxiously at her.

She'd been offered a home with people who seemed very kind, and a job she knew she could do, that would allow her to save some money. A feeling of warmth crept through her. And excitement. On only her second day in New York, she'd taken the first step towards returning to James.

'I'd be very pleased to live here and work for you,' she said. 'Thank you.'

19

HAMPSTEAD

Sunday afternoon, the end of July

Robert leaned forward in his chair, and stared at his parents and uncle and aunt, his face pale and drawn.

'I appreciate what you're saying,' he said, 'and I'm really grateful for all the help you've been giving me, but nothing – I repeat, nothing – will ever stop me from feeling desperately guilty about what happened. In fact, guilty doesn't even come close. I can't describe how awful I feel, and how responsible, and how unhappy. I loved Lily so much, and I still do. I'll never get over this, and I don't deserve to. Poor Lily – she must've been so very unhappy, but didn't feel she could tell me. It's killing me to think I let her down so badly. What sort of husband does that make me?' His voice caught in his throat.

'You're being too hard on yourself, darling,' Maud said. 'We saw you and Lily together a number of times and you were always very attentive. You were clearly a devoted husband.'

'We'd had a couple of arguments before the party,' he said miserably. 'But it didn't mean I didn't love her.'

'Of course, it didn't. All married couples argue,' Sarah said firmly. 'That's normal. You should hear Charles and me.'

Maud nodded. 'Sarah's right, darling. As we've all told you, the most likely thing is that Lily felt out of her depth among our family, and couldn't face the future feeling like that. We tried to make her feel welcome, and include her in conversations, but she never really joined in. I wish now we'd made a greater effort with her, but we couldn't know the depth of her misery any more than you.'

'She couldn't join in, as she put it. She wasn't like you so she was ill at ease with you,' Robert cried in despair. 'And that's partly because she'll have sensed you didn't like her. She may not have been well educated, but she wasn't stupid. And my attitude won't have helped, either. I should have taken much more notice of how increasingly uncomfortable she felt among the family. Instead, I was actually impatient with her at times. How could I have let her down so!'

'You're only human, Robert,' Sarah cut in. 'It's hard for any two people to adjust to each other. But listening to you, I'm wondering if perhaps Lily did what she did as she thought it would be best for James. She might not have wanted him to be caught between the two of you, and the different lives you wanted to lead. It's not impossible – she was besotted with the baby.'

Robert frowned. 'I hadn't thought of that. But I suppose you could be right.'

'That's a good point, Sarah,' Charles said. 'From what you've told us, Robert, Lily's early years weren't easy. She'll have wanted things to be so much better for James, and could have been fearful that she'd hold him back.'

'For whatever reason, Lily's done something she thinks will benefit you and James, you can be sure of that,' Joseph said, 'and you mustn't let her sacrifice be wasted. I never liked the woman,

I'll admit, but I realise it's a tremendous loss for you. Fortunately, we've a lot of ongoing projects at the moment, and if you throw yourself into your work, it should help you get over this.'

'Not forgetting that there's more to life than just work, though,' Charles said.

'That's true, of course.' Joseph frowned at Charles, and then turned back to Robert. 'You're obviously still in shock – after all, it's barely been a month. But at some point, you'll have to force yourself to take an interest in life again, for young James's sake, if for no other reason. Fortunately, he's a happy little thing, helped no doubt by the extra fuss we've been making of him, and by the fact that he's clearly very fond of Annie. But when he's a little older, he'll be more aware of what's happening around him, and he'll need a father who's living, not mourning. Not that you'll ever forget Lily,' he added quickly. 'You obviously won't.'

'Presumably you won't hear from the police again until they've something to tell you, Robert, darling,' Maud said.

'You mean, not until her body's turned up?'

'Well, I wouldn't have put it quite so bluntly,' Maud remarked. 'But yes.'

Joseph cleared his throat. 'With drownings, bodies aren't always found. Tides are unpredictable. Obviously, the police and coastguard will do their best, but there's an outside chance that Lily will never be found.' He cleared his throat again. 'I had a word with our solicitor about that, and apparently there's nothing you can do about your status until after seven years.'

'Every day I dread there'll be a body, but at the same time, I want a body for the finality of it. Does that sound mad?' Robert asked.

'No, it doesn't,' Sarah said gently. 'It's entirely understandable. You're bound to have an element of hope until Lily's found.'

'While that's true,' Joseph said, 'finding Robert's car near the seafront, and some of Lily's clothes on the beach, is, I'm afraid, pretty suggestive of what happened. And of course, her short note. I think it'll help you if you accept what's clearly happened, son.'

'And I do. It's just, I keep hoping she'll walk through the door at any minute.' His voice broke. 'I love her and I don't want her to be dead, and I don't want to believe she is till I know for certain.' He put his head in his hands.

Maud leaned forward and put her hand on his shoulder. 'I'm afraid you're going to have to force yourself to believe it, darling. You'll ruin your life and James's if you don't. Babies sense an atmosphere, and it wouldn't be good for him if you were constantly unsettled and unhappy. You're stronger than that. As your father said, you must make sure that Lily's action wasn't in vain.'

'You told us you'd asked Mrs Bailey not to touch Lily's clothes or personal effects,' Sarah said. 'I wonder if they aren't too much of a reminder of her, and if you wouldn't do better to ask Mrs Bailey to clear Lily's cupboards and dressing room. She could put everything in suitcases, and store them in the attic. They can always be got down again. Or Nellie could do that, if you'd prefer. She and Walter are only in the next room.'

Joseph nodded. 'That's a good idea, Sarah. If you want, I'll have a word with Mrs Bailey, Robert.'

Robert stood up. 'I'll go and speak to her myself. But whether or not her clothes are in the wardrobe, I know that I'll always love Lily, and I will never ever forget her. And I'll never forgive myself for what happened.'

* * *

From her seat on the sofa in the rear reception room, Nellie listened to the sounds of talking coming from next door.

They were still talking about Lily, she told Walter with a groan, and she'd no intention of joining them until they'd changed the subject. She was genuinely sorry about what had happened, but she was also very sorry that Robert had met Lily in the first place. His life would have been so much better if he hadn't. And whatever he claimed to feel about Lily in the aftermath of her death, she'd seen enough of them both together to know that while he was still clearly head over heels about her, there was a strong chance that her father had been right and he could have come to regret his marriage.

Walter shook his head. 'The whole thing's tragic. It's impossible to think of her as dead.'

Nellie leaned against his shoulder. 'Father's very grateful to you for all your help since it happened. He seems much friendlier towards you now.'

Walter smiled at her. 'Maybe it's because he's come to realise how much I adore his lovely daughter.' He leaned down and kissed her lightly on the lips. She glanced swiftly towards the door, and then flung her arms around his neck, and pulled him on top of her.

At the sound of movement outside, they sprang apart.

'Oh, Walter, I do love you,' she whispered, as their eyes lingered on each other. 'I can't wait to marry you.'

'Nor me you.' He settled back against the sofa, put his arm around her shoulders and hugged her to him. 'As soon as this tragedy is behind us, I'm going to ask your father for his consent. I just hope you're right that I've won him over.'

'I am.' She nestled into the crook of his arm, her fingers playing with the buttons on the front of his waistcoat.

He moved closer to her. 'I can't wait to be able to whisk you up to a room of our own, and have my wicked way with you. It's only my awareness of those formidable Linfords in the next room, and that they could come in at any moment, that's keeping your clothes intact and my hands where they should be.'

Nellie giggled. 'Lucky Dottie – she's long been able to do what she wants with the man she loves.' She straightened up. 'My goodness, I'd completely forgotten Dorothy! She won't know about Lily yet. I'll have to tell her.'

'I thought you didn't have her address.'

'Actually, I have. I found her letter to Father a while ago and wrote down the address. It's funny, he's always so organised about filing his correspondence, yet he left Dottie's letter on his desk. I wondered at the time if he'd deliberately left it out for me to see. I know he's said he's cut her off, but you don't stop loving someone just because you don't approve of who they marry. Look at Robert and Lily. Father stayed close to Robert, despite Lily, and he even seemed to be getting used to her.'

Walter coughed.

'And anyway,' Nellie went on, 'apart from telling Dottie about Lily, I'm curious to know if I've got a German nephew or niece. She'll have had her baby ages ago.'

* * *

In the sitting-room in Kentish Town, Alice looked up from her sewing. 'I wonder how it went this morning with Robert.'

Thomas shrugged. He folded the newspaper and put it on the table beside him.

'They can say what they like,' he said, ignoring Alice's remark, 'there's trouble ahead. How on earth do the lunatic Allies expect Germany to be able to pay the gigantic sum of money they're asking for! Whatever David Lloyd George says about Germany deliberately evading the disarmament clauses in that ridiculous Versailles treaty, it'll continue to evade them, regardless.'

Alice nodded. 'That's a frightening thought.'

'Unfortunately, our complacent Government doesn't seem to think so. They don't seem to notice that Germany's still got an air force, and hasn't abolished conscription or given up their weapons. The Government should stop worrying about the riots in Londonderry, and pay attention to what's happening in Germany. Or rather, to what *should* be happening, but isn't.' He changed his position in the chair. 'Mind you, I don't know why I bother to follow the news. I don't have anything to contribute – the army's never going to need a one-legged man with half a hand missing.'

'The army might not need you, but your family does. At the moment, Robert needs all the support he can get. You should've let Joseph take us to see him this morning.'

'I don't think so,' he said sharply. 'They'll say everything that needs to be said. And it would've made me sick to hear them trying to sound as if they really cared about Lily. They didn't. You can be sure that they're extremely glad she did what she did.'

'That's ridiculous, Thomas, and you know it,' she said. 'Whatever they might have thought of her, no one would be pleased that she's killed herself.'

'You're welcome to your opinion. Mine is that Lily was worth any number of them, and family get-togethers will be more boring than ever because of her absence.'

20

LONDON

Late September 1920

Joseph stood at the front door, waiting for Maud.

His son had done well in the past few months, he thought, coping with what had inevitably been a terrible shock, a shock that had been intensified by Robert's overwhelming feeling of guilt.

That Robert would take so much of the blame on himself had been a huge surprise to him, and a very unwelcome one. Had he anticipated that Robert would feel as guilty as he did, Joseph wasn't sure that he would've persisted with his plan. But really, how could he have known that just a few days before Nellie's birthday weekend, Lily had seen Robert talking to another woman, and had been tremendously unsettled by it?

That woman had been Marian Ames, Robert had later told him when they'd gone to the Club about a couple of weeks after Lily's supposed death. It had been a perfectly innocent chance meeting, but when he'd got back home, Lily had confronted him and all but accused him of preferring Marian to her.

From her mood in the following few days, it had been obvious to Robert that he hadn't been able to allay her fears, and he'd been torturing himself that Lily's sudden sense of insecurity may have been what triggered her suicide. Instead of showing irritation at her anxiety, he should've shown her how deeply he loved her by an even greater display of affection than usual.

Joseph had attempted to give Robert some peace of mind by taking a share of the responsibility for Lily's death upon himself. He told Robert that he, too, felt somewhat guilty about what had happened. His opposition to their marriage might well have aggravated Lily's unhappiness and made her feel unwanted by the family.

That may be so, Robert had told him, but that wouldn't have driven her to suicide. Lily had known from the day she met him that Joseph disliked her, and while she wished it could have been otherwise, she'd learned to live with it. And anyway Joseph hadn't been quite as unpleasant towards her since they'd married and James had been born.

No, it had been seeing him with Marian that had been the catalyst, Robert insisted.

But later, in the solitude of his home once Maud had retired to bed, Joseph had felt a strong sense of discomfort at what he now knew, and was weighed down with guilt and remorse for causing his son such misery. He'd had to remind himself more than once that his motives had been well-intentioned, and that'd he'd sought only to spare Robert the lifetime of suffering that an ill-judged marriage would bring.

Even a month after Lily's death, Robert's anguish was still so great that he couldn't bring himself to celebrate James's first birthday. But now, another month having passed, there were early signs, such as the invitation to lunch that day, that Robert was finally starting to look to the future again.

But the healing process wouldn't be totally complete until Robert had someone else in his life. Of that Joseph was sure.

And as he'd lain in his bed last night, he remembered how Robert had mentioned enjoying his short conversation with Marian Ames, and he thought back to how well they'd seemed to get on during Robert's month in London. In sudden excitement, it occurred to him that she would be just the right sort of someone else for Robert.

Furthermore, during the month in which Robert and Marian had seen a great deal of each other, her father, too, had felt the suitability of a match between them, and both he and Joseph had contrived to bring Robert and Marian together as frequently as possible. Unfortunately, the machinations of Lily had put a stop to their hopes.

But now that Marian had reappeared, and was still unattached, as Joseph had swiftly ascertained, he'd been pondering all morning how he could bring them together again. Apart from Marian being just the kind of wife Robert needed, an alliance between Linford & Sons and a successful builders' merchant would be an added bonus, an opinion that Marian's father had shared the last time around, and quite probably still would.

As the person responsible for his son's mental torment, the least he could do was try to put Robert back on a path to the happiness he deserved, Joseph told himself, and he'd contact Henry Ames in the coming week, and invite him to dinner one evening at the Club. That would be the first step.

He'd have to tread carefully with Robert, though. Although he'd begun to make progress since the first nightmarish days, it would be a long time before he was ready to contemplate marrying again. And anyway, he wouldn't be legally able to do so for seven years. But those years would pass more easily if he had the right woman waiting patiently at his side.

But he'd be honest with Henry Ames from the start, and tell him about the timescale involved. It was always possible that despite the many advantages of having close ties with Linford & Sons, Ames might consider that a seven-year wait was too much to ask of his daughter.

It was also possible that Marian herself might feel the same way.

She could, quite justifiably, refuse even to meet with Robert again. After all, only a very special person would be willing to wait for so long to be married. But then he recalled how well she'd got on with Robert when first they'd met, and how his instinct had told him that Marian's feelings for Robert ran deep. But if he were wrong, the sooner he found out, the better.

But assuming that neither Henry nor Marian was deterred, Joseph would look for the earliest opportunity – one that wouldn't appear contrived – to invite the Ames family for dinner. And Robert, too.

With a sense of hope that had almost become a stranger to him, he moved to the foot of the stairs.

'Do hurry up, Maud,' he called to her. 'Thomas will think we've forgotten to pick him up, and the longer we leave it, the more disappointed he'll be when we finally *do* turn up.'

* * *

'Don't fuss so,' Thomas snapped.

Alice stepped back and held up her hands in the air. 'All right. If you don't want me to help you stay upright, that's fine.'

'I don't. They'll be here any minute now, and I don't want to look like a scarecrow propped up in a field, do I? When we get to

Robert's, I'll let Joseph help me out of the car and into the house, but after that, I'm on my own. Is that clear?'

'Perfectly, thank you.' She hesitated. 'I hope you're going to be pleasant today.'

'I'm always pleasant.'

'No, you're not, and you know it. And when you're unpleasant to me, it embarrasses everyone else. As it's the first time we've been to Robert's since the accident—'

'Since she killed herself, you mean? Drowning yourself is not what I'd call an accident.'

'Well, *I* prefer to think of Lily's death as an accident, as a cry for help that wasn't heard.'

'Anyone on the beach would've needed amazing hearing to pick up the cry of a woman out at sea. Waves are pretty noisy, you know.'

'You have your opinion and I have mine. But let's get back to today. We must make it as easy for Robert as we can, and that means you being nice to everyone, including me. It's the least we can do to help.'

He turned awkwardly on his crutches and glared at her. 'Don't presume to tell me how to behave towards my nephew. I'm very fond of him, as it happens, and I know exactly how to conduct myself. And what's more, I intend to be nice, as you put it, to Walter and Nellie, too. Walter seems a sharp lad – he's won Joseph round which can't have been easy – and Nellie's got some spirit in her. Must have got it from her mother as it certainly didn't come from her cowardly father, who hid behind a building company rather than fight for his country.'

She gave a theatrical sigh. 'Don't you think you should drop that line, Thomas? I've heard it so many times that I can no longer be bothered to argue with you.'

A slow grin spread across his face. 'You know, Alice, just

recently you've begun to sound quite spirited yourself. You've started answering back instead of standing there, nun-like in demeanour, while I wipe my feet on you. Or rather, my foot. The new you is much more fun. Don't climb back into your shell again, will you?'

She laughed. 'I promise I won't. If I'd known the effect it would have on you, I'd have broken that shell a little sooner.'

'I'm not sure you *do* quite understand the full effect of your new-found spunk. If we weren't off to Robert's at any moment, I'd show you just how powerful it is. In fact—'

Their eyes met.

The roar of an engine filled the street, and both turned sharply to face the window as Joseph's pale grey Austin Twenty drew up outside the house. They saw Joseph get out and approach the front door, and Maud move from the front seat into the back.

'So much for that idea,' Thomas murmured ruefully as he heard the maid letting Joseph in.

'Sorry to keep you waiting,' Joseph said, coming into the room.

'We'd have been happy to wait a bit longer – wouldn't we, Alice?' Thomas replied. For a long moment, he stared into Alice's face, and then he smiled, turned on his good leg, and with the aid of his crutches, manoeuvred himself towards the door.

As Alice waited for Thomas to get through the doorway, a buzz of excitement fizzled deep within her, and she realised that for the first time in a very long while, she was actually looking forward to returning home.

* * *

As the sun sank slowly towards the blue-grey horizon, and the shadows thrown by the trees lengthened across the grass, a stillness descended upon the garden, broken only by the occasional crackle of a bird as it landed on one of the few dead leaves that had yet to fall from the branch, or by the sharp clap of a pigeon shutting its wings.

Joseph settled more comfortably in his garden chair, and glanced at Walter.

'Thomas was in a better mood today,' he remarked, raising his whisky glass to his lips. 'When Charles said that he and Sarah were ready to leave, I was amazed when Thomas asked Charles to drop him and Alice at home. I thought he'd wait to go with us. And he was nicer today towards Alice than he's been for a long time.'

Walter nodded. 'He *can* be a difficult man.'

'Don't be afraid to say what you think, son. Thomas can be bloody rude. It's a constant source of amazement to all of us that Alice has put up with him for so long. And a constant source of concern – God knows what we'd do if she left! Fortunately, if today is anything to go by, we need not worry.' He took a sip of his drink, put his glass down, and gave Walter a wry grin. 'But I don't think you've joined me out here to talk about Thomas, have you? Nor that Nellie was happy to let you leave her side for that reason.'

Walter cleared his throat. 'You're right, sir.' He coughed and changed his position. 'As you know, my period as an articled clerk has come to an end and I'm now fully qualified and in a good practice. I'm sure I don't need to tell you, sir, that I love your daughter very much, and now that I'm able to support her, I want to marry her more than I can say. May I have your permission to ask Nellie for her hand in marriage?'

Joseph leaned forward and clapped Walter on the shoulder.

'Of course, you have it, dear boy. I couldn't be more delighted to give my consent. You've grown into a fine young man, and I know I'll be entrusting Nellie to a safe pair of hands. And to someone able to keep that strong-willed daughter of mine in check.'

They both laughed.

'We'll toast the news with champagne later – I imagine you'll be proposing as soon as possible. If you haven't already done so,' he added with a smile. 'Or if she hasn't already proposed to you.' Both laughed again. 'For the moment, though—' He held out his glass to clink it against Walter's.

'Thank you, sir. I must say, that's a great relief.'

'Why don't you come for dinner tomorrow evening and we can talk about dates, and the announcement for the papers? I imagine Nellie will want a June wedding – most girls do. Assuming she says yes, of course – we're taking rather a lot for granted.'

They laughed again.

Joseph turned slightly to look more directly at Walter, his face suddenly serious.

'There's something I ought to make clear, Walter. It's actually the reverse of what you said to me a while ago. I'm not consenting to the marriage because of your help and discretion over what happened with Lily. Thanks to Nellie pushing you into my path – almost literally at times—,' he added ruefully, 'I've come to know you well, and I like you. I would've said yes with the greatest of pleasure even if you'd no knowledge at all of the Lily situation. I hope you believe that.'

'I do, sir. Thank you. I really appreciate your reassurance.'

The sound of doors slamming, followed by voices and laughter, drifted through the windows into the garden.

'It's getting somewhat chilly,' Joseph said, rising to his feet. 'I think I'll go in. And we ought not to keep Nellie in suspense for much longer. If I know my daughter, she'll be waiting for me to disappear, and as soon as I do, she'll be out here in a trice, wanting to know what I said.'

'I can't disagree with that, sir.'

'And I've known her long enough to know it'll have been her recommendation that you speak to me this afternoon. She'll have calculated that I'd be so pleased about the improvement in Robert's spirits that this would be the ideal moment.'

Walter smiled. 'You do, indeed, know Nellie, sir.'

'If I bump into her on my way in, I'll assume a neutral expression and leave it to you to tell her that her scheming's worked. The champagne will be ready when you come in.' He paused. 'Welcome to the family, son – it's about time you officially joined it.'

* * *

Robert stood at the nursery window, a cup of coffee in his hand, and stared down at the garden. A grey mist was creeping across the grass, leaching the bronze from the leaves that had gathered at the foot of the trees. As he stood watching, twilight deepened into the dark of night, and a dun mantle fell across the world.

Every so often, he turned and glanced at the cot, and smiled at the sleeping James. The family had certainly tired James out that afternoon, encouraging him to take a few wobbly steps on his own before he collapsed. And after that, he'd sat there gurgling happily, looking at everyone and everything, as if keen to discover the world for himself. It was no wonder that he'd fallen asleep as soon as Annie had put him down that evening.

If only Lily had been there to see James take his first steps! How excited she would have been. She'd loved James so much. No one could've been a better mother. Or a better wife.

For a heady moment, he could almost feel her come and stand quietly beside him. Motionless, he held his breath, waiting for he knew not what.

The moment passed, and he started to breathe again.

For the rest of his life, a part of Lily would remain alive for him, in his heart, in his mind, and through their son.

Realising this was helping him find a degree of inner peace.

He'd finally had to accept that she'd gone, that when he turned over at night she wouldn't be there, that his day would never again be brightened by her smile, that she'd never again face him across the dinner table, bringing his day to an end with such joy.

His beloved Lily was gone.

But his deep love for her would live on, whatever happened in the years to come.

He'd invited the family over that day because they'd all been so kind at the time of Lily's death and in the weeks after that. Not one of them had blamed him, and they'd all done their best to help in whatever way they could. Nevertheless, he'd fully anticipated that the lunch that day would be a painful reminder of the last family lunch in Hampstead when Lily had still been with him.

Yet it hadn't been. To his great surprise, it wasn't only James who'd enjoyed the day – he had, too.

After the first few nostalgic moments, he'd found himself relaxing for the first time since losing Lily, and he'd actually been able to laugh. Looking back, he realised that it was because, although she'd never been far from his thoughts throughout the day, he'd finally accepted that he could never bring her back.

And what surprised him almost as much was his reaction to the news of Nellie and Walter's engagement. Instead of the idea of an impending wedding plunging him back into grief about his own situation, he'd wholeheartedly welcomed Walter into the family, and had been genuinely delighted to do so.

He liked Walter enormously, and he knew of the effort that Walter had made to convince Joseph that he was worthy of Nellie, which Nellie had confided in him some time ago. Also, he appreciated the friendship that Walter had shown him, and the advice he'd received from him on more than one occasion.

Walter would be the perfect companion for his sister, whom he loved dearly, but who was quite the most headstrong woman he knew. Whatever Nellie wanted, Nellie was always determined to get. It was fortunate for the family that Nellie had clearly wanted quiet, logically thinking Walter from the day she met him. And she'd never looked happier than when she'd announced their engagement that afternoon.

If there'd been any remnants of sadness and gloom lurking in the corners of the Hampstead house, Nellie's joy had driven them out.

And he knew that he was now ready to start living again.

But not to get married. It'd be a very long time, if ever, before he'd even think of marrying again.

21

LOWER EAST SIDE, NEW YORK

October 1920

'I was thinking this morning,' Ruth said, who was perched on the edge of the parlour sofa, watching Lily finish a seam by hand, 'that we ought to go out this evening. The next lot of orders won't come in till Monday, so we should make the most of a Saturday evening without anything to finish. And we've got things to celebrate.'

'Such as?'

'Well, for a start, you've only been here for three months, but you're already getting orders for dresses.'

Lily glanced across to the dressmaker's mannequin, and her eyes skimmed the lace-trimmed shirtwaist bodice, with its long sleeves and pleated front, and the lace-trimmed ankle-length skirt, all in silk. She turned back to Ruth and smiled happily. 'It was so lucky that Mrs Goldstein mentioned to your father that she needed a dress, and he recommended me. And then that she told everyone how pleased she was with her dress. It was such an easy style, too.'

'It was beautiful, Lily.'

'I don't know about beautiful, but it was neat and tailored, which was what she wanted for committee meetings. And I don't think I told you, but she came by this morning and ordered two more for the cold weather – this time in cashmere. And a couple of her friends want the same thing, too.'

'So we've got that to celebrate. And also, that Pavel's going to work for the bakery,' Ruth went on, beaming. 'They told him this evening that he'd got the job. *Abba* said he's got to keep on going to school, though.'

'Isaak will be pleased. That wagon he made Pavel out of that old packing crate, and using the baby-carriage wheels he got from Mrs Abelman, was really clever.'

Ruth nodded. 'He wouldn't have got the job without it. But it's going to be a long day for him. He starts at four thirty every morning, loading the first of the day's orders, and then he's got to deliver them. He'll go backwards and forwards till everything's delivered, and he'll have to be quick if he's going to get it done before school. They're giving him a dollar seventy-five for the week, and a couple of rolls, coffee and milk every morning before he starts. I wonder if he'd have wanted to be a baker if we were still in Kishinev. We'll never know.'

'He certainly sounds keen on being a baker one day.' She paused. 'I don't mean to pry, Ruth, but I'm curious why you left Russia. It's just that you've got so many Russian things in the apartment, and you often mention Kishinev. I imagine you're living pretty much as you would've done there. It's not an easy life here, so I was wondering why you came. I hope you don't mind me asking.'

'Not in the least. I'd have told you sooner if I'd known you were interested. Basically, we didn't have a choice,' Ruth said bluntly. 'If we hadn't got out, we'd almost certainly be dead by now. Thousands of Jews have been massacred in the pogroms over the years. You can't imagine the horrors that *Abba* and *Momma* have seen, such as little babies torn to pieces while the local police stood by and watched. No matter how hard *Abba* and *Momma* try, they can't bury the memories, but they never talk about it.'

Lily stared at her in disbelief. 'But why would anyone do such terrible things?'

'The Russian Government needed to blame someone for everything wrong in the country, didn't they?' Ruth said with bitterness. 'So they blamed the Jews. The worse things got in Russia, the worse life got for the Jews. They passed laws to stop us working, travelling, living where we wanted. But *Momma* and *Abba* kept hoping things would improve because despite everything, they loved Russia. We held on till Isaak was fifteen. The Russian army conscripted boys at sixteen, and that's why we finally left. Lots of families never saw their conscripted sons again.'

'But that's awful!'

'It was. People did everything they could to stop their boys from being taken. One of the mothers in our village cut off her son's finger so he couldn't fire a gun. Another hid her son in a wagon heading for Germany. She gave him enough money to buy a passage from Germany to America, and then buried him under a pile of wood. And it wasn't just dangerous for boys. My friends and I weren't allowed to stand or walk together in a group of three or more. If we did, the soldiers would rough us up. Year after year, people we knew fled to America, and in the end we followed them.'

'How did you know where to go when you got here?'

Ruth shrugged. 'From letters. People wrote home once they'd settled here. And from some of the people who'd been sent back home by immigration officials at Ellis Island. They'd heard on the boat that in Lower East Side people spoke the same language, and would help you. And if they gave you a job, you wouldn't have to work on the Sabbath.'

'That's where *I* heard about Orchard Street – on the boat.'

Ruth nodded. 'I remember you saying that. So, although we work very hard, we don't live with the daily fear of being murdered. And we're all together, which is the most important thing.' Her face broke out into a smile. 'But we don't go out enough – so, how about tonight?'

Lily shrugged. 'Why not? Where shall we go?'

'Well, there's Leow's Avenue B Theater, on the corner of East 5th Street. We could see a movie if there's one playing – we haven't done that for a while. Or there's the Sunshine Theater on East Houston Street? You've never been there, and I think you'd like it even if you didn't understand a word they were saying. It's a Yiddish vaudeville house,' Ruth added with a laugh. 'And afterwards, we could get a knish from Yonah Schimmel's, which is almost next door to the theatre.'

'What's a knish?'

'Think of *Momma*'s *piroshki*, but larger. A round piece of dough with a filling inside. Mashed potato and onions is my favourite, and it's Isaak's, too.'

'Then I'll get one of those, and also one for Isaak.'

Ruth moved from the arm of the sofa to the seat.

Lily glanced at her, and promptly put down her sewing.

'What're you not telling me, Ruth? You've gone bright red.'

'Just that Isaak would like to come with us. Actually, the Sunshine Theater and knishes were his idea. Would you mind?'

'And that's made you blush? Because your brother wants to go somewhere with his sister?' She laughed.

Ruth wriggled in discomfort. 'I don't think it's me he wants to be with.'

'Oh, I see.' Lily's laughter died away. She looked down at her sewing.

'You told us you were married, and that your husband died,' Ruth said, a trace of awkwardness in her voice. 'And we know you've a son who's with family in England, and that you're saving up to go back and see him. But England's far away and it will take you a long time to save enough, even though you work hard. And you do seem to be settling here. Isaak is twenty, and he likes you very much. He wants you to know that he'd like to walk out with you.'

Out of the corner of her eye, Lily saw Isaak appear in the doorway, and stand quietly there, leaning against the wooden door jamb, his dark eyes on her.

Avoiding looking directly at him, she kept her eyes on Ruth. 'Your parents wouldn't like that, Ruth,' she said quietly. 'Isaak is a fine-looking man and a hard worker, and he'll make someone an excellent husband, but that someone can't be me. It must be a Jewish girl, ideally Russian, too, like you. It's what your *abba* and *momma* will want for him, and it's right that they do. Every time you leave the apartment, or come into it, you touch the *mezuzah* by the front door. All of you do. Always. Your beliefs are at the heart of your lives, and Isaak needs a wife who shares them.'

'You could learn those beliefs, if you wanted.'

'It's not the same. And I don't really want to. I'd be marrying someone whose parents were against it, as yours would certainly be, and that could lead to a lot of unhappiness. I know all about that. As I told you, Robert's father was violently against us marrying and made things really difficult. That's a bad way to start a marriage. And apart from that, your parents have been extremely kind to me – giving me a home, a job, making me feel part of the family – and I'd never willingly do anything that would upset them.'

There was a movement in the doorway.

Lily glanced towards the kitchen and saw Isaak turn and walk away, his head down. A minute later, she heard the front door close behind him.

For a moment, she felt a wave of regret for what might have been, for the security she might've had, but she shrugged it off. Compared with seeing Robert again – just to see him once more was all she asked for, even though she couldn't live with him – and compared with going back for James, security mattered little. Nothing was going to stop her from returning to England.

'All I know for certain is that one day I'll go back for my baby,' she told Ruth. 'Not till I've got him will I be able to think about anyone else, and maybe not even then. Will you tell Isaak that I'm very sorry?'

Ruth nodded slowly. 'And I'm sorry, too. You would've been my sister.'

Lily smiled at Ruth. 'It wouldn't at all surprise me if you didn't have a sister before too long, though it won't be me. I think your mother's realised that Isaak's now thinking about his future – I saw her talking to the matchmaker a few days ago, and the search to find him a wife is probably already under way.'

Ruth nodded. 'Isaak knows that *Momma*'s spoken to the *shadkhan*. But before it went any further, he needed to find out if there was any chance with you. That's why he asked me to speak to you.'

'I see.'

Ruth bit her lip. 'I hope you won't let this drive you away – I'd really miss you.'

Lily laughed. 'Don't worry, I'll be here for some time yet. But once you're a telephone operator, you'll make so many friends, you won't notice whether I'm here or not.'

Ruth hugged her knees. 'I'd always notice. But I do hope I get a job with them. I intend to apply very soon – I'm sure they need more operators. D'you know, so many houses have telephones now that people don't use their names any longer – they've got numbers instead? And the numbers are getting longer all the time as more and more telephones are being added. I've worked so hard on my English that I've hardly any accent, and I'm definitely over five feet tall, which you have to be to sit at the switchboard. I'd much rather work there than plough through endless garments. I hate sewing. And I'd get more money, too.'

'Why don't you apply now? Pavel's now working, and I'm bringing in better money, Alexei can surely manage without you. You're always talking about the Cortlandt Exchange, so you should try there. If you like, I'll come with you next week when we've finished the new orders.'

'I *would* like that, thank you. I bet I'll be nervous.' Ruth smiled gratefully at Lily. 'You're a really good friend, you know. In fact, you're more than that. Even though you don't want to be with Isaak, you're still part of this family now, and whatever happens in the future, you'll never again be on your own.'

* * *

But she wasn't on her own, Lily thought, when later she stood at the window and stared at the sleeping street. Robert would always be her husband. She would never, ever stop loving him, and he would always live deep in her heart.

As time had passed, though, she'd had to force herself to face what his absence from her life said about the depth of his feelings for her. If he'd loved her a fraction as much as she'd loved him, he'd have instantly hired someone to look for her. Any detective would have discovered in no time at all that a Lily Brown had sailed to New York, and any American investigator would almost certainly have started his search for her in Lower East Side, the district for which most new arrivals headed, especially as Robert would have told him that she could sew.

And he would have found her.

But he hadn't. There'd been no communication from either an investigator or from Robert, and a deep sense of hurt had taken a seat alongside love.

Once or twice in the early days in New York, when the pain of not being with Robert had been almost unbearable, and her burning desire to contact him had been overwhelming, she'd been on the verge of writing to him, but at the last moment, fear had stopped her from doing so.

She didn't know what Joseph had told Robert about her disappearance, but he was a clever man and he was bound to have come up with a convincing story that would've presented her in a bad light. The fact that Robert hadn't looked for her was an indication of that, and he might now be deeply regretting their marriage.

She was absolutely certain, too, that if she warned the family that she'd be returning for James, they'd find a way of preventing her from getting anywhere near him.

Rather than risk that, she'd had to force herself to accept that Robert, unable to marry anyone else because he was still married to her, and unable ever to communicate with her as he didn't know where she was, would be feeling the pain of loneliness, just as she was, and that much as she desperately wished it weren't the case, that was the way it would always have to be.

22

HAMPSTEAD

June 1921

To the strains of the Wedding March, wearing a slim white gown of beaded-lace upon silk, with a round neckline and full-length beaded-lace sleeves, Nellie walked slowly down the aisle of St John-at-Hampstead on Joseph's arm. A line of tiny bead-buttons ran down the back of her bodice and led into a skirt that gently filled out at the back as it fell to the floor. Her sleek dark hair had been cropped in a modern style, and a tiara slid into it, from which there floated a veil of filmy white lace that just covered her face, but behind her reached to the floor. For jewellery, she wore a small diamond stud in each ear, a present from her parents the evening before.

On either side of the aisle, clusters of white roses had been fixed to the ends of the pews, and were filling the church with their fragrance. In her hands, she carried a posy of the same flowers, full-blown, loosely tied with a ribbon of *eau de Nil* silk. She'd wanted one bridesmaid only, her cousin Louisa, who walked behind her in a mid-calf dress in the same *eau de Nil*, a single white rose in her hand.

Christopher and James walked behind Louisa, each in an *eau de Nil* pageboy waistcoat suit. Christopher held James's hand very tightly as James toddled unevenly down the aisle, an expression of intense concentration on his face.

His eyes never leaving Nellie, Walter stood at the front of the church in a black evening tailcoat over a cream silk waistcoat, with an *eau de Nil* tie and a matching pocket handkerchief. In his lapel, he wore a single white rose, as did Charles, who stood next to him, visibly delighted to have been asked to be best man, Walter's way of thanking him for the introduction to Nellie.

When she reached the steps leading up to the altar, Nellie stopped in the circle of red-gold brilliance that flowed from the midday sun through the stained-glass windows above the altar, and handed her posy to Louisa. She turned to her father with a nervous smile. He took her hand in his, held it a moment and then put it into Walter's and stepped away.

She looked up at her groom through the milky haze of the veil.

'You look really lovely,' he said quietly. 'I knew you would, but you're beyond anything I could have dreamed of.'

Her face broke out into a radiant smile, and hand in hand they turned and faced the vicar.

* * *

The speeches over, Joseph started circulating among the white-covered tables in the large marquee that had been erected in his garden.

He'd offered to book a hotel for the reception, but Nellie had been adamant that she wanted her Wedding Breakfast in the

Primrose Hill house that had always been her home, and he'd given in to her wishes. After all, the garden could easily accommodate the family and all the other guests, and with the brightly coloured flowers that bordered the lawn being in full bloom in June, he'd known there'd be a highly attractive background for the photographs.

Yes, Nellie had definitely chosen the right venue, he thought as he moved from table to table, exchanging casual words with one group of guests after another. And it was a lot cheaper than a hotel, which he appreciated, although he strongly suspected that saving him money hadn't been part of her motivation. Knowing Nellie, it was more likely to be that she'd wanted to spare Walter's family any glaring evidence of the imbalance between the two families' financial situations.

Not that Walter's background mattered at all.

He was already a high-earning lawyer, and Joseph had seen for himself how shrewd and quick-thinking his new son-in-law could be. Walter's talents, along with his natural enthusiasm for the law, and his strong work ethic, was going to prove invaluable to Linford & Sons.

And there'd been no reason for Nellie to economise on his behalf, anyway, he thought. She knew full well that the company was booming.

As he'd predicted, the firm had been in a strong position to profit from the explosion in the demand for houses at the end of the war, and owing to the scarcity of building materials, coupled with rising inflation, the houses they'd been building in and around London had sold at a very high price. Like all builders, though, he was well aware that the situation was changing – building costs had started falling, and house prices were dropping. But the high number of units they were able to sell was more than offsetting the reduction in price. Demand was still growing, and there was no reason to think it would dry up at any point soon.

On the contrary, in fact.

Increasingly, people at management and administration level were clamouring to buy a house, and also teachers, civil servants and those in retailing. It was true that demand was falling among workers in factories, shipyards, coal mines and on the land. But the company was still building houses for rent, in addition to those for sale, so Linford & Sons was able to meet the demand at both ends of the market, and Nellie could have had her reception wherever she'd wanted.

* * *

'I'm so glad you and your parents could make it today, Marian,' Joseph said, reaching the table where Marian was sitting with several of Joseph's business colleagues. 'When I saw your parents go across to Nellie, I thought I'd come over and say hello. It must be quite some time now since you got back from that finishing school of yours, but I do believe this is the first time I've seen you since your return. Your father's kept me up to date with your accomplishments, though.'

'How extremely boring for you,' she said with a laugh. 'If today has done nothing more than put an end to such a tedious outpouring of information, it will have achieved something.'

Joseph smiled broadly. 'Oh, I'm sure it will achieve more than that.'

'Hello, Marian,' Robert said, coming up behind his father. 'I glimpsed you earlier, but I was waiting for the speeches to finish. There was one speech in particular that I thought would never end,' he added, with a sidelong grin at his father.

'In that case,' Joseph said in amusement, 'I won't inflict any more words on either of you, but will leave you to talk to each other.'

'If I may,' Robert said, and he sat down on the empty seat next to Marian.

Swivelling in his chair, he turned to face her.

Her dark brown hair, tapered short at the back and drawn into a single curl on each cheek, emphasised the long black lashes that fringed the clear blue eyes that shone out of her smiling face.

'I hope you don't mind me saying that you're looking lovely, Marian,' he said.

She shook her head. 'I don't mind at all. It makes a happy change from Father looking at me as I stand before him in my finery, and saying that he's just remembered that he needs to check a delivery of concrete!'

They both laughed.

'I could understand it better if he was inspired to think of a shortage of shingle,' Robert remarked. 'That's the name for the way you've had your hair cut, isn't it? It suits you.'

'Very neatly done, Robert,' she said with a smile. Then her smile faded, and she leaned forward and rested her hand lightly on his arm.

He felt a sudden urge to cover her hand with his. It was so long since he'd felt the touch of a woman's hand on his in such a way. Not since Lily. With difficulty, he forced himself not to move.

'This is so happy an occasion,' she said, 'that I hate to bring up anything sad, but I can't not tell you how terribly upset I was to hear about your wife. I feel so desperately sorry for her and for all of you.'

'Thank you, Marian,' he said quietly. 'It's something one never really gets over, but I'm doing my best. I have to – there's James to think of, apart from anything else.'

They turned towards the small boy, who was sitting on Annie's lap, pushing her hand away in irritation as she tried to stop him from cramming a *petit four* into his mouth. Both his face and his white shirt were smeared with chocolate. Annie looked harassed.

As she glanced up from James, Robert caught her eye. He gave her a wry smile and pointed his finger upwards. She nodded, stood up with James in her arms and ignoring his loud wails of protest, carried him out of the marquee and towards the house.

'Oh, dear,' Robert said, turning back to Marian. 'I'm afraid you're not seeing him at his best. He'll be two next month. In his defence, I understand that his behaviour's fairly normal for that age.'

She smiled. 'I'm sure it is. And it's been a long, very exciting day for him. He made a sweet little pageboy. Did you see the look on his face as he walked down the aisle? He was trying so hard to get it right, even though he probably had no idea what was going on.'

'He was, wasn't he?' he said, brightening up. 'It's kind of you to say that. But I always knew you were a lovely person.'

Their eyes met. Both looked quickly away.

'And the other two attendants did very well, too,' she said presently, breaking the awkward silence that had fallen. 'The bridesmaid's a very pretty girl. She'll be quite stunning when she grows up.'

'They're my cousins – Uncle Charles and Aunt Sarah's children. Louisa's quite strong-willed like her mother, but Christopher seems a gentle boy. He's got a good grip, though. James didn't stand a hope in hell of getting away from him.'

He inched his chair slightly towards her.

'I'm sorry about the awkwardness just now, Marian—' he

began. She gave a dismissive wave. 'No, don't deny it – we both felt it. On my part, it was because I know I should like to see you again, but I also know that I'm not properly free. It means that I don't feel I can ask you out to dinner.'

'Oh, what a shame, Robert, because I enjoy our conversations, and it just so happens that my diary's clear next Saturday evening.'

His face broke out into a broad smile. 'Well, in that case, I'll pick you up at seven thirty, if that suits you.'

* * *

'And what did Henry Ames want with my darling husband?' Nellie asked, sitting back down at the table. She laid her cheek against Walter's arm. 'I saw him bending your ear after he'd spoken to me, but I couldn't hear what he was saying.'

'Next time, I'll ask him to speak more loudly. But don't worry, it wouldn't have interested you. It was about one of his premises. Trouble seems to be brewing, and he wanted advice. I've agreed to meet him when we get back from our honeymoon.'

She stretched up and kissed him on the cheek. 'Everyone can see what a clever man I've married.'

'It was certainly clever of me to marry you, Nellie,' his voice thickening as he gazed at her. 'You're beautiful, and there's nothing you can't do. It amazes me how you organised this wedding, right down to the colour of my handkerchief. It's been absolutely perfect.'

'Hasn't it all been wonderful! And what's also made me so happy is seeing Robert talking to Marian. They met before he married Lily, you know, and we all liked her then. We thought he did, too, but unfortunately he went back to Lily. But with no Lily...' Her voice trailed off, and she shrugged.

'I hope you're not—'

At the sound of the band starting up by the dance floor, he stopped speaking.

A smile played across Nellie's lips. 'Oh, dear, this is the moment you've been dreading, Walter.'

'What must be, must be, dear wife.' He stood up and held out his hand to her. 'This is our dance, I believe.'

Gathering up her skirt, Nellie rose with a smile, gave him her free hand and let him lead her to the polished parquet floor that had been laid down at the end of the marquee. As they passed between the tables on the way to their first dance as husband and wife, the guests rose to their feet and closed in behind them.

Walter led her to the middle of the floor, took her in his arms and looked deep into her eyes. 'I love you, Nellie Shawcross,' he said. 'I love you even more than I loathe dancing, and that says a lot.'

And with a confident sweep of his arm, he began to move her around the floor to the strains of 'I'll Be With You in Apple Blossom Time'.

* * *

Standing near the entrance to the marquee, Charles watched Thomas balance himself with the aid of his crutches. Given that Thomas had been snapping at him and everyone else all day, he didn't relish the prospect of driving him home.

'I don't envy you your passengers,' Joseph said drily, coming to stand next to him.

'I don't envy myself! It's going to feel a much longer journey than it actually is. At least on the way here, I had Sarah with me, and her daunting presence kept him in check. It'd take a braver person than Thomas to risk Sarah's tongue. But Sarah's busy chatting, and Thomas insists on leaving now, so I'm having to undergo the forthcoming ordeal on my own. It doesn't bear thinking about, especially as he's had a few drinks. Perhaps I should appeal to Sarah's better nature and ask her to keep me company?'

Joseph stared across the marquee to the table where Sarah was engrossed in conversation with Maud. 'She doesn't look like a woman who'd welcome an interruption.'

Charles followed his gaze. 'I'm afraid you're right,' he said mournfully. 'I'll just have to turn a deaf ear to Thomas and return as soon as I've dropped him off.' He turned back to Joseph. 'Maud looks stunning, by the way.'

'So she should! I won't tell you how much that bit of lilac silk set me back.'

'I'm glad to hear that the business is doing so well, despite your fears,' Charles said with a smile.

Joseph glanced sideways at him. 'Ah, yes. I'd forgotten the concerns I expressed a few months ago. But that was before the railway and transport unions decided at the eleventh hour not to strike along with the miners, and a national strike was averted.'

A gale of laughter reached them from the far end of the marquee. They looked towards the dance floor, and saw that Nellie was dancing with Christopher, who clearly had no idea what he was doing.

'You'll miss her,' Charles said. 'She's a great girl, full of life. Your house is going to feel very quiet with her gone.'

'That won't happen for a bit. Walter's moving in with us while we're doing some work on their house. We gave them a small house in Camden Town as a wedding present. But you're right, we *will* miss her when the time comes.'

'D'you ever think about Dorothy at times like this? You never mention her these days, but a firstborn's always special. She was such a serious little thing.'

'The stock answer is no – she cast herself out of the family when she married a German, and that's that. But the honest answer is yes. How could I not? But that's just between us. Maud and I don't talk about her, though I know she must think of Dorothy, just as I do.'

'She's bound to.'

'As I may have told you, I'm certain that Nellie writes to Dorothy, which I'm glad about. I don't know if Maud's aware of that – she hasn't said she is. But then she wouldn't, would she, after what I said about disowning Dorothy. But if anything happened in Germany that made Dorothy anxious about her safety, although I can't imagine that anything would, not now that Germany's agreed to pay war reparations—'

'They didn't exactly have a choice!' Charles said mildly. 'If they hadn't, the Allies would simply have marched into Germany and occupied it, and that's the last thing the Germans would've wanted.'

'—but if it did,' Joseph continued, 'I'd want Dorothy to feel there was someone here she could contact. It's why keeping a link to her through Nellie is important. Despite what I said in the past, if Dorothy were vulnerable, I'd want her back in England, and her child, German or not. I've separated one baby from his mother, and I'd never do that again. But she couldn't bring her husband. I wouldn't do that to Thomas.'

'That sounds very fair, Joseph.'

'And talking of daughters,' Joseph said cheerfully, 'I think I'll go and dance with the bride. I'll see you when you get back.' He nodded towards Thomas and Alice, who were heading towards them. 'My timing's spot on – your charges are on the way. Good luck, old chap!'

Clapping Charles on the shoulder, he moved off.

23

THE FOLLOWING SATURDAY EVENING

Robert smiled at Marian across the table. 'I'm very glad you agreed to dinner this evening, and that your parents didn't object, given I'm still technically married.'

'Yes, I wondered if they would, but after all, we're just two friends catching up with each other. Having said that, I *did* get a lecture from Mother that friendship was one thing, but it should not be allowed to develop into "something too dreadful to mention". The colour of her face spelt out the nature of that "something too dreadful to mention",' she added with mock gravity. 'But to my great relief, she left it at that.'

He smiled. 'And what about your father? He's always struck me as a determined sort of man.'

She giggled. 'I agree, he *can* be belligerent. He hummed and hawed, as you'd expect, but as it was completely impossible to construct a coherent sentence out of his grunts, I made a wild guess and responded with an "I'll take your advice, Father". He seemed content with that. It helps that he likes your father. They meet quite a lot these days, I believe.'

Robert nodded. 'They do seem to get on.'

'Indeed, it's amazing how friendly they've become over the past couple of years. They were on good terms before I first met you, but only in a business capacity. But now, they're as thick as thieves.'

'That month in London when we first met feels so long ago. So much has happened since then. And it's hard to believe that it's over a year since Lily died.'

'It will have been such a difficult year for you,' she said quietly. She hesitated. 'A year's not that long, Robert. You must still miss Lily enormously.'

He nodded. 'I do. But not in the way that I used to, thanks to the help I've had from my family. I can truthfully say that I've finally emerged from a dark tunnel, and I'm ready to start living again. Lily will always have a special place in my heart, and not just because she's James's mother, but because I loved her so much. But life has to go on, as they say.'

'Yes, it does.'

They fell silent for a moment or two.

'I'm very glad we met again at Nellie's wedding, Marian,' Robert said quietly, breaking the reflective mood.

'Me, too.' Marian blushed and looked down at her side plate.

He coughed. 'I feel I ought to tell you, even though it might not be a matter of interest, that I won't be free for another six years. I really enjoy your company, and I'd hate to think my situation might put you off coming out with me again, but I'd completely understand if it did. Six years is a long time.'

'It hasn't,' Marian said, blushing more deeply.

Robert smiled broadly. 'That's a relief! I would have hated it if we'd had to stop meeting. And it's also a relief that your father didn't insist on a chaperone.'

'I know – I was really surprised about that.'

Marian took a slice of bread from the plate in the centre of the table.

Robert looked around the room. He cleared his throat. 'I've always liked the Spaniard's Inn – it's so full of character. Did you know that Dickens mentioned it in *The Pickwick Papers*, and Keats is supposed to have written *Ode to a Nightingale* in here over a glass of claret or two? And the garden's lovely. When the three of us were little, Father and Mother used to bring us here and we'd climb on to the artificial mound in the garden and stare out across London. You can even see Windsor Castle on a clear day.'

'Let me guess! You're now going to tell me that Dick Turpin is thought to have been a regular here?'

They laughed.

'I'm sorry,' Robert said, sitting back. 'You can probably tell I'm a bit nervous.'

'You're not the only one. But I, too, used to come here as a child,' she said.

'So we may have played in the garden at the same time, but not known each other.'

'It's possible.'

They smiled across the table.

'I often wonder what would've happened if I hadn't met Lily before I came to London for that month,' Robert said a few minutes later, breaking the silence that had fallen again. 'I really liked you.'

She stopped buttering her bread, and shook her head. 'You don't have to say that, Robert.'

'But it's true. I know you'll have realised long ago that I was already with Lily by the time we met, and she was all I could see in my head. As a result, I'm now responsible for a home and a child. I'm married but don't have a wife, and I feel much older than my years.' He smiled. 'But I'm not complaining. No one can ever complain about loving someone, and feeling loved by them. It's a wonderful thing. But all that's in the past, and it's the future I'm now interested in. So, what shall we talk about? We seem to have exhausted the history of Spaniard's Inn. Tell me about your finishing school.'

The waiter put a plate of sole fillet in front of each of them, and after ensuring they had all they wanted, left the table.

Marian stared down at her plate, but didn't move.

'When we said goodbye,' she said quietly, 'I knew I very much wanted to see you again, even though we hadn't known each other for long. I desperately hoped you'd write to me while I was at my aunt's, even though you hadn't said you would. And I confess that when I didn't hear from you, I was quite miserable.'

'I'm so sorry, Marian.'

'And then the war ended, and I heard you'd married, and that she was very beautiful, which I'm not, and that you were going to be a father. I was distraught.' She looked up at him, her face pale. 'Distraught,' she repeated. 'It's not too strong a word for how I felt, yet I'd only known you a month. I was sure that going away to school would help me forget you, and I thought it had, but then I met you in Hampstead that day, and I knew those feelings were still there.'

Robert leaned across the table and took her hand. 'Oh, Marian, I could so easily do something really unmanly and cry. I could cry for the situation we're now in. But they'd be tears of frustration as I'm powerless to do anything about it.'

She looked up at him. 'So many tears, indeed! You'd be in danger of causing a flood. Mind you, that would win you the gratitude of Mother. She was saying only this morning that the garden's sorely in need of rain.'

She gave him a watery smile.

He squeezed her hand, and then released it and picked up his knife and fork. 'I think we'd better start eating. I don't want to get you back home too late, otherwise your father might not let me take you out again. I'd suggest a walk on the Heath tomorrow, but perhaps you'd think it too soon after this evening. But I'd like to make another arrangement before we go our separate ways, if you'd like that, too.'

'I would.'

'Good.' He hesitated. 'I know it must seem selfish of me, given my situation, not to walk away and let you get on with your life, but I wouldn't find it easy to do that. Not if you were still willing to see me again.'

'I am. And actually, a walk on the Heath tomorrow sounds most agreeable.'

He beamed at her. 'I'm looking forward to it already.'

She picked up her knife and fork. 'Then as you say, we'd be wise not to be late back this evening,' she said, her voice shaking.

And both turned their attention to their fish.

* * *

The milky white crescent of the moon was high in the velvet black sky above him when Robert returned to the house, having seen Marian home.

He went straight through the house and out into the garden, and sat down on the garden bench that had been placed beneath the nursery window on the very spot where he used to stand and listen to Lily singing to James, and where, in the past year, he'd sat so many times, wishing that he could hear her sing again.

Loneliness stabbed deep within him.

It was more than a year since her death, but she was still so real in his mind that he could close his eyes and see every detail of her face, so real that at times he felt as if she were standing next to him.

But he knew, beyond doubt, that the time had come to lock away his memories of Lily, and to accept with his heart as well as his head that she'd gone and wouldn't be coming back.

He knew that he would never stop loving her – she was a part of him and ever would be – but he also knew that he must now try to love another woman, both for his sake and for James.

And his every instinct screamed at him that Marian could be that woman.

But he wouldn't use Marian as a way of trying to dull his memory of past happiness – that would be completely unfair to her. She was worth better from him than that.

She deserved to be loved for the good person she was.

When he'd first met Marian, he'd liked her enormously, but not, he'd realised long before the month was out, in the knee-trembling way that he'd felt about Lily. He'd never for one moment felt a fire blaze deep within him at the very sight of Marian, and he wasn't sure that he ever would.

But he'd had that sort of love once, and he wasn't unrealistic enough to expect to have it again.

He'd need to feel something more for Marian than the warmth of friendship, though, and if he couldn't, in all fairness to them both, he'd walk away.

But the way he already felt about her, it was possible that he could truly love Marian, and that they could be very comfortable and happy together. And if she were to agree to be his wife when he was free to marry, he'd force himself to not think about Lily so much, but would be the best husband he could be, and he'd certainly never let her down.

He stood up and walked slowly through the darkness back into the house, unaware that his cheeks were wet.

24

CAMDEN TOWN

August 1921

'Well, I can certainly see what influenced you,' Sarah said, strolling around the room, her fingers grazing first Walter's enamel cigarette box and then the mother-of-pearl letter opener on the table that stood beneath a large, black-framed mirror. 'It's very *Good Housekeeping*, with your rectangular fireplace, your single pieces of furniture, rather than ornate suites, and having plain walls without any decorative plasterwork.' She glanced across at Nellie, and smiled. 'As you can tell, I had a look at the magazine after you spoke so highly about it.'

She stopped in the centre of a large round rug with a geometric pattern, which covered a part of the polished parquet floor, and glanced down at the rug.

'Some of our friends have got tiled floors, but we preferred parquet,' Nellie said quickly. 'Well, d'you like the way the room looks?'

'You can take that anxious look off your face, Nellie, darling. I love it. It reflects your warmth and vitality. It's absolutely right for you and Walter. Well done for thinking for yourself, and not just replicating your childhood home.'

'We certainly haven't done that,' Nellie said with a laugh. 'You should see Father's face whenever he comes here! Personally, I would've gone even further with the modern look, but Walter wasn't keen. Some friends of ours have got a hall that's silver, black and chrome – it's got a silver-leaf ceiling and a glossy black floor. I suggested that, but it was a bit extreme for Walter. His face was a picture!'

Sarah smiled. 'I think I'm with Walter on that. It's perfect as it is now, or as it will be when everything's done.'

Nellie clasped her hands together in glee. 'I'm so glad you like it. We can't wait to move in. Mother and Father have been wonderful, putting up with us as they have, and helping us find our domestic staff, and arranging for them to move in ahead of us and get settled, but we want to be on our own now. And the sooner the better.' She hesitated, and a haze of pink spread across her cheeks. 'I'm not sure it'll be just the two of us for much longer.'

'Oh, Nellie!' Sarah clapped her hands, went quickly to Nellie and hugged her. 'I'm so thrilled for you.'

'We don't know for certain, but it looks like it.'

'We must get you off your feet, then. Let's relax in your new armchairs while we wait for our coffee, and have a proper chat. It's been far too long since we've done that – not since before your wedding, in fact.'

'I know, and that's awful,' Nellie said, sitting down. 'It's just that I've been so busy, what with the house, and thank-you letters, and everything else. I haven't even told you yet that I had a letter from Dottie. She sent us best wishes for our wedding. It's funny to think my own sister hasn't met my husband and probably never will.'

Sarah sat down in the armchair next to Nellie's. 'Did she say anything else?'

'It was actually a terribly sad letter. I know you think she was very wrong to marry Franz, but even you would've felt sorry for her. She recently lost the baby she was carrying, and she's clearly still devastated. Elke must be about a year and a half now, and they'd wanted a brother or sister for her before she was much older. But that's not to be. At least, not yet. I know she really loves Franz – you can tell that from every sentence – but you can also tell that she misses us all. And although she doesn't go into detail, it's obviously not easy, living in Germany at the moment.'

'I'm naturally sorry to hear about the baby, but harsh though it sounds, I can't forgive her for marrying a German. Not when you think of the suffering the war has caused. She let her feelings cloud her judgement, and that's a form of weakness. Sometimes we have to take hard decisions because it's the right thing to do.'

'Well, *I'm* sorry for her, and also for Robert.'

Sarah raised her eyebrows. 'Indeed? And what's Robert done to earn your pity? I thought he seemed to be coping remarkably well.'

'In some ways he is, but I can tell that he's ever so lonely. I'm so glad he's met Marian again. I think they'd be good together, and Father would be delighted at a connection with such a successful builders' merchant. Father's not exactly subtle – he checked almost daily that Marian and her parents had been invited to our wedding. But Robert's going to have to wait six years before he can marry again, unless Lily's body suddenly appears, which doesn't seem very likely now.'

'I agree. It must be awful, being trapped in an invidious situation that's not of his making. A young man like him shouldn't have to be alone, and James needs someone, too. A nanny is all very well, but as he gets older, he'll need a mother's influence. Ah, here's our coffee!'

A housemaid came in carrying a tray with a cup of coffee, and an empty cup, a silver teapot and pot of boiling water, a small jug of milk and a plate of custard cream biscuits. She set everything out on the occasional table between the armchairs.

Nellie passed Sarah the coffee. 'As you can see, I'm having tea, not coffee,' she said, pouring milk into the empty cup. 'I seem to have gone off coffee.'

'You'll like it again in a few months' time,' Sarah said with a smile, and she sipped her drink.

Nellie took a biscuit from the plate and leaned back in the armchair. 'Having to wait so long could be a real problem for Robert. I'm sure that Marian likes him, but I can't see her wanting to wait six years to marry. No one would.'

'I wonder. You'd expect her to have married by now, but she hasn't. Joseph thought a few years ago that something was developing between her and Robert. Obviously, he'd underestimated the strength of Robert's feelings for Lily, but maybe he was right in picking up that Marian felt attracted to Robert. If so, and if she still does, maybe she'll be prepared to wait for him to be free. Stranger things have happened.'

Nellie laughed. 'How romantic of you, Sarah. But I think it's highly unlikely. I expect she'll marry someone else before too long, and the only person who'll be almost as sad as Father will be Henry Ames. And maybe Robert, too, of course. But Henry and Father have become great friends, and apparently Henry's even thinking of investing in the business.'

'Perhaps he'll do that, anyway. I believe he's even met Charles a few times to discuss the possibility. In fact, it seems that he and Charles get on rather well, which is surprising, considering how different they are. But don't let me get started on Charles! Have you and Walter thought about names yet?'

25

HAMPSTEAD

October 1921

The light of day was starting to fade, and the warm evening air thickening as Robert and Marian walked beneath a line of horse chestnut trees, their feet crushing the spiky green husks that littered the ground, discarded by children who'd removed the conkers from within.

With Jack Straw's Castle receding into the distance behind them, and the dense wooded slopes of the Heath on the opposite side of the road, they strolled past Whitestone Pond in the direction of West Heath Road, where Marian lived.

'I love this time of day,' she said as they stopped by the pond and looked at the sparkling water.

She glanced towards West Heath Road, which bordered the southern edge of the pond, and looked swiftly back at the water. Tucking her arm into Robert's, she rested her cheek momentarily against his shoulder. Then she straightened up.

He put his hand lightly on top of hers, and left it there.

'You can almost touch the stillness that settles on the place as night begins to fall,' she said, acutely conscious of the weight of Robert's hand. 'It was a really good walk this afternoon, as were all the other walks we've done in the past three months – I always enjoy the time we spend together.'

'And I do, too,' he said, and he smiled warmly at her. 'Very much.' He glanced at his watch. 'You know, it's still quite early. We could walk into Hampstead, if you aren't tired of walking, and perhaps have supper there. But we're not far from your house, and you might prefer me to take you straight home.'

'Personally, I'd be very happy to go further, but I don't want to keep you from anything you've got to do. We've been out for a while now, and you must be keen to get back to James.'

'Not in the least bit,' he said cheerfully. 'And anyway, James will be tucked away at the top of the house, in bed by now. His nanny will be with him, probably knitting or doing whatever it is that nannies do when their charges are asleep. I'm reluctant to let you go until I absolutely have to, if I'm truly honest.'

'And I'm reluctant to go, even if it's greedy of me to want to hold on to you for longer.' She laughed in embarrassment. 'I'm afraid you must think me very forward, being so obvious. According to my finishing school, maidenly women are meant to flutter a fan and be coy. The last thing they're meant to do is say what they honestly feel.'

'I've met plenty of woman who'd leave your finishing school with flying colours,' he said, slightly increasing the pressure on her hand, 'but they're not the sort of women who'd interest me. Not in the way you do. Don't ever change.'

'Well, in that case, and if you're sure there's nothing you'd rather be doing, a stroll through Hampstead would be lovely.'

'Perhaps next weekend, we could take James out with us,' he said as they started walking again, Marian's hand still under his arm. 'We could come up here and let him sail the paper boat that

Father gave him for his birthday. But that's only if you'd like to spend some time with him,' he added quickly. 'You don't have to.'

'I'd love that! I'd really like to get to know him. He seems such a dear little boy. And it means a lot to me that you've suggested it.'

'Well, if we're going to carry on seeing each other…'

Their eyes met, and both looked instantly away.

They crossed West Heath Road, not even glancing towards her house, and headed down Heath Street. When they reached New End, which led to the road where Robert lived, they both automatically turned left, and continued walking.

Ahead of them, Robert's house came into sight.

Marian tucked her arm more tightly into Robert's.

Reaching the steps that led up to his front door, they stopped.

Robert moved slightly back, and Marian's hand slipped to her side. 'I'm not quite sure how we've ended up here,' he said, his voice reflecting a sudden discomfort. 'I think I'd better take you back to the high street.'

'May I use the water closet, please?' Marian asked.

'Oh, of course,' he said hastily. 'Follow me.'

He went up the steps, unlocked the door, opened it and stood aside to let Marian go into the house. Giving him a slight smile, she went into the entrance hall and straight through the doorway on the left that led into the front reception room.

'It's just up the stairs,' he said, coming into the room behind her, and pointing back towards the flight of stairs that led up from the entrance hall. Then he gave an embarrassed laugh and dropped his arm. 'But you know that, of course. You've been here before.'

'That's right,' she said, turning to face him. 'But it seems that I don't need it, after all. I was mistaken.'

And standing with her back to the mantelpiece and the large gilt-framed mirror that hung above it, she pulled off her gloves and her cloche, slipped out of her long ivory cardigan and threw them all on to the nearest armchair.

Motionless, her arms at her side, her flimsy dropped-waist dress skimming her slender body, its low-scooped back reflected in the mirror, she stood there, her eyes on his face, waiting.

He hovered in the doorway, his heart pounding, unable to drag his gaze from the face that had come to seem very beautiful to him, unsure whether to trust his interpretation of what she was suggesting. Unsure of what her body seemed to be saying. What he hoped it was saying.

She gave a nervous laugh. 'Don't just stand there staring, Robert – you're making me uncomfortable. Say something, anything. It doesn't matter what.'

He put his hands to his head in despair. 'God, Marian, you don't know what I'd give for things to be different! But they're not. I know exactly what I'd like to say. And I know the question I'd dearly love to ask. But I can't ask it. It's breaking my heart, but I can't.'

'I love questions – they're often the start of a lively discussion. Pretend you're not married and ask me anyway.' Her voice was silk-smooth.

He shook his head. 'I can't. It's impossible.'

She stepped closer to him. 'Nothing's impossible, Robert,' she said. 'Nothing.'

She took another step towards him.

A smile playing across her lips, she raised her arms, and fluttered her fingers in the air above their heads. 'There you are. I've sprinkled some invisible fairy dust on both of us. Fairy dust has the power to magic away all problems. So the way is now clear for you to ask your question.'

The air was so heavy he could hardly breathe.

'If you say that there's fairy dust in the air, I have to believe you,' he said at last, his voice seeming to come from somewhere far away. 'After all, you *are* the daughter of a builders' merchant, so you'd know better than anyone else where to get your hands on it.'

'That's right,' she said liltingly, and she tilted her face towards his.

He moved even closer, looked down into her eyes, and took a deep breath. 'Dear Marian. I've no right at all to ask you this, fairy dust or not, but I've come to love you. I know it's impossible – but with all my heart I want to marry you. There now, I've said it.'

He stared anxiously into her face.

'That was a question?' she asked, raising her eyebrows in mock surprise. 'If I'd been writing out such a sentence, I think I would've ended it with a full stop, not a question mark.'

'And you'd have been right.' He took another deep breath. 'Will you marry me?'

A smile spread across her face. 'Yes, of course, I will. I love you, Robert Linford. I think I fell in love with you the day we met, and I've never been able to stop myself loving you, no matter how hard I tried. No one I've met since then has come near to making me feel the way I feel when I'm with you. I would love to spend the rest of my life with you.'

He pulled her to him, but she slid from his arms, caught hold of his hands, took a step back and faced him.

Her eyes suddenly serious, she gazed up at him. 'I do believe you've come to love me,' she said. 'If I didn't, I wouldn't agree to marry you, however much I loved you. But I know that I'm not beautiful like Lily – my face is an ordinary one – and I realise you'll never feel about me as you felt about Lily. You should know that I accept that. But I think that the love we have for each other is a strong, true love, and that's enough for me. I believe we can be very happy together.'

'Oh, Marian!' he said with a heartfelt sigh. 'So do I. And you're wrong – I think you're very beautiful, and I do, indeed, love you.' Slowly, he ran his fingers down the side of her face. Then he suddenly dropped his arm and pulled back, despair and dismay clouding his face. 'What on earth am I thinking of? I can't possibly ask you to wait for me for such a long time. What would everyone say? It would be completely selfish of me.'

She looked up at him, her face colouring. 'I think we should forget about the rest of the world – this is just about us. I don't mind waiting six years for you to put a ring on my finger, but I don't want to wait six years to be a proper wife to you.'

He gazed down at her in misery. 'I don't want to, either, but we have to. Your parents would rightly never forgive me – and I'd never forgive myself – if you became pregnant before I was free to marry you.'

'That need not happen,' she said quietly.

'I don't understand.'

She went a deeper shade of red. 'Please, don't think I'm too forward, but I knew you wouldn't risk compromising me, so I took matters into my hands. I think six years is a long time for someone who's already been married to wait, and it's a long time for the woman who loves him, too.'

He caught his breath.

'Hoping very much that you'd ask me to marry you,' she went on, her voice trembling, 'I've been to see a doctor about such things. Not the family doctor, of course,' she added with a nervous laugh. 'I told the doctor I was getting married, but that we didn't want a family yet. So now there's no need to be concerned about James having a brother or sister before we're ready for that to happen.'

He released his breath in a long low sigh of joy. 'I can't believe this. How can I be so lucky? I don't deserve you, Marian. I have to ask, how long must we wait before we can test this?'

'About as long as it takes for us to get to your bedroom,' she said, a tremor in her voice.

'I love you, Marian,' he said.

And he cupped her face in his hands, and brought his lips hard down on hers. Then he slid one arm around her back and swung her legs up with the other.

'I'm carrying you upstairs as every new bride should be carried,' he said, turning towards the stairs as he cradled her in his arms. 'After all, in my head, you're already Mrs Robert Linford.'

Her heart racing, she leaned against his chest and let him take her up to his bedroom.

26

PRIMROSE HILL

November 1921

Charles pushed his chair slightly back from Joseph's dining-room table, crossed one leg with the other, and began talking.

Joseph's mind started to wander.

Gazing along his mahogany table, he admired the rich sheen of the polished wood, the crisp whiteness of the starched napkins, the gleam of the silverware, and the sparkling crystal wine glasses and chandelier, and he felt an inner glow of satisfaction.

He hadn't been looking forward to the conversation he needed to have with Charles, so he'd asked Mrs Morley to use the best tableware that evening, even though it was just the two of them for dinner. Being surrounded by the visible trappings of his success would give him the confidence he needed, as head of the family, to confront a difficult issue.

And now that they'd finished eating, and the frequent sharp bangs from the local firework displays that had punctuated the early evening had slowed, he couldn't put it off for much longer.

Indicating the open curtains to Charles, who was still in full flow about internal changes to the bank's structure, Joseph got up and went across to the window that looked out over his front garden. Putting a hand up to each curtain, he paused to stare out into the night.

Ahead of him, the orange-red glow from the numerous bonfires across the town had lit up the sky. Occasional showers of silver and gold soared through the amber-red halo into the darkness above, splintering there into a myriad glittering shards that were swallowed up by the black mouth of night as they fell to the earth.

One could almost smell the burning wood and smoke through the glass, he thought, as he pulled the heavy floor-length brocade curtains across the window, and shut out the November night.

Returning to the table, he sat down, poured himself a brandy, and started listening to Charles again.

Charles had moved on to the subject of family. Maud's suggestion that she and Sarah should take Christopher and Louisa to Chorton for the bonfire weekend had been very welcome, he was saying as he reached for the port. He paused, holding the bottle mid-air. 'You don't mind, do you,' he said, 'me making free with your port?'

Joseph shrugged. 'Not in the least, but I'll stick to brandy.' He sat back in his chair. 'I just hope the weather in Oxfordshire has been as good as it has here. Maud was keen on the children going to the village fireworks' display. She feels we should be seen to support such events. Or rather, the children should – I don't think she's ever been to such an event in her life. Our Maud's a complete stranger to the joys of standing in a muddy field, brandishing a sparkler. And Sarah, too, I should imagine.'

'Indeed, it's a difficult picture to conjure up,' Charles said with a smile. 'I would've thought it more up Nellie's street, though not necessarily Walter's. Have they gone to Chorton, too?'

'No, they've gone to some friends they've made in Camden Town.'

'Sounds fun.' Charles took a sip from his glass. 'The girls won't be back till tomorrow evening, will they?'

'That's right. And that's the reason I've asked you here tonight. There's something I want to talk to you about – well, two things, actually, one with potentially more worrying consequences than the other – and I wouldn't want Maud to be privy to either. Or Sarah, for that matter.'

'That sounds serious, old chap. I'm glad I'm well-fortified with port.'

Joseph swirled his brandy in his snifter. 'How d'you think Robert's doing these days? Generally, I mean – not work. He's obviously well on top of everything relating to the business.'

'I assume you're referring to Marian?' Charles said, with a wry smile.

'Ah, so you've noticed it, too. For a man who's supposedly living like a monk, and who believes he must do so for years to come, Robert's in extremely high spirits. In fact, I'd say they're the high spirits of a young man whose needs are being most satisfactorily met, despite his circumstances. As he's not the sort of man to pay for a woman, and he's clearly very close to Marian, I would imagine they've come to an unofficial understanding. Anything more at this time would be impossible.'

Charles nodded. 'My thoughts, too. Does it bother you that they may have somewhat jumped the gun?'

'Not at all. Robert needs someone in his life, and Marian's absolutely delightful. She's the perfect woman for him in every single way – the complete opposite of Lily. And James is going to love her, too. She'll be a wonderful mother to him, and to any children that she and Robert may have. I have to trust they're ensuring those other children don't arrive until she's got a wedding ring on her finger.' He took a drink.

'What about Marian's father? Having seen them together, presumably he's come to the same conclusion that we have. Is he as content with the situation as you, and presumably Maud?'

'Indeed, he is. Once I'd assured him we were in complete agreement about them being left unchaperoned so that they could reach an understanding between themselves, he made it clear how delighted he was that they were together. And given the unusual situation, he wasn't about to reproach either of them. I wasn't surprised. From the moment he saw their interest in each other, he's favoured them marrying, for business reasons as well as out of friendship.'

Charles sighed, and took another sip of his port. 'It's a shame they can't marry sooner.'

Joseph nodded. 'I agree. But clever though Walter is, not even he can rewrite the law, and we're just going to have to be patient. One stroke of luck, though, is that Henry's now so confident that there *will* be a wedding that he's definitely putting some money into the business in the New Year. A sort of advance dowry, if you like. That's one of the things I wanted to tell you this evening.'

'That's good news indeed.' Charles hesitated. 'Does it concern you at all that when Robert marries Marian, as we both think he will, he'll be marrying bigamously? Whatever any certificates might say, we both know that Lily isn't really dead.'

'She might as well be, as far as we're concerned. She'll never come back. But I won't pretend it's the ideal situation. You make a decision at the time, and you think you've covered every angle, and then later, when it's impossible to undo it, you find that there're potential repercussions you hadn't thought of. This is one of them. But you have to live with it.'

'If you could turn the clock back, would you do the same thing again?'

Joseph stared at the glass in his hand. 'I honestly don't know,' he said at last. 'But the answer to your question is probably no – or certainly not in the same way. I hadn't for one moment anticipated the pain it'd cause, which was made even worse by the guilt Robert felt. But also because, I have to admit, he seems to have truly loved her. It was a little more than the infatuation I'd thought it to be.'

He put his glass down on the table and turned slightly towards Charles. 'But let's go on to the second matter. Robert and Marian aren't the only ones who've been doing what they shouldn't, are they? But they're the only ones who've got what most people would consider a valid excuse. You haven't.'

Charles leaned forward and ran his finger around the rim of his water glass. 'What're you talking about?'

'You're playing away from home, Charles. Sarah told me about the meetings you're supposed to be having with Henry Ames. We both know that you aren't in any way involved in Henry's investment plans, and won't be for some time, and there's no other explanation for the lies you've been telling to cover your whereabouts. Such dishonesty has a way of getting out. Look at how visible Robert and Marian have become without them being aware of it.'

'You're mistaken,' Charles said, colouring.

'I'm not. One whiff of you looking at anyone else, no matter how casual your interest, and you and Sarah would be finished. Do you honestly think a proud woman like Sarah would carry on as if nothing had happened? She wouldn't, and you know it.

You'd become a ship without a captain, and you'd soon be lost at sea.'

'You don't know what you're talking about,' Charles said, his face sullen.

Joseph stood up. 'Think about it, Charles. I would say that you had considerably more to lose by casual dalliance than you have to gain. I'm going to bed now. You can see yourself out.'

27

LOWER EAST SIDE, NEW YORK

Last day of April 1927

Sitting across from each other, Lily and Ruth stared at the items spread out on the kitchen table – a salt-and-pepper set made of glass, two oval china dishes, a china bowl, a collection of silver cutlery tied with a faded green ribbon, the Sabbath candlesticks, a metal samovar and two framed pictures of a cottage surrounded by fields.

Ruth indicated the array in front of them. 'As that's virtually all that's left to be packed, I'll be finished by the time the others get back from the synagogue. The last thing will be the *mezuzah*, but we'll leave that till we're actually walking out.' She glanced across at the small scroll on the wall by the front door, and then looked back at Lily. 'I won't be able to believe we're really leaving till the *mezuzah*'s down.'

'I can't imagine being here without you,' Lily said, her face drawn. 'The Abelmans are signing the lease for another year, I know. D'you know if any of the other tenants are?'

'As far as I know, we're the only ones leaving.' She paused. 'I hate to say goodbye, Lily,' she said, a break in her voice. 'In the almost seven years you've been here, you've become like a sister to me.'

'And you to me. You've made me feel a part of your family since the moment I met you, and I'm really going to miss you all.' Her eyes filled with tears.

Ruth leaned forward and grasped Lily's hand. 'Then come with us. You know we want that.'

Shaking her head, Lily withdrew her hand. 'I can't, Ruth. You know I'm going back for James as soon as I've got enough money. There hasn't been a single day when I haven't thought of my baby first thing in the morning and last thing at night, and I won't rest till I'm with him again.'

Ruth straightened up. 'But he's not a baby any longer, is he?' she said gently. 'He must be seven or eight by now. He was so young when you left – he won't remember you.'

'Which is why I must go back as soon as I can. With business as good as it is, I need two more years at the most. Maybe less than that.' She glanced through the tubercular window to the deep pink dress on the mannequin stand in the parlour, its round neck and long sleeves trimmed with black lace. 'Mrs Welsch brought three of her friends to see her dress this afternoon. They loved my design, and all want one, but they have to be in a different colour from hers, she told me. I'm starting on them tomorrow, A few more orders like that and I'll soon be on the boat for England.'

'It *is* gorgeous,' Ruth said, her voice wistful.

'And I don't know if I've told you yet, but when Mr Abelman heard I was taking over the apartment, he asked if I'd let his sons use my third room to make cheap cigars. He's going to pay me, so naturally I said yes.'

It was going to prove possible in the limited space, she told

Ruth, because cigar-making didn't require much room – it was just a matter of pushing tobacco into moulds. With ten grooves in each strip, they could make a large number of cigars very quickly. And if ever there was an increase in demand and they had to take on temporary workers, Mr Abelman was going to pay extra for her to let the workers sleep in the third room. Since she'd already decided to carry on sleeping in the kitchen as she'd been doing for the past few years, she'd readily agreed.

She really ought to think about making America her home, Ruth urged her. She'd be able to make so much money if she stayed there, and then she'd be able to visit them in Massachusetts.

What's more, it would be the perfect time for Lily to open a shop of her own.

Lower East Side had changed since the Immigration Act three years before, which aimed to reduce the number of Jewish and Italian immigrants. The Act had worked, and with it being much more difficult now for such immigrants to enter America, there were too few of them moving into the garment district to replace those who'd left, and there was a large number of empty properties, and plenty of work going.

There were lots of rich women in New York, Ruth reminded her, and women always needed dresses. With the flair Lily had shown for design as well as for every stage of making a garment, she'd soon have a thriving business, and would be able to keep all the money for herself. And then she could go to England, get James and bring him back.

Lily shook her head. 'It wouldn't work. This life is fine while it's just me, but not when I've a child to consider. He's used to a very different sort of life. Also, he has a family in England, and it wouldn't be fair to cut him off from them.'

'You're right. They'll be the only family he knows, and he'll love them.'

'But I'm his mother,' Lily said sharply. 'He'll love me, too.'

'That's true,' Ruth said hastily. She smiled with regret. 'You're obviously doing the right thing for you and James, but we'll miss you. Every time we wear something you made for us, we'll be reminded of you. Unfortunately, it's an ugly stove that will make you think of us!' They both laughed. 'But I'm glad that *Momma* and *Abba* have given it to you. It's nice to think of you having something that was central to our lives for so long.'

'It means a lot to me,' Lily said.

Ruth looked around her. 'I'll miss living here – it's been twelve years, which is longer than most people stay. But it's time to move on. And with so many from our synagogue already in Massachusetts, we'll be surrounded by friends. And we'll have more space and be closer to the countryside. Closer to *Momma*'s dream,' she added with a smile. 'And Isaak and Golda will get the large apartment they need, with a second child on the way.' She laughed. 'It sounds as if I'm trying to convince myself, but I'm not. I know what we're doing is right.'

'You'll write to me, won't you, when the baby arrives. And I want to hear how Pavel gets on. Seventeen's very young to own a shop, however much he wants it. And I hope he finds a wife – I know he'd like to be married.'

'You can be sure that *Momma* will be off to the matchmaker before we've even unpacked.'

Lily smiled. 'And you, Ruth. What about a husband for you?'

Ruth shrugged. 'I didn't want to marry any of the men the *shadkhan* suggested. I know the sort of man I'd like to marry, and I intend to look for myself. I'm afraid I've become too American to leave it to a matchmaker. *Momma* is shocked at the very idea, but that's the way it is.' She picked up the candlesticks with both hands and stared at them. 'We're Americans now, as well as Russians, and I don't want a husband who'll live only in the Russian way. But nor do I want to forget where I came from, no matter how they treated us.' She put the candlesticks down again.

Looking around her, her vision misted. Impatiently, she wiped her eyes.

Lily pulled her chair closer to Ruth's, and put her arm around her shoulders. 'It's all right to cry, you know. You're bound to be sad at leaving.'

'It's not really about leaving. It's all these things.' She indicated the objects on the table. 'They remind me of our family in Russia, of visiting each other, of eating together, of Friday nights together. Although I'm very happy in America, it still hurts to think of the friends and relatives we left behind and will never see again.'

She picked up the samovar and looked at it.

'Remember when I used to wonder what that was?' Lily said with a smile.

Ruth nodded. 'We haven't used it since *babushka* died, which was a year after we got here. But we'd never leave it behind. It kept the tea hot from morning till night, and *babushka* would always sit at the table here,' she tapped the table next to where she was sitting, 'and sip a cup of hot tea through a sugar cube between her teeth, and she'd tell us stories about life back in her home village.'

'Would you ever go back to visit?'

Ruth vigorously shook her head. 'Never. It wouldn't be safe – we might not be allowed to leave again. They'll always hate us, whatever they say.'

'Then you must look only to the future,' Lily said. 'Just think, you'll soon be answering telephone calls in Massachusetts.'

'No, I won't,' Ruth said, and she wiped her eyes again. 'I'm not going to be an operator again.'

'Why ever not? I knew there were things you didn't like about the job, but I didn't think you actually disliked it.'

The job had changed so much, Ruth told her. Now that customers had dials on their telephones, they made their own connections, and operators rarely had contact with the customers, which had been Ruth's favourite part of the job. Before dials, the operators and customers had recognised each other's voices, and operators would give out information, such as the latest news, weather, sports results, the correct time of day, and would even gossip with customers. Now, on the rare occasions when an operator spoke to a customer, the operator had to follow a script issued by the company. Massachusetts was bound be the same, Ruth said, so she was going to look for a different job.

'Such as?' Lily asked.

Ruth shrugged. 'I'll find something, but I don't yet know what. Maybe in a department store. I wouldn't have to be as alert all the time, and as silent. We'll see. But for now, I'd better finish packing. The others will be back at any minute, and then it'll be time to go.'

Taking a deep breath, she picked up an end-cut of material and carefully wrapped it around the samovar.

* * *

Lily walked slowly back along Delancey Street, a bag of knishes in her hand. As she turned right into Orchard Street, she stopped abruptly and stared down the length of the street.

Her mind rewound to the day she'd arrived in New York and had stood on that very spot, tired, hungry and scared. Too scared to enter the noise and the bustle that burst from the street, too scared to propel herself into a world that was like nothing she'd ever seen before.

And then she'd met Ruth and the Erlikh family, and from that moment on, with their support, she'd taken her first steps into the frenetic life of the Lower East Side.

How long ago that seemed.

How alone she'd felt at that time, and how lonely.

And now, when she went back into the apartment, she'd be alone again. But this time, she wouldn't feel lonely.

The Erlikhs had cocooned her in a warmth and friendship that she knew she'd feel for a very long time. And they'd been so generous with their knowledge of the area and its people, and had shared with her the names of their contacts, and had advised her on the best places in which to do business, that she felt no trepidation about her situation. They might have left, but they would continue to be with her in spirit, and she with them, every step of the way in the exciting venture ahead of her.

From now on, she'd be working for herself, and the money she earned would be hers alone. In two years' time, she'd return to England, able to take care of James. She'd know how to run a successful dressmaking business and would start one in England so that she'd have regular money coming in. Her heart overflowed with joy at the very thought. It was thrilling to hold her life in her hands, and to know that every cent she made would bring her closer to home.

But she wouldn't be seeing just James again when she returned to England, she'd be seeing Robert, too.

For so long, she hadn't allowed herself to think about him – it would have hurt too much. So much had happened over the years that she felt a different person, and he must feel that way, too. But her misery and disappointment at his failure to seek her out would always remain, and she would never again be able to live as Robert's wife.

But at the thought of seeing him again... just to see him once more...

Her heart beat fast, and she felt a sudden breathlessness.

And in that moment, she knew that whatever she'd told herself over the past few years, she would desperately love to feel Robert's arms around her again.

Her eyes glazing with unshed tears, she started walking again, but she found her path suddenly blocked. She stepped aside, but the blockage stepped aside with her.

'Extra! Extra!' the newsboy in front of her shouted. He pulled a *New York Times* from the pile under his arm and waved it in front of her face.

She exclaimed in exasperation, but he wouldn't move out of her way.

The front page stared at her. Headlines screamed that the sale of new cars was down, that farmers were earning less, that unemployment was creeping up, that fewer houses were being built.

She wondered if the same problems were being experienced in England, and for an instant the image of Joseph filled her mind. The hatred she felt for him surged up, a hatred that had lain dormant within her, waiting for the day when she could expose him for the cruel and manipulative man he was. Well, that day was considerably closer now.

Again, she stepped aside.

Again, the newsboy stepped aside with her.

Speculators were buying shares in the stock market with the same enthusiasm as they'd been doing for the past few years, she couldn't avoid reading.

For a moment, she wondered what all that meant. Then she inwardly shrugged. Whatever it was, it was nothing to do with her. She'd be signing the lease on Rent Day one more time, but if the clothing orders continued to flood in, in 1929, two years from now, she wouldn't be signing the lease again – she'd be boarding a boat for England.

She turned to her right, half ran from the newsboy, and continued towards her tenement block. When she reached the steps that led up into the building, she smiled to herself as she walked up to the evening of sewing that awaited her, which would hasten the day when she saw James again.

And when she saw Robert again.

Her stomach did a somersault.

28

PRIMROSE HILL

The end of June 1927

'Good God, Maud! Have you read today's headline article? It's rather alarming.' Joseph lowered his newspaper and stared across the breakfast table at Maud.

'I'll thank you not to blaspheme, Joseph. As for reading the article, how could I have done? You've monopolised the paper since the boy delivered it.' She touched her napkin to her lips, and held out her hand. 'If you care to pass it over, I'll read it now.'

'In a moment. I haven't quite finished with it yet. And anyway, I'm not sure it's the kind of article that would interest you.'

America had recently lent a considerable sum to Germany, he told Maud, so that Germany could pay its debts, firstly to the rest of Europe, and after that to America. Borrowing to such an extent from America had made England and Europe highly dependent on America, and if anything happened to the American economy, Europe would be in danger of collapsing like a stack of dominoes.

'But nothing's going to happen to it, is it?' Maud interrupted, a trifle impatiently.

'I hope not. But have you heard Charles on the subject? He was worried as far back as a year ago that everything was booming too fast in America, which could have devastating consequences. Well, land prices in Florida have just dropped through the floor, and it looks as if that might be only the start of it. As Charles has always said, there's too much of everything over there – too many goods being made for the number of people to buy them; too much food being produced by farmers, so prices are steadily falling, and too many small banks with insufficient funds.'

'I admit, that *does* sound worrying.'

'It is. If everybody wanted to withdraw their money from the banks at the same moment, America would probably have to call in its loans, and heaven help Germany and the rest of Europe if that happened. This article is only saying what Charles has been saying for quite a while now.'

Maud gave him a languid smile. 'I must say, it makes a pleasant change to hear you praise Charles, Joseph, instead of criticising him for one failing or another. You and Sarah used to make quite a chorus, although she seems to have quietened down, too. Whatever the trouble between the two of them a few years ago, I'm glad that that seems to have passed.'

'It certainly seems to have done. Charles has his faults, but believe me, to give credit where it's due, he's been taking a lot more interest in his work these days, and I trust his judgement.'

'Since Sarah's obviously worked some magic on Charles,' Maud said drily, 'or something has, perhaps she'd now work some on her daughter. Louisa's in urgent need of disciplining – her behaviour's an utter disgrace. It's completely beyond me why Sarah tolerates such rudeness. Or Charles, for that matter.'

'Give the girl a chance – she's only seventeen. Both Nellie and Dorothy knew their own minds at that age, and Robert, too.

What's more, I suspect that Nellie's Emily is going to be just the same as Louisa. She's got a good pair of lungs on her, that child, and she's certainly inherited Nellie's strong will. You've just forgotten what young children are like.' Joseph folded the paper and handed it to her. 'That's the article,' he said, pointing to it. 'There's something about inflation in Germany, too. And you might want to read about the sun. Apparently, there's going to be a total eclipse on the 29th, and we're advised to protect our eyes.'

Maud took the paper from him. 'If you recall, Joseph, I suggested a while ago, when you mentioned that German inflation was sky-high, that we got in touch with Dorothy and asked if she'd like to come home, but you refused. You told me that you didn't know where she was, but I didn't believe you at the time, and I still don't. There's nothing you don't know about this family. In case Charles proves to be right about the economy heading for trouble, I suggest we contact Dorothy now, and tell her she can come back, if she wishes.'

'I admit I'd feel happier if she were back in England, but not that husband of hers. I dread to think what the sight of him might do to Thomas, and also how he'd react if he saw Dorothy again.'

'That doesn't mean you can't ask her if she wants to come home. Thomas may be your brother, but she *is* our daughter, after all.'

'If Dorothy wanted to return, I'm sure she knows she could.' Joseph pulled his fob watch from his waistcoat pocket, glanced at it, put down his napkin and stood up. 'It's time I left. Every day, there seem to be more cars on the road, and it's taking longer than ever to get to Kentish Town. When I've finished in the office, I'll have lunch with Thomas, and maybe sound him out about Dorothy.'

They heard a knock at the door.

'Who on earth can that be?' he exclaimed, and he sank to his seat again.

A moment later, Robert appeared, a wide smile on his face. 'I was hoping I'd catch you before you left,' he said, crossing to the table and sitting down.

Joseph leaned back in his chair. 'Good gracious, Robert! What brings you here at this early hour?'

Maud leaned across to her son and put her hand on his. 'Before you tell us, darling, help yourself to whatever you want from the sideboard. I'm sure that whatever you have to say can wait a moment.'

Robert stood up, went across to the sideboard, took some scrambled eggs and grilled tomatoes from the electric heaters, and returned to the table. Maud picked up the silver pot from the salver next to her and poured him a cup of coffee. He took a sip, and then put his cup down.

'You're wrong,' he said. 'It can't wait a minute longer. It's over – I'm a free man!'

'Oh, darling!' Maud rose to her feet and Robert stood up, too, beaming at his mother. She hugged him tightly.

'I couldn't be more thrilled that it's finally come to an end.' She hugged him again, her eyes moist, and then released him.

A sudden feeling of warmth swept through Joseph's body, and he felt close to tears. He got up and shook Robert's hand. 'I'm sure you know how pleased I am for you, son,' he said, his voice catching, and he clasped Robert on the shoulder.

'Thank you.' Robert smiled at them both, and sat back down again. He picked up his knife and fork. 'The Court Order was granted yesterday, and my marriage has been ended on account of Lily being dead. I can't tell you how grateful I am to Walter for his advice and for dealing with the whole thing.'

'I'm delighted, dear boy,' Joseph said, sitting down, followed by Maud. 'So, when's the wedding to be?'

Robert laughed. 'Subtle as ever, Father. Very soon, in fact. Walter confirmed the Order yesterday evening, and I went straight around to Marian's and spoke to her parents. We both want the same thing. Out of respect for Lily, we want a quiet wedding in the church near us, with just a few close friends and family, and a meal somewhere nearby afterwards. Henry and Edith have invited me to dinner tonight to talk about dates. I think they plan to contact you, too, in case you're free this evening.'

Joseph nodded. 'Well, I have to say I couldn't be more pleased. She's a lovely girl, and she'll be an asset to the family, son. I'm sure you'll both be very happy. And James, too. It's plain to see how much he's come to love Marian over the years – she's already like a mother to him.'

Robert's smile broadened. 'She is, isn't she?'

'When will you tell James?' Maud asked. 'I wouldn't let him hear it from anyone else.'

'As soon as possible. And we both want to be there. I thought I'd take this afternoon off, if my boss agreed.' He grinned at Joseph. 'We can collect James early from school, take him out on the Heath, and find a good moment to give him the news. I doubt he'll be that surprised. After all, he's eight now, and he knows that his mother drowned years ago and isn't coming back.'

* * *

The Heath was quiet in the absence of all but a few very young children, who'd been brought in their prams and pushchairs to see the ducks in the warmth of the late June afternoon.

James ran on ahead, weaving his way between the trees that

grew alongside the path, and tearing across any open patches of heathland, flattening as he did so the profusion of daisies and bright yellow buttercups that had sprung up between the blades of grass.

Robert and Marian dawdled slowly behind him, hand in hand.

When they came to a wooden bench at the side of an empty stretch of path, Robert stopped walking. 'How about here?' he suggested. 'It's as good a place as any.'

She glanced ahead at James. 'Yes, let's do it now. To be honest, I'm feeling quite nervous, and the longer we leave it, the worse it'll get.' She looked at Robert and pulled a face.

'He loves you, Marian,' Robert said. 'He's going to be very pleased.'

'Oh, I do hope so.'

He called to James to join them, and they sat down, leaving a space for James between them.

'Come and sit here, son,' he said, patting the bench as James came running up to them. 'Auntie Marian and I have something to tell you.'

Marian glanced down and smoothed her skirt. Robert sent her an encouraging smile.

'What's that?' James asked, standing in front of them, hopping from one foot to the other.

Robert coughed. 'Well, you know that I loved your mother very much, but that she died some years ago.'

James stopped hopping, took a step back and stood quite still.

'Well, since then I've got to know Auntie Marian, and you have, too, and she's got to know us. She's come to love us, in fact. And I know that I love her, and I think you do, too, so I've asked her to marry me.'

James turned his head and stared at Marian.

'And I'm delighted to say that she's agreed.' Robert smiled at Marian, and then looked back at James. 'It means that when we're married, she'll move into the house. Nanny will continue looking after you, just like always, but Auntie Marian will also care for you. As she's been doing for a while already.' He paused. 'Do you understand, James?'

James nodded.

'Good boy. It doesn't mean I'll love you any less, because I won't. But it means that the three of us will be living together as a family.' He paused again. 'Well, what do you think?'

James moved to his other foot. His head down, he took a couple of steps closer to Marian, and stopped.

She leaned forward and took his hands in her hers. 'Dear James. You needn't worry that I'll attempt to take your mother's place – no one could do that. But your father's right – I love you both very much, and I'd like to live with you and Daddy. Would you be happy about that?'

He bit his lower lip, and nodded slowly.

A wave of relief washed over Robert, and he stood up, followed by Marian. 'Then I suggest we go home and celebrate. A little bird told me that Mrs Bailey has asked Cook to make your favourite treacle tart, James.' He smiled down at his son, and then at Marian, and held out his hand to her.

She took it. Turning to James, she held out her other hand.

His eyes on the ground, he took it.

And they started walking along the path towards their home, Robert and James with Marian between them.

'You know I call Auntie Marian Auntie Marian?' James began as the road that ran down the side of the Heath came in sight.

Leaning slightly in front of Marian, Robert glanced at him in amusement. 'I do.'

'Well, when you're married to Auntie Marian, do I have to call you Uncle Robert?' James asked, and he giggled.

Robert grinned at him and straightened up. 'I think Daddy will do very nicely, thank you.'

They walked a little further.

'If I call you Daddy, shouldn't I call Auntie Marian Mummy?'

Marian stopped walking. She dropped Robert's hand, and turned to James, tears brimming. 'Oh, James,' she said. 'I should like that very much. Very much, indeed.' Her voice caught, and she leaned forward and kissed the top of his head. Then she stood up and smiled at Robert through a mist of unshed tears.

He put his arm around her. 'That would be perfect, son,' he said quietly.

And with Robert's arm still around Marian's shoulders, and James's hand still in hers, they headed for home.

29

PRIMROSE HILL

Late September 1927

Thomas leaned back, feigned horror on his face. 'What have you done with the real Joseph? You've not said anything dictatorial all evening. Such joviality's not like you at all.'

Joseph laughed. 'That's because I'm in a good mood.'

'Presumably it's because Robert got married last week.'

'You presume right. He's had to wait a long time to be able to marry Marian, but at last the wait is over.'

'She seems a very pleasant woman, and not unattractive,' Thomas said, glancing towards Marian, who was talking to Charles, while holding James's hand. 'But she doesn't have that extra something that Lily had, does she?' He paused. 'I know Robert rarely mentions Lily these days, but I'll bet he still thinks about her.'

'I doubt that he does,' Joseph said tetchily. 'There'd be no point. The woman's gone and she isn't coming back. Robert's a young man who needs a wife for himself and a mother for his child, and in Marian he's found the perfect person.'

Thomas shrugged. 'As I say, she's a nice woman, and I'm sure she'll make him an excellent wife. But she's hardly the sort of woman to erase the memory of someone as stunning as the first Mrs Robert Linford, is she? But at least, he can look forward to a life without surprises. I suspect that life with Lily would've been very different.'

'Not everyone wants a life full of surprises,' Joseph snapped. 'Aha!' he exclaimed, breaking out into a smile as Robert approached them. 'Here's the man himself! We've just been singing the praises of your wife, Robert. Just saying that word wife fills me with pleasure – I still can't believe you're a married man again.'

Robert smiled. 'Perhaps we should've made a more noticeable splash when we tied the knot, then.'

'Not at all. It was perfect as it was, and very suitable in the circumstances.'

'That's what we thought. I came across to tell you that we'll be leaving shortly. We must put James to bed – it's a school day tomorrow.'

Joseph nodded. 'Before you go, I thought of popping into Kentish Town tomorrow morning,' he said. 'There're one or two things I want to discuss. If you could be around at eleven, Robert. You, too, Thomas. I know we're all here now, but this isn't really the time or the place.'

Thomas gave him a sly grin and nudged him with his elbow. 'Oh, go on with you, Joseph. You know you want to.'

Joseph glared at him.

'I've got a few minutes now,' Robert said. 'So, if Thomas has, too, why don't the three of us sit down and you tell us what it's all about?'

'Fine. Let's do that, then,' Joseph said, and they grouped three chairs together and sat down.

It was about the new estates, Joseph explained. The requirements for estate houses were very different from those for individually sited houses and, like other companies, Linford & Sons was employing a panel of architects to design their estate homes. But people buying estate houses came from the lower end of the market, and with the widespread competition to attract them, their sales had started to level off.

But this wasn't the experience of all builders, and he'd had a team looking into the reasons for the strong sales enjoyed by their competitors. It seemed that a large number of them were concentrating on the externals of their houses. Buyers saw mock Tudor beams, imitation leaded lights, pebble-dashed brickwork, tiled bathrooms, curved staircases, and assumed that as the house looked architect-designed, it must be good. They didn't look at the actual quality – the handmade bricks and tiles, stone and hardwoods, the cavity wall insulation – at all the signs that a house was built to last.

Linford & Sons had always built quality homes, but with their competitors attracting buyers with gimmicks, they were having to think about whether to drop their standards and focus on appearance in order to maintain the strong market position they'd always enjoyed, or cut down on costs by designing estate houses themselves. If they did that, they'd have to vary a standard plan according to the size of the plot and the amount they could charge for the finished house.

'So, you don't want to compromise on our standard of work, but can't see an alternative,' Robert summed up when Joseph had finished talking.

'In a nutshell, Robert,' Joseph said. 'I must say, though, I'm reluctant even to think about lowering our standards.'

Robert nodded. 'And I would be, too.'

'Is this between the two of you,' Thomas interrupted, 'or do you want to open out the discussion and include me? I may have lost my leg, but my leg didn't do much of my thinking because, funnily enough, my brain is located elsewhere.'

'Go ahead, Thomas,' Joseph said, with an apologetic smile. 'I wasn't excluding you, or certainly not intentionally.'

'Don't worry, Joseph, I'm used to it. You'd be amazed how often someone will look at my missing fingers and promptly stir my coffee for me. Yet how many people, I ask you, stir their coffee by holding their spoon in two hands?'

'Point taken,' Joseph said. 'So, what d'you think?'

'That gimmicks come and go,' Thomas said bluntly. 'What appeals to people one day, won't do the next. Having the sort of visible external features you're talking about will soon have the opposite effect from the desired one – they'll make the houses look uniform, rather than individual in design.'

'That's absolutely right, Thomas,' Joseph said slowly.

'So, you need to do two things,' Thomas went on. 'First, the sales team must focus their selling specifically to address this. It's not enough to assume that weekend house-hunters, trawling from one show house to another, will see the strong points in the construction of a house, or the way in which superficial designs make houses resemble each other – they must be told.'

Joseph nodded. 'Good thinking.'

'And the rest is up to me. I must see that my team looks for something less obvious than mock Tudor beams and the like. There'll be accessories around that aren't merely superficial and showy, but nor are so pricy that we have to think about sacrificing quality, and we'll just have to find them. For example, old timber could be used with some ingenuity, old bricks could be mixed with new handmade tiles, and so on. There are a number of interesting things you could do that wouldn't be too costly.'

Joseph stared at him. 'D'you think you can come up with sufficient ideas like this, Thomas?' he asked at last.

'I can give it a try.'

'Thank you,' Joseph said, a sudden lump in his throat. He coughed. 'I should watch out, Thomas,' he added. 'You're beginning to sound horribly like a builder.'

30

SOUTHAMPTON, ENGLAND

May 1933

At last she was back in England!

Lily stepped on to the docks at Southampton, and stopped. Behind her lay New York. Ahead of her, the future. She drew in a deep breath. She was on the same soil as James, breathing the same air as her baby.

Breathing the same air as her husband.

She took another deep breath. What would she feel when she saw Robert again? And what would he feel?

With butterflies frantic in her stomach, she picked up a bag in each hand and started to make her way out of the docks.

Her life, on hold for the past thirteen years, was finally moving forward again. New York already felt way back in the past, although it was only nine days since she'd opened the apartment door, glanced at the discoloured patch on the wall where the *mezuzah* had hung, stared at it for a moment and then walked out of the apartment and closed the door for the very last time.

She'd been overjoyed to leave.

Not because she hadn't been happy there, because she had, despite the difficulties of the last four years.

She'd felt a particular contentment living alongside the Erlikhs, who'd shown her a kindness she'd rarely known before, and she'd keenly felt their absence when they left. Instead of being surrounded daily by the warmth of their friendship, solitude became her companion.

Her dressmaking had helped her through the first few weeks after they'd left, and had given her genuine satisfaction. But New York was on the wrong side of the ocean from where she wanted to be, and on several occasions in those first few weeks after Ruth and her family had left, she'd come close to packing her bags and leaving for England.

Each time, however, she'd reminded herself that if she could carry on earning in the way that she was for a couple more years, she could go back for James, able to provide for both of them. Her skill with a needle had given her a reputation, and no sooner had she finished one order than she was starting another. And not only was she making dresses to standard patterns – increasingly, she was designing them herself.

She found the whole process of making a dress immensely satisfying, and as she'd lain in bed at night, she'd gradually formed the plan of opening a shop in England in which she could sell the dresses and blouses she'd made, some from a standard pattern, some from her own design. It was an idea that filled her with great excitement, and she was confident she could make a success of it.

With thoughts of leaving New York increasingly in the forefront of her mind, she began to feel that she should be making an effort to see more of the city while she still could.

In the past, she had regularly eschewed invitations from the women who lived in the neighbouring tenements, with whom she'd occasionally stop and chat, to go with them to a speakeasy or the Sunshine Theater. She'd preferred to save every cent for her return home, and she didn't need their company – she had Ruth.

But with Ruth now gone, it was down to her alone to make the most of her last two years in the city.

With such thoughts in the back of her mind, she'd been going down the stairs one afternoon as Mrs Abelman had been coming up. Mrs Abelman had been unusually smiling and communicative, and had all but forced Lily to stop and look into her basket. Despite her limited English, she'd been able to make Lily understand that she herself had cooked the American food she was carrying.

She'd then thrust a leaflet into Lily's hands, and Lily had felt obliged to stand and read it while Mrs Abelman stood next to her, nodding. It was from a place called Settlement House, in Henry Street. They were teaching people to cook the American way, and regardless of age, everyone was welcome to go along to a domestic science class, or to learn new skills, or take classes in art and theatre. And for those who couldn't speak very good English, they'd help them to improve.

Lily should come with her the next time, Mrs Abelman managed to indicate, and then they'd gone their separate ways.

As Lily had walked along the street to the bakery, she'd thought about Settlement House and the classes there. It wouldn't be sufficient, she realised with a sudden jolt, to have the money to look after James – she needed also to educate and improve herself so that he wouldn't feel ashamed of her. Furthermore, it would stand her in good stead when she started her business in England if she was able to talk about general matters to the women who came into her shop.

Fired up, she'd had a word with Mr Abelman the following

morning, and asked that Mrs Abelman call for her the next time she went to Settlement House.

To her surprise, she'd found the classes both enjoyable and useful, and she'd started going weekly. It took only a small amount of time away from her sewing, but she was sure that the value of what she gained by going there considerably exceeded what she could've earned in that period.

And it wasn't just the classes that drew her there – it was the friends she'd made. There were a number of women there, all of them also eager to better themselves, and she'd very much enjoyed their company. She'd even let them persuade her into going with them to venues like the Henry Street Music Hall and the Neighbourhood Playhouse, places she wouldn't have dreamed of going to before.

But much as she'd enjoyed the classes and outings with her new friends, she'd never been remotely tempted to accept any of the many invitations extended to her over the years by the men she met.

From the moment she'd set foot in New York, she'd deliberately given wide berth to any man who'd shown an interest in her.

The only men she'd allowed in her thoughts were the Linford men.

Her hatred of Joseph would return to England with her.

His threats of prosecution if she ever returned had long since ceased to hold any fear for her. The woman who'd been cowed into a panicked silence, unable to think clearly, no longer existed. The Lily Brown she'd become was more than able to face the Linfords and reclaim her child.

Her dislike of Charles lived alongside her loathing for Joseph, although she recognised that Charles had most likely been forced by Joseph to assist, and she'd sensed a degree of regret for his part in her banishment. Also, he'd given her James's shawl, which he needn't have done. He was probably just a weak man, she'd concluded, unable to stand up to his stronger brother.

As for Robert, quite simply she loved him, and she always would, even though she'd long ago realised that his failure to pursue her showed that his feelings for her were not equally strong. But her love for him left no room in her heart for anyone else. And loving James as she did, there was no question of her not returning to England.

Just two more years, she'd daily thought, and she'd return to England and would see both Robert and James again.

But then, in what she'd intended to be her last October in America, everything changed.

* * *

When the stock market crashed, it took numerous banks with it.

Overnight, businesses went bust, and For Sale signs became a familiar sight on shop windows. Thousands of people lost their jobs, and started roaming the streets, looking for work.

Unable to pay their rent or mortgage, many lost their homes and found themselves living in desperate conditions, close to starvation. One New York family moved into a cave in Central Park, Lily heard, and it became common to see people living in shacks made out of scrap metal and boxes, concentrated in groups called Hoovervilles after their President Hoover, who seemed to be doing little to ease the suffering of his people.

Bread lines and soup kitchens opened up everywhere.

Apple sellers became a regular sight on street corners, selling their apples for five cents apiece. One of them, a young boy with a babyish face, stood every morning on the corner of Orchard Street and Delancey Street. He reminded her in a strange way of

James, and she took to buying an apple from him every now and then.

Over the weeks, she and the boy began to exchange a few words, and one day she asked him where he got the apples he sold. From a house in Harrison Street, he told her. Early every morning, thousands of unemployed people went there and bought apples below the market price. The fruit growers subsidised them so that street vendors could make a few cents on each.

Looking back at that time in the years of hardship that followed, she'd tried to remember why she hadn't taken the money she'd saved and returned to England immediately after the Wall Street Crash, but had stayed on. After all, her orders had dried up almost at once, so her savings had instantly stopped growing.

She decided that it must've been because she'd failed to realise the scale of what had happened, and had been mistakenly confident that things would soon improve. And she'd also failed to appreciate the effect that the growing demand for ready-made garments would have on her business.

The few woman who still had money were no longer choosing to spend it on handmade garments, but were turning instead to the cheaper ready-made clothes churned out by factories. It meant that the garment factories that had survived the Crash were thriving, but her order book was empty.

She'd also been worried that it might be the same in England, in which case it would be a risky time in which to start a business there, especially with James to support. In New York, she knew the systems and she had contacts, so she'd thought it wiser to stay put until things improved.

While she was waiting for that to happen, in desperation she'd started collecting garments from a thriving local shirtwaist factory and finishing them in her apartment, although the money was paltry. Fortunately, Mr Abelman's sons were still making cigars and he was paying her rent for the room. But she'd feared that his need for her room might not last, and a few months after the Crash, she was proved right.

There would always be a demand for cheap cigars, Mr Abelman had told her, but with an end to the demand for luxury cigars, all the luxury-cigar manufacturers were shifting to the production of cheap cigars. Made by machines, their cigars could be sold for as little as five cents each, and his sons would never be able to compete with that.

Given that, and with his jewellery business having folded, they were thinking about going west to join other members of his family, he'd said. And not long afterwards, they'd moved to California.

The week after they left, she'd had to dip into her savings in order to live, and she'd considered again the offer of work as a draper that the shirtwaist factory owner had thrown her way on several occasions. While factory owners preferred to hire young children, whose small hands and nimble fingers were good for working with the machinery, a draper's job was skilled, and few could turn a design drawn on paper into a pattern that could be used to cut the different parts of the garment. Because of this, drapers were in demand, and their wages were higher.

Until then, she'd refused to work in any factory, having heard about their unpleasant working conditions, but she'd realised in despair that if she was ever to go back to England, she'd have to take up the offer.

She'd hated working there. The hours were long and the conditions unhealthy, confined as they were to a room where the air was full of fluff, there was a constant din from the sewing machines, and everywhere stank of cigar smoke, machine oil and unwashed bodies. And all the time, she'd been anxious about the safety of the large number of children who were clearly younger than ten, the legal age for starting work.

Walking back to Orchard Street with one of her co-workers after a factory inspection one afternoon, she'd expressed her disappointment that the inspector hadn't properly searched the place. If he'd done so, he'd have found the children hidden in boxes. He was in the pay of the foreman, she was told. And besides, her fellow worker had added somewhat acidly, those children's families were desperate for their wages, and everyone working there needed the factory to stay open for exactly the same reason.

From then on, she'd kept her thoughts to herself, resolving that the minute she could, she'd leave.

But instead of that day coming closer, it seemed to be getting further and further away.

The last winter had been the hardest so far. Despite her wages from the factory, she'd found herself digging more frequently into her savings to pay her rent and eat. If she carried on doing that, she'd realised in fear one evening as she'd peered beneath the floorboards into the hiding place she'd made for her savings, she'd soon have too little to be able to go back for James, let alone start the business she dreamed of.

And in that moment, she'd decided to leave for England at once.

* * *

Her fellow workers had tried to persuade her to stay on, assuring her that everything was about to get better. The recently elected President Roosevelt was talking about a New Deal, they said, which would get people working again, and Congress was being asked to pass the Beer Act, which would finally kill off Prohibition. And there was going to be more money for the poor. For all those reasons, it was the wrong time to leave, they'd insisted.

But she'd no intention of risking everything she had left by gambling on the success of the president's plans, she'd thought as she climbed the stairs to her apartment the day after she'd made her decision. And she was more than ready to go home, anyway.

And two days later, she'd boarded a boat for England.

31

As she walked away from the docks, a bag in each hand, she allowed herself for the first time in ages to wonder how Joseph had explained her absence, and what the Linfords had said about her after her disappearance, and whether they still talked about her or if she'd long been forgotten. She wondered in particular what they'd told James as he'd grown older, whether he ever mentioned her, what he looked like.

And she wondered if Robert ever thought of her.

Now she was back on English soil, she found herself increasingly curious about what Robert would look like after thirteen years – whether he'd filled out, had lines on his face, had gone grey.

She wondered, also, what he'd think about her appearance when he saw her. She was still slender, but the years had been hard, and the bloom of youth that had so attracted him must have long gone. Would he find that what remained held any appeal? Not that they could ever live together again, but it would be interesting to know.

And would they still feel, as they always used to, that stirring sensation low in their stomachs when they looked at each other?

She mentally shrugged off the question – she was being silly. Of course, they wouldn't.

Her butterflies giving way to a mixture of trepidation and suppressed excitement, she reached a signpost, stopped, put her bags on the ground to give her arms a rest and looked up at the directional arrows. One of the arrows was pointing towards Southampton Terminus railway station. Turning to look in that direction, she saw a large building in the distance, fronted by arches. Smiling to herself, she shook her arms a few times to get rid of the ache, picked up her bags and made for the building.

She'd had eight days on the boat in which to consider what to do when she got to London, and where to go. During that time, one person stood out in her mind – the one Linford, apart from Robert, who'd ever shown her any warmth – and she'd decided that he would be her starting point.

Hurrying as fast as her heavy bags allowed, she headed for the first of the trains that would take her to Kentish Town.

* * *

Sitting in his wheelchair in front of the sash window, a glass of whisky on the table next to him, his prosthesis thrown on the floor, Thomas stared idly across the road at the line of derelict shops that were partly obscured by the plane trees.

As he sat there, a slender figure emerged between the two trees directly opposite his window, and paused. The figure moved closer to the edge of the kerb and stood still, a bag in each hand, staring in his direction.

Thomas blinked a couple of times.

The figure stepped into the gutter, and stopped again, facing his window.

He straightened up in his chair. 'Good God!' he exclaimed. 'It can't be!'

The figure started walking across the road towards the house.

His whisky glass crashed to the floor as he lunged clumsily forward to grab at his crutch. Staggering to his feet, he moved to the window, leaned against the glass and stared out.

'Good God, it is!' he cried.

32

KENTISH TOWN

Later that day

The stillness of the late afternoon crept through the windows and settled in Thomas's small sitting-room. Shadows deepened in all four corners of the room.

Thomas found a more comfortable position in his armchair, and stared in amazement at Lily.

'So, you're alive,' he said, shaking his head. 'I still can't believe it. And you've been in America all this time when we thought you were dead. Who'd have thought it of Joseph? The sly old dog.'

'Sly's hardly strong enough!' she retorted. 'It was cruel – downright cruel – to tell Robert and James I was dead. Worse than that – that I'd killed myself! Robert must have felt terribly guilty. That was a really mean, unpleasant thing to do. Why not just say I'd left? That would've been kinder.'

'The answer's obvious – he wouldn't have wanted Robert to look for you. It wouldn't have taken a detective long to discover that a Lily Linford had boarded a boat to New York, and Robert would know at once that you hadn't gone of your own accord.

You'd never shown any signs of being the adventurous type. But more important than that, he'd know that you'd never have willingly left James.'

She sat back. 'It was a Lily Brown that got on that boat, not a Lily Linford. Lily Linford died the moment she was dragged from her baby.'

'And you say Charles knew, too?' Thomas said. 'There's no love lost between us, but nevertheless, I'm surprised he'd get involved in something like that.'

'And I think Walter might've known, too. I'm sure I heard him talking to Joseph when I came downstairs after saying goodbye to James.'

He nodded thoughtfully. 'You could well be right. He and Joseph became thick as thieves after you left.' He paused, and gazed at her curiously. 'But all that was years ago, Lily. You've told me a little about your life since then, and about the successful business you built up and what happened after the Crash. But the worst of the Crash seems to be over, and I imagine you could've revived your business if you'd stayed there. And I'm certain you could've married again. You were a beautiful woman, and you still are. So why didn't you marry and settle there? Why come back to England?'

She looked at him in surprise. 'For my baby, of course. There hasn't been a single day since I left England that I haven't thought about James. I love him and I want him back.' She hesitated. 'And I want see Robert, too. I missed him so much.' Thomas gave a slight start. 'Don't worry, I don't have any feelings for him, and I don't expect him to love me. But I'm curious to see what he looks like now. I'm still his real wife, after all, not Marian.'

'I'm afraid you're not. Your marriage to Robert was ended by a Court Order. Marian's legally his wife now.'

'But now I'm back, they'll know I'm not dead, and it'd alter things, if I wanted them altered. Not that I do. I just want to see him.'

Thomas shook his head. 'I'm afraid you're not quite right about that, either. Apparently, it's possible to go to Court and ask to have someone declared dead. The Court Order doesn't result in a death registration, but it brings the marriage to an end, and that person can marry again.'

'Oh, I see,' she said slowly.

'From what you've said, Walter knew you were alive, and he will have done it that way to protect Robert, and make sure that should you ever return, Robert's second marriage was valid, and he couldn't be accused of bigamy. Also, presumably any children from the second marriage would have been legitimate, but there aren't any, so that's not relevant.'

She nodded. 'I understand.'

'Robert and Marian don't deserve the devastation that your return would bring about,' he said gently. 'And it would throw James into utter turmoil. He loves Marian.'

'I didn't cause the situation,' she said sharply. 'That's down to Joseph. James is *my* son, not hers. I love him and I'm going to see him. I take it they still live in Hampstead?' She made a move to get up.

Thomas waved his hand impatiently at her. 'For heaven's sake, sit down, will you, and take that look off your face. I can't pretend that I think it's right for you to go to James, as I don't, and that rather amazes me. I've been known to complain about my family in the past, and I would've expected to be rejoicing at the prospect of their imminent misfortune, but strangely I'm not. That doesn't mean I won't help you, though.'

Lily sat down. 'You complained quite often, if I remember rightly.'

Thomas gave a half-smile. 'I suppose you *could* say that. But surprisingly this time, I feel I want to protect the family. Robert, James and Marian are happy. I firmly believe it'd be wrong to disrupt their lives.'

'But I can't hide away, even if I wanted to. Being registered dead, it might affect me starting my business. I'll need a bank and all that. So I'll have to reappear. And they should know how cruel Joseph was. It's only fair.'

'But you aren't registered as dead, Lily. You were declared dead, but that's not the same thing. There was no death certificate. But as I say, I'm prepared to help you.'

'If you're so against me doing this, why would you?'

'Because you're going to barge in there, anyway, whatever I say. And if you rush blindly off to Hampstead, the damage could be even worse for all involved. I need to think about the best way to do this. While I do so, you could make yourself useful. My housekeeper's already gone home, but she always leaves my dinner in the kitchen. You could see what there is in the pantry that'll make the dinner stretch for two.'

'I'll do that,' Lily said, and she got up and went to the kitchen. After a short period of time, she returned with a tray on which there were two plates of food, a glass condiment set and some cutlery. Thomas had moved to a gate-legged oak table next to the wall, so she laid everything on the table, stood the tray against the wall and sat down opposite him.

'Well, this makes a change,' he said, picking up his knife and fork. 'Now there's no Alice, I've eaten alone, with just the wireless for company.'

'So have I,' Lily said. 'But without the wireless.'

They smiled at each other and started eating.

'So why come to me, rather than, say, Charles, for example?' he asked after a few minutes. 'After all, he was in it up to his neck.'

She paused, her knife and fork in her hands. 'I wasn't quite ready to face them all. And you were the only one I used to like talking to. I never felt you looked down on me.'

'That would've been difficult on one leg.'

She laughed.

They finished their meal in silence. Lily put the plates back on the tray, lifted it up and turned to leave the room.

'Leave the tray on the kitchen table,' he told her. 'Mrs Carmichael will deal with it in the morning. When you come back, I've a suggestion to make.'

When she returned, he was back in his armchair next to the fireplace. Perching herself on the edge of the chair opposite him, she looked expectantly at him.

'First of all, there's an empty room upstairs. You can stay there for a few days. No one ever goes up there, so you could keep out of the way if Joseph or Charles dropped by before they knew you were back. Or Louisa, for that matter. She's Charles's daughter, if you remember. She comes here every so often. I'm afraid I've become her worthy cause – being nice to grouchy old me is her way of atoning for her past misdeeds, of which there were plenty.'

'That's really kind of you, Thomas. And what about seeing Robert and James?'

'We've got one of those dreary gatherings in Chorton this coming weekend to mark Joseph retiring as Chairman and Robert taking over, and also to celebrate Walter becoming a full partner in his practice. Marian and James will be going to Chorton with Maud and Joseph on Friday morning, I believe. But Robert won't be going till Saturday, and that's when I intend to go, too. I could invite Robert for dinner on Friday, and you could speak to him then.'

She thought for a moment. 'I don't want to give him the

chance of telling everyone before I do. I've a better suggestion – I'll go with you on Saturday.'

'That's not a good idea.'

'Yes, it is – it'll be perfect. The whole family needs to know what Joseph and Charles did, and that they're liars. And they'll understand that it's only natural I want James back – they can't have forgotten how much I loved him. And Robert won't have, either. And when he knows what Joseph did, he'll see that I deserve to have James. And even if he wanted to stop me taking him, he'll know I've got rights. I shall take James away with me at once.' She paused, and sat back heavily against the chair.

'And what about James? Do his feelings matter in any of this?' Thomas asked quietly.

She hesitated. 'Of course, they do. I'm his mother, aren't I? It's bound to be very strange for him at first. But Robert will tell him who I am, and what child wouldn't want to be with his mother?'

'He thinks of Marian as his mother.'

'She isn't his real mother; I am.'

'And Robert's his father, and a very good father, at that.'

'He's lucky he's had the chance of being James's parent – I didn't.'

'Have you any money?' he asked after a few minutes' silence.

'A bit. I've been saving for years. I had to use some of it to live after the Crash, but I made sure I came back while I still had enough to make a start here.'

'Good, because that's important. If you're seriously planning on taking James to live with you, he's used to there being a car, so you'll need one. I know you can drive. Unless you intend to cut him off from the whole family – and I don't think you're planning on being that unkind to him; at least, I hope you're not – he'll have to go to Chorton for occasional weekends, for example.'

She nodded. 'I haven't driven since I left England, but it's bound to come back to me.'

'James is growing fast, and even if they give you his clothes, he'll soon outgrow them and they'll have to be replaced. And he'll need food – lots of it.'

'That's obvious.' She bit her lip.

'And you'll have to find somewhere to live. Remember, he's still at school and he'll want to stay at the same one, so you'll have to live close enough for him to get there each day. Finding a car, sorting out accommodation, buying everything James will need, stocking a larder – that's quite an amount to do in a few days, don't you think?' he asked, raising an eyebrow.

She stared at him, frowning in concern. 'It does sound a lot.'

'And you'll need to work out what to say to James. I don't know if you've thought that far ahead yet, but he won't recognise you, you know. He was much too young when you left. It might be wise to think about the ways in which he might react.'

She nibbled the inside of her cheek. 'You're right. It's funny, but over and over again in New York, I imagined the moment I'd see James again, but I didn't fill in any of the details. I just saw me holding my arms out to my baby, and him reaching up to me. I never saw beyond that.'

'That's understandable.'

'And as for Robert, I thought he wouldn't be able to marry, so him having another wife is a shock. Not that I expected us to live together again – too much has happened. I was always so angry with him, and so upset that he didn't look for me. But now I know why he didn't, and that it wasn't his fault.' She stared at Thomas in anxiety.

'So what *are* your feelings for Robert, now that you know about the lie?' Thomas asked. 'You said that wanting to see him was just out of curiosity. And you didn't think he'd still love you. But you didn't actually say that you didn't love him.'

'Well, obviously I don't. I've changed and he'll have changed, too. We're different people now. I've come back for James, not Robert,' she added firmly.

'Are you sure? Just as you're still very lovely, Lily, he's pretty good-looking, too. That's not changed.'

'We're different inside, and that's what matters. But I don't want to talk about Robert, I want to talk about James. You're right, I must work out exactly what to tell him, and what he might say to me. Just so's I'm prepared.'

'If you insist on going to Chorton, you need to consider where it's best to speak to Robert. You don't really want to do the whole thing in front of the assembled family, do you?'

She hesitated. 'I thought I did, but perhaps it's better not to.' She thought for a moment. 'You could go into the house and tell Robert that someone wants to speak to him, and bring him out to the car. I'd insist on seeing James, but Robert could go in ahead of me to explain to James who I am before he sees me. He could take James to an empty room, perhaps, and tell him that his real mother is back. And then I'd go in. After I've seen James, I can then tell the rest of them just what Joseph did.'

'Good girl. Now you're thinking like a mother.'

'I'll ask Robert to have James ready to come with me in two weeks' time. James will have had time to get used to the idea, and by then, I'll have got a car and found somewhere to live. I think that's a better idea, don't you?'

'I definitely do. So, we've now got a strategy. I'll take you with me to Chorton – it'll certainly add some spice to what would've been just another dull family weekend – and we'll take things from there. But I don't think we'll let you do the driving,' he added with a smile. 'I've now got a car, and also a driver, which gives me some independence. You can come back here after Chorton, and stay for the time it takes to make your arrangements for James.'

Tears filled her eyes. 'I'm so grateful to you, Thomas.'

He waved away her gratitude. 'There's no need. You look shattered, by the way. I suggest you go to your room and get some sleep. It's on the right at the top of the stairs. I'm afraid that like the rest of the house, it wouldn't score much in *Ideal Home*, but I've never taken any interest in what's on the walls. All I need is a roof over my head, a room where I can work, and a place to sit.'

She stood up.

'Just before you go up, though,' he said, 'would you pour me a whisky? My last one fell on the floor at the shock of seeing you.'

She went across to the sideboard, picked up the crystal decanter and half-filled a glass, which she took back to Thomas. 'Thank you seems so inadequate,' she said, giving it to him. 'But thank you, anyway. Good night.'

She went across to the door, opened it and then hesitated a moment. She looked back at him, a question in her eyes.

He gave her a wry smile. 'I know what you're thinking, Lily, and no, I won't expect to be allowed into your bed in return for my help – nor will I require you to come down to mine, for that matter. I avoid the stairs whenever I can. You're quite safe. The hand I'm offering is out of friendship, not lust. Sleep well.' He raised his glass to her in salute, and drank deeply.

'Goodnight, Thomas,' she said, and quietly closed the door behind her.

33

THE FOLLOWING SATURDAY

The black Morris Ten rounded the bend in the country lane and Chorton House came into sight. Her heart racing, Lily leaned forward in her seat and stared at the part of the house that was visible above the low dry-stone wall surrounding the house and gardens.

The bright light of the early afternoon sun was bouncing off the front-facing windows with a dazzle of light, and the stone walls of the house gleamed with a golden sheen. A profusion of flowering wisteria hung from wooden espaliers fixed to the walls, and tumbled down on top of each other in drapes of shimmering lilac.

'What a wonderful place to grow up,' she said, almost as if to herself. 'I'd forgotten how lovely it was, if I'd ever noticed.'

'You can stop here, George,' Thomas told the driver as they passed the wrought-iron gates at the bottom of the drive and reached the foot of a narrow dirt track that led up a slope that was bordered on one side by the garden wall and on the other, by the fields of the neighbouring farm.

'That's the way Robert used to get to the farm where I

worked,' Lily said, staring up the track. 'He'd climb over the wall and run across the fields.' She paused. 'As there's no one around, I think I'd like to get out here, and walk a little way up the track for old times' sake. It might help me to settle down. I don't think I've ever been as nervous as I am now.'

'If that's what you want.'

'I've been doing what you said – trying to anticipate what James might say to me – but it's so difficult, and I'm getting more and more frightened that it won't come out right.' She gave a nervous laugh.

'Don't worry; I'm sure you'll be fine,' Thomas told her. 'George and I will go a little further along the lane, and wait for you there. When you've been as far as you want to go, come back to the car and tell me what you want to do. We'll drive up to the house, if that's what you still want. They'll all be there now – they'll have come in time for lunch. I always arrive in the afternoon, so I'm only doing what I usually do. Or you can suggest something else. It'll be your decision, Lily.'

'I know, and I appreciate it. I won't be long. I'll just have a quick look round.' She opened the door and climbed out. Still holding on to the door, she turned and gave Thomas a tremulous smile. 'It's a funny feeling, knowing my son's in that house,' she said, her voice shaking.

Thomas smiled reassuringly. 'Like I say, you'll be fine.'

Biting her lip, she closed the car door and stepped back.

She watched the car drive further down the lane, and come to a stop, and then, taking a deep breath, she turned and started walking up the dirt track.

With her every step, she stared above the wall at the house. Halfway up the path, to her great annoyance a dense thicket of trees and bushes on the other side of the wall blocked the house from sight, and she walked more quickly to get to a place where she could see the house again. And see the upper windows, too, just in case James was standing at one of them.

But before she'd completely cleared the thicket, she heard an explosion of laughter on the other side of the wall, and she stopped abruptly. Robert used to tell her how much he and his sisters had always enjoyed playing among the trees when they were young. Perhaps James did, too.

The laughter sounded again.

She stared at the wall, her heart pounding.

There were children behind it, only inches away. And James might be among them. She might be about to see him again.

Her heart thudding, she moved closer to the wall, trying not to make a sound. Resting her hand against the stone, she raised herself on the tips of her toes and tried to peer over the top, desperate to have the first glimpse of her son that she'd had for years.

But would she recognise him, she suddenly wondered. There might be other boys there too.

And would she be able to see him without him seeing her?

Because he mustn't see her. Not yet. Not peering over the wall, like an outsider looking in, as if she didn't belong.

She'd look like a strange woman. Yes, that's how she'd appear to him, she thought with a jolt. A stranger. Not his mother.

But she wouldn't want him to look at her and not know who she was. That would hurt, really hurt.

She hastily lowered herself on to her heels, stepped back on to the track and turned quickly to face the way she'd come. She'd go back to the car and leave it to Thomas to bring Robert out as he'd said he'd do. It'd be easier for James if Robert had prepared him before he saw her again.

Of course, James might look at her and recognise her, just like that. Yes, he'd been very young when she'd left, but there was a special bond between mother and child that nothing could break. He might feel that bond the moment he saw her.

That's what she hoped, more than anything. But in her head, she was coming to accept that the chances were that he wouldn't. Thomas had tried to prepare her for that.

And when he didn't recognise her – she closed her eyes, she didn't want to imagine that – but when he didn't, it would be better that Robert was there, assuring James that she *was* his mother and that all would be well.

Robert would make everything right.

Yes, that was the best way to do it.

She opened her eyes and started back down the track. The sooner she got back to Thomas, the better. She began to run.

And something hurtled into her from behind.

A powerful jolt slammed through her and her feet slid from beneath her. With a sharp cry of shock, she was thrown forward on to the ground.

She lay still for a moment, winded, the world revolving.

'Gosh, I'm sorry,' she heard a boy say from somewhere above her. 'Really I am. I couldn't stop in time. Are you all right?'

She rolled over on to her back, and struggled into a sitting position, shaking her head to clear her vision. Then she looked up at the boy.

Robert's dark eyes stared anxiously down at her. Robert's lips were parted in concern.

She caught her breath. The world stood still, and everything blurred again.

'I'm really sorry,' she heard him repeat, his voice muffled.

Shaking uncontrollably, she clambered to her feet, and tried to steady herself. 'I'm fine,' she said.

Hearing the tremor in her voice, she gave a slight cough in the hope of stilling her trembling, and started to brush the dirt from her dark blue skirt, all the time staring at the boy – but not too obviously, she hoped.

He was almost as tall as she was, she saw in surprise. Not a baby.

She was suddenly aware that her hand was hurting, and glancing at it, she saw that she'd grazed her skin in the fall. She pulled a handkerchief out of her pocket, and tried to wipe away the dust and blood.

'You *are* hurt,' he said. 'Daddy will kill me.'

'It's just a graze, nothing serious. Don't worry about it. We won't tell him.' She attempted a smile.

'Phew, thanks!' Robert's smile came back at her.

She didn't need to ask, but she knew she had to. She had to know for certain. So much time had passed. Her memory of Robert was bound to be hazy, and she could so easily be imagining what wasn't there. She had to make sure.

'What's your name?' she asked.

'James Linford,' he said, and he smiled at her again. Then he shifted to his other foot, and his eyes strayed to the bicycle that was lying at the side of the track, its rear wheel spinning.

She sensed that he wanted to be off, but that he didn't want to look rude or uncaring. But she wasn't ready to let him go. She hadn't yet spoken to him. Not properly. She couldn't leave it just like that.

What would he think when she was introduced to him later on?

She certainly couldn't introduce herself now. This was completely the wrong moment – she was still shaken from the fall, and he was clearly anxious to get back to what he'd been doing before he'd hit her.

But her mind was a blank, and she couldn't think what to say. She'd never really spoken to any boys of his age. There'd been

Ruth's brother, Pavel, but he'd always been out, working for the bakery or at school, and she'd never had a proper conversation with him.

James switched to the other foot, and made a visible effort to hide his restlessness.

'That's a nice bicycle,' she said with a feeling of desperation.

He nodded vigorously. 'It's a Raleigh. It's an early birthday present – I'll be fourteen soon. I was told to stay on the drive till I'd got used to it, and not come out here.'

'Did your father give it to you?'

'And Mummy. She and Grandfather persuaded Daddy to let me have it. He thought it'd be too big for me. But it's not. Well, maybe it is a bit.' He paused, and his shoulders slumped. 'I *did* hurt you, didn't I? You're crying.'

With the back of her hand, she wiped away the tears she hadn't known were there, and shook her head. 'No, you didn't, or not much, anyway. It was just a bit of a surprise, you crashing into me like that. These are tears of shock.' She tried to make her watery smile a reassuring one.

'I'm ever so sorry,' he said again. 'I was practising, you see. Christopher's got a Raleigh, too, and we're having a race later on. He's my cousin. He's a few years older than I am, but I'm sure I can beat him.'

He glanced again at the bicycle on the ground. Then he looked back at Lily. 'I wonder what Christopher's doing now,' he said. 'I bet he's been practising, too, even though he said he wouldn't. He'll have sworn the others to secrecy.' He laughed in delight.

'You'd better go and see what he's up to, then,' she said, trying to smile.

'Are you sure you're all right?' he asked awkwardly. 'You're still crying. Is your hand hurting a lot?'

'Just a little bit. But it's not your fault. You weren't to know I was here. And look.' She held up her hand. 'It's stopped bleeding now, and it looks quite clean. What d'you think?' She held out her hand for him to inspect. He took a step forward, tentatively took her fingers and glanced at the graze. Then he let her hand fall and moved back.

He nodded, his face serious. 'It looks clean to me, too.'

She smiled at him. 'We're agreed, then. So, you can go off and find Christopher.'

'If you don't mind,' he said in obvious relief.

'I don't. Goodbye, James.'

She started to say something about possibly seeing him again, but before she could think up a suitable sentence, he'd picked up his bicycle, got back on the saddle, shouted goodbye and was pedalling furiously down the track.

She hurried after him, oblivious to the pain in her knee. When he reached the bottom, she saw him turn left into the lane and cycle in the direction of the wrought-iron gates. She ran out on to the lane after him, and watched him pedal up to the gates and turn into the drive.

At no point did he look back. Not so much as once.

* * *

She sat in the back of the car next to Thomas. 'He didn't know me,' she said, tears streaming down her cheeks. 'I could've been anybody. He was sweet, and polite, but it was clear that he was dying to get off and carry on with what he'd been doing.'

'He's just a normal boy, Lily. That's all.' He handed her a handkerchief.

'Yes, he's a boy. You tried to tell me that, Thomas. And Ruth did, too. He's not a baby any longer. But he was to me. He'd stayed in my mind as he was the last time I last saw him – just a little baby. I still love him as much, of course I do, but I don't know what to do. I didn't know what to say to him. He seemed so happy, and I don't want him to be unhappy. Yet at the same time, I do, because then he'd need me. I know that sounds awful, but it's the truth.'

'It doesn't sound awful. I do understand what you mean.'

'Having seen him as he is today, I don't know that he'd ever forgive me if I took him from everything he knows. In fact, I'm not sure he'd even come with me. I couldn't drag him kicking and screaming out of the house. As a baby, he wouldn't have known what was going on. But as a boy... as a boy, he's got a life. That's what I saw today. He's got a life, and I'm not part of it.'

Her tears fell into her lap.

'It might be best to go back to London now, Lily,' he said gently. 'I'm not sure that you're in any state to be introduced to James as his mother at the moment, or to see Robert again.'

'Oh, God! I'd forgotten Robert in all that's happened.' She put her uninjured hand to her cheek. 'I'd hate for him to see me now, when I'm looking like this. I want to go back to London at once.'

'Very wise. This whole thing has been a huge shock for you, and you need time to absorb it all, and decide what's best to do. I suggest that I join the family now, which I can't avoid, and that George takes you back to Kentish Town. I'll tell Charles the car was playing up and that George has taken it to be fixed. Charles can drop me off on Sunday evening.'

'Yes, that's the best thing to do. I'm so grateful to you, Thomas.'

'I'll see you on Sunday, then. Make yourself at home, and try to relax.'

Lily nodded.

Refusing her offer of help, Thomas got out at the foot of the drive, and then George turned the car and headed it back to London.

Not once during the journey to Kentish Town did Lily's eyes stray from the place where James had taken hold of her hand to look at her graze.

34

CHORTON HOUSE

That evening

Thomas beckoned to Charles to join him near the fireplace in the main reception room at Chorton House.

With surprise written across his face, Charles went across to him, a glass of wine in his hand. 'You'll forgive me if I can't believe my eyes, Thomas. After you've all but ignored me for years, you're now seeking out my company.' He gave Thomas a tentative smile. 'I'd like to think this indicates a thaw in our relationship.'

'I wouldn't count on it, if I were you,' Thomas said coldly. 'I've called you over because there's something I need to tell you now, and for no other reason. I suggest you sit down.' Looking slightly bemused, Charles took the seat next to him, and Thomas turned to face him. 'I had a surprise visitor a few days ago. Mind you, it was a far greater surprise for me than it would've been for you.'

'Have you become an aficionado of riddles, Thomas? If so, I must confess I prefer plain talking, if only for the simple reason that I might have some idea what you're getting at.'

'Lily Brown,' Thomas said. 'I can't talk plainer than that.

Though plain's not an apt word when referring to Lily. She always was extremely pretty, and she's aged even better than the fine wine in your glass.'

Charles went white.

'Yes,' Thomas went on, taking a sip of his whisky. 'You can imagine my amazement when I saw her standing across from the house. Returned from the dead, I thought. Like a phoenix rising out of the ashes, you could say. Except, of course, that New York is a heap of concrete, rather than ashes.'

'Good God!' Charles's voice was a whisper of horror.

Thomas stared at him in icy contempt. 'You and Joseph robbed Lily of her child and husband, and Robert of his wife. That makes you the lowest of the low.'

'Robert!' they heard Marian exclaim across the room, with laughter in her voice.

Both Charles and Thomas turned towards Marian, and saw that she was offering Robert an apron. James was standing next to her, and he was laughing as much as she was.

'Put it on, Daddy,' James urged.

His shoulders hunched, his arms crossed in front of his face, Robert was acting out despair.

'What's Lily planning on doing?' Charles asked, his eyes still on Robert and Marian.

Thomas's features twisted into theatrical surprise. 'Well, she obviously wants James back, of course. It's all she's thought about since you forced her to leave, and it's all that she's worked for during these past thirteen years or so. And she wants the family to learn what despicable, amoral bastards you are.'

Charles turned to Thomas, panic on his face. 'Have you thought what it'd do to Robert and Marian, not to mention James?'

'Actually, I have, and that's why, much as I despise what you've done, and would dearly love to see you pay the price, I'm trying to stop her from going ahead. But you're going to have to help.'

'Whatever it is, I'll do it.'

'You're going to sell me that house you bought in Kentish Town for your use. I'll pay the princely sum of one pound for it.'

'Why d'you want it?'

'I'm giving it to Lily. It's the very least we can do for her. She came here with me today—' Charles gave a sudden start. Some of the wine spilled from his glass on to his trousers. 'Don't worry, she's gone,' Thomas went on. 'She didn't say anything to James, although she'd intended to. She saw him, though – he ran into her with his bike. It gave her quite a shock – he wasn't the baby she'd been expecting, and that rather disorientated her.'

'Thank God for that!'

'With a bit of prompting, I think she'll decide not to identify herself to him right now, and hopefully not to the family either, although I can't be sure about that. Fortunately, she doesn't seem to want Robert back, but again I may be wrong about that. But I'm pretty sure she'll only hold off telling James for a while if she's living somewhere that allows her to follow everything he's doing. If she's in Kentish Town, she can do that through me.'

'The house is empty so you can take it.' Charles sat back and looked at him curiously. 'Why're you helping us like this? You've always treated Joseph and me with disdain as we didn't fight in the war, while you were risking life and limb, et cetera, et cetera. I'd have expected you to be rubbing your hands in glee, knowing the damage that woman could inflict on us.'

'How gratifying to know that your brother holds you in such high esteem,' Thomas murmured.

'You know what I mean.'

'The answer is that, despite what you think of me, and despite my contempt for you, I don't want to see the family torn apart.

Because that's what would happen. And I like Robert and Marian. I dread to think what would happen to their marriage if they knew that Lily was back in the land of the living. I'm not worried about its legality – Walter will have seen that all was as it should be – but I worry how both would cope, knowing that Lily was living nearby. The thing with Lily happened a long time ago, and I think it should be left in the past as far as it's possible.'

'Thanks, Thomas. I appreciate that. And Joseph would, too, if he knew. Are you going to tell him?'

'Yes, but not for a bit – he doesn't look terribly well, as it is. But if Lily's living in Kentish Town, which she will be, he's sure to see her at some point, and he needs to be prepared for that. Of course, Lily might not go along with my proposal. If so, he'd have to be told as soon as possible. And Robert, too.'

'I'll get the deeds to the house drawn up next week, and everything else that has to be done,' Charles said. 'Walter will do it.'

'I assume that Walter knows what happened.'

Charles nodded. 'He'd been in the library and heard the whole thing, which was just as well as he proved a great help.'

'You can send me the key, but leave drawing up the deeds till Lily's decided what she wants to do. There's no need for Walter to know she's back, or not yet at least. If the house is empty, she can move in at any time, and the deeds can be done later. I wouldn't want Walter spreading word of her return from the dead.'

'I'll hold off telling him if that's what you want, but he's shown himself to be the soul of discretion. He wouldn't say a thing to anyone.'

'I'm sure he wouldn't,' Thomas said drily. 'Nellie wouldn't be best pleased, to say the least, if she knew that Walter had been active in something that caused her brother years of guilt and misery.'

'That's true.'

Thomas gave Charles a cold smile. 'There's a kind of irony in the fact that the house you bought, I presume, to screw women in, will be used by another woman who, one could say, was somewhat screwed by you.'

Charles clapped him on the shoulder and stood up. 'Now that's more like the Thomas we've come to know and love.'

* * *

'Are you sure you don't want to go up for a rest, Joseph?' Maud said. 'You look quite exhausted, my dear.'

He shook her hand off his arm. 'Quite sure, thank you,' he said testily. 'Leave my own retirement celebration? Never. In fact, I was about to have a quick word with Robert, and this could be your moment to talk to Nellie. She's anxious to discuss Emily's schooling. But Emily's a bright girl, so I can't imagine what Nellie's worrying about.'

They glanced towards the French windows, where Nellie was standing with her daughter, her arms outstretched, barring her from going out.

'...or you'll go straight up to bed,' they heard Nellie say in exasperation.

'Things are so different now,' Joseph mused, turning back to Maud. 'Gone are the days when most families had five or six children, or even more. Look at *our* family, for example. Nellie and Walter appear to have stopped at Emily, and Robert and Marian at James.'

'Why not, if they can do so and don't want more?' Maud said smoothly. 'Children aren't dying as young as they used to, so there's no need to have replacements in reserve.'

Joseph chuckled. 'You never did mince words, Maud. That's one of the many things I love about you.'

She inclined her head. 'Thank you, darling.'

'But it's not just the number of children,' he went on, 'it's how they behave. These days, they seem to be downstairs all the time. And you don't just see them, you hear them as well! Particularly Emily!'

'That's down to circumstances. Domestic staff who want to live in are now a rarity, so it's harder to hide the children away. But I wouldn't say that that's a bad thing. Parents today will know their children better than we knew ours. And husbands and wives will know each other better, too. Robert doesn't sit in one room, while Marian sits in another – they sit together. They talk to each other, listen to music together, read books together. That's a good thing, I'm inclined to think.'

'I suppose you're right.'

'And some of the changes are good for the business, too,' she added with a smile. 'Only the other day, you were telling me that with people living longer, there's a growing demand for smaller houses for parents to move into when their children have married and moved away. That should put a lift in your step.'

He smiled at her. 'Oh, it does. And smaller families and retired couples also want smaller houses. In fact, that's what I wanted to talk to Robert about. So, if you'll excuse me, my dear.'

* * *

'I think we ought to focus more on bungalows, Robert,' Joseph said, moving him slightly away from Marian and James. 'They're increasingly in demand now, and not just as holiday homes or a weekend home for the rich, but as a permanent residence.'

Robert looked around him in feigned amazement. 'I must be

confused,' he said, turning back to Joseph, 'but I could've sworn we were here today to celebrate your retirement. But obviously I'm mistaken, and it's only Walter's partnership we're here for.'

'I take your point,' Joseph said, laughing. 'But as you yourself will find, it's hard to let go of the reins.'

'All right, then. I can't resist the woebegone expression you're trying to assume. Talk to me about bungalows.'

'What I said just now is about all I wanted to say. I think we should explore this aspect of the market more than we've done in the past. That's all.'

'I agree, Father. And that's why I've drawn up plans for a bungalow division. I want us to look at all possible styles of bungalow. And I want us to start buying up cheap land for this in the outer suburbs, as well as in coastal towns and retirement districts. In fact, I'd really like to run my plans past you at some point soon, if I may.'

Joseph beamed at him. 'I'd be delighted, dear boy.' He glanced across at Marian, who was sitting with James, Christopher and Louisa. 'You've been a good son to me, Robert, and you're obviously a good husband to your lovely wife. And Marian's a wonderful mother to James.'

Robert smiled at him. 'I can't really comment on the first part of that, but I can certainly agree about Marian.'

Joseph turned back to him. 'D'you ever think about Lily? Although James closely resembles you, there's something of Lily in his expression at times. It must make it impossible to forget her completely.'

'I've never tried to forget her – she's James's mother, after all. I was desperately sad about what happened, and I still am, and I'll always feel responsible for her death.' He hesitated. 'I'll always love Lily, you know, Father. I love Grandfather and Grandmother, too, even though they're no longer with us, and I love Lily in the same way. You can love more than one person at a time, and there's no reason why I should ever stop loving her, even though I know I'll never see her again.'

'When you put it like that, I can see what you mean.'

'But loving Lily doesn't stop me from loving Marian,' Robert continued. 'It's a different sort of feeling, though, from the way I felt about Lily. But I've grown to love Marian very much. I'm so glad you brought us together, Father – I know you were behind me meeting her again.'

'It was obvious that you two were meant for each other.'

'And James loves Marian, too. While I very much wish things could've been different for Lily, I feel lucky every day that Marian's at my side.'

Joseph nodded. 'I'm glad you feel that way, son. Your mother and I couldn't be more delighted at the happiness you've found, despite the dreadful circumstances that led to it. And I know that Henry and Edith feel the same.'

'What are you two looking so serious about?' Charles asked, coming up to them, still ashen-faced.

'God, you look dreadful, Charles!' Joseph exclaimed. 'I hope you're not sickening for something. We've just been singing Marian's praises, if you want to know. Louisa gets on particularly well with her, I've noticed.'

Charles looked across at the small group with Marian. 'Yes, she does,' he said thoughtfully. 'I wonder if I should ask Marian to have a word with Louisa. I still worry about her. She lost her spirit because of the trouble, and that's not good. At twenty-three, she should be causing me all kinds of anxiety, but she isn't – she just sits at home most of the time, reading or helping Christopher with his various collections. It's not natural for a girl of her age.'

'What about a job?' Robert suggested. 'I know she doesn't need the money, but it'd get her out of the house.'

'I thought of that, too, but she says there's nothing she can do. I've told her she's bright enough to turn her mind to anything she wants, but will she listen to me? No.'

'I've an idea,' Robert said. 'I know she visits Thomas occasionally—'

Joseph threw back his head and laughed. 'You should hear Thomas on the subject! She's made him a cause. She's putting herself through the trials of visiting him as a way of showing contrition for her past misdemeanours. Fortunately, it appeals to Thomas's weird sense of humour.'

Robert grinned. 'No wonder he never encourages her to sit by him on family occasions, which I've seen her try to do more than once. Quite the reverse, in fact. He's probably afraid she'll cut up his meat. But I'm sure he could be persuaded to let her join his team. He sorted out the estate houses, and at a cost-effective price, too, and we'll need him to repeat his magic on the bungalows. For that he'll need more people in his team.'

Charles nodded slowly. 'Well, it's certainly an idea. I'll put it to her. Thanks, Robert.'

He turned to Joseph. 'You must be relieved to know that you're passing the chairmanship into such capable hands.'

'Yes, I am,' Joseph said. And he beamed at Robert.

As he turned away, he caught sight of James spinning round on the spot, his arms outstretched. He watched for a moment as James came to a stop, laughing.

'See, Christopher. I said I could beat you,' he heard James say, his voice triumphant as he turned towards his cousin.

For a brief moment, Joseph caught sight of a Lily expression.

Thank God, I did what I did, and she's gone, he thought.

35

KENTISH TOWN

Sunday evening

Thomas opened the door to his sitting-room, paused for a moment and stared at Lily, who was sitting in the armchair next to the fireplace, entombed in the fast-fading light of the day.

A brass coal scuttle and a set of wrought-iron fire dogs stood on the hearth between her chair and the fireplace, and there was an unlit lamp with a fringed parchment shade on the small table at the other side of her chair. She was twisting a handkerchief in her fingers as she gazed in the direction of the green-glazed tiles of the fire surround.

He suspected that her mind was miles away.

Moving awkwardly to the chair on the opposite side of the fireplace from her, he sat down, switched on the lamp next to him, and waited.

'I'm going to tell James who I am,' she said at last, 'but not yet. You're right. He's too young. He could resent me for breaking up the only family he knows, and it would be selfish of me to try. He's clearly a happy boy, and I don't want to destroy that.'

Thomas nodded approvingly. 'That's the right decision, Lily.'

'And Joseph is part of his life. In the few minutes I spoke to James, I could tell he was fond of Joseph. If I tried to explain my disappearance, I'd have to tell him what Joseph did, and it'd only confuse him. For James's sake, I shall wait till he's older, and better able to understand. But in future, I want to be able to watch him from afar. I'll want to know what he's doing, and everything about him.'

He smiled warmly at her. 'Now you're talking like the mother you are, Lily, putting James's welfare ahead of your own. I'm proud of you.'

She gave him a wan smile.

'Because I thought you might make that decision,' he continued, 'I've been giving the matter some thought, and I've come up with an idea. Joseph will have to be told and—'

Her sharp cry of fear silenced him.

'He'll try to get rid of me again,' she said, her body trembling, her eyes wide in alarm. 'He'll want to do that before James finds out.'

He shook his head. 'No, he won't. Joseph's a different person now. He won't do you any harm or attempt to send you away again. Those days are long gone. But we need to tell him you're back or there's a risk that he'll literally die of shock if he sees you. He's not as strong as he used to be.'

'If you're sure he won't try anything,' she said, her voice filled with doubt.

'He won't. But to go on to where you'll live, I guessed you'd want to stay in touch with what was happening in James's life. That won't be difficult. I can keep you up to date, but it would be easier if you lived near here.'

'Whereabouts?'

'I spoke to Charles yesterday. He owes you for the part he played in Joseph's plan—'

'You can say that again!'

'What's important is that he's accepted his responsibility. He's got a small house not far from here, and he's agreed to sell it to me for a nominal sum. Much as I enjoy having you here, you need a place of your own, and I'm giving you the house. You won't pay rent – you'll own the place. Any annual costs will be paid by the company. If ever you want to sell it, the money you get from the sale will be yours. You and I will meet from time to time, either here or in your house, so that I can update you on James. And I'll take you to see him occasionally, but only from a distance.'

'Would I be able to run a business from the house?' She leaned forward in her chair in a burst of sudden excitement. 'When I was in New York, I was wondering how to support James when I got back, and I decided to start a dressmaking business. Like I had in New York. I'd start off by taking orders and making the clothes at home, and then if things went well, I'd like a shop where I can sell what I make. I think I can make a success of such a business. And if I do, it'll make it easier for James to accept me, won't it?' She looked at him hopefully.

'It sounds a great idea, Lily. The house should be ideal for starting you off. We can think about a shop later, when we see how things go.'

'Thank you.' She sat back and started to twist her handkerchief again, her face taking on a troubled air.

He sat quietly, waiting for her to tell him what was bothering her.

'I hate to say this, Thomas, you being so kind,' she said after several minutes' silence, 'but there's something else, and you're not going to like what it is.'

'Try me.'

She took a deep breath. 'The things I said about James don't apply to Robert. I want Robert to know I'm alive, and I want to see him as soon as possible. I didn't know I'd feel that way, but I do. I don't want him back, I really don't – you've told me he's married and he loves his new wife – but I need to see him. To explain, maybe. It's strange, knowing he's now so close to me… It's unsettling… I just want to see him… I don't really know why… But I do.' Her voice trailed away.

She stared at him, her eyes glistening.

'I understand, Lily,' he said quietly. 'In your place, I'd probably feel the same. And anyway, telling him soon would be the wisest thing to do. He could easily bump into you when he comes into the office.'

'I want to see him before you tell Joseph I'm back.'

'If that's what you want.'

'I only want to see him once. I won't need to see him again. I want *you* to keep me in touch with how James is getting on, not Robert.'

'I'd be happy to do so.' He paused. 'You wanting to see Robert again rather changes things, you know. I think you're going to have to tell the family sooner than you intended. As I've said, we'll have to tell Joseph, and make that as soon after you've spoken to Robert as possible. Robert's bound to head straight for Joseph's house as soon as he knows the truth. And before long, Charles will have to tell Walter that you're back as Walter will be dealing with the deeds of the house. So they'll know, and also Robert and Marian – he wouldn't keep this from her.'

'I wouldn't ask him to.'

'Louisa may be starting to work here, so she's likely to see you. She was ten when you left, so she'll probably remember you.

Within a day or two, several in the family are going to know you're back, and things have a way of getting out.'

'I don't mind. I want the whole family to know what he did.'

'I understand that. You'll see their disapproval of him as the punishment he deserves.'

'It's actually less than he deserves, considering what he put me and Robert through.'

Thomas glanced around the room, and then returned his gaze to Lily. 'I suppose I could ask everyone to go to Robert's next Saturday afternoon, obviously having checked first with Robert that he's not doing anything that would make that impossible. I could say I've got something to tell them. That'll rouse their curiosity, and they'll certainly all turn up.'

'That's a really good idea, Thomas.'

'As to who we want there, I don't think we need Nellie and Walter's Emily – she's about eleven now, and wasn't even alive then – or Charles's children, Christopher and Louisa. I know Louisa's twenty-three and Christopher nineteen, but I don't think they need to hear all the details.'

'Why not? I doubt that anyone thought them too young to be told the terrible thing I was supposed to have done. It's only right they hear the truth.'

'And I'm sure their parents will tell them. But next Saturday should be about you and those who were involved, one way or another, and their wives, don't you think?'

'Not really, but we'll do as you suggest.'

'And James shouldn't be there. Whether or not you stick to your plan of holding off telling him, he shouldn't learn that you're alive in such a way. I can ask Henry Ames if he'd invite James to go there for the day. I can tell him that Annie will be out that day, and that we'll be discussing business matters, which would bore James. But after Saturday, you might want to think again about what would be best for James. It'll be harder to keep it from him once everyone else knows.'

'I understand that.'

'And I think we should get to Robert's ahead of the others. Robert should see you before anyone else does.'

She nodded. 'It'll be such a shock for him.'

He gave her a wry grin. 'I'd say that was an understatement.'

She stared at him, her brow creasing in a frown. 'Why are you helping me like this, Thomas?'

'I've always liked you. Some of my family have treated you appallingly, and I want to help you. That's reason enough, isn't it?'

'It was your brothers who did it, not you. But you're doing far more for me than you need, getting me a home and all that.'

He gave a loud sigh, and leaned his head back against the chair. Then he straightened up.

'Look at me, Lily,' he said, gesturing to himself. 'I'm an almost fifty-year-old cripple. I've lived on my own for years. After Alice, I had a nurse, but I drove her away with my moods and I've never felt any desire to replace her. With the aid of a housekeeper, I've managed by myself, and I thought I was fine, living in my friendless way. And then you walked over the road and into my house, and in that moment I realised that my life had lacked something. It had lacked excitement, for want of a better word. Your return has woken me up, and I look forward to having your company on occasions in the months to come, if only to discuss James.'

She made a slight movement, and opened her mouth as if about to speak.

He held up his injured hand. 'And to prove that this is just about helping you, and that I've no intention of trying to win the sort of affection that I imagine you fear you might be expected to give at some point as a payback, I'm going to be brutally honest with you. I prefer to sit in the evenings with my false leg on the floor next to me. It's more comfortable. And that's how I intend to sit in future, whether or not you're here. That should convince you I've no lascivious designs on you.'

Turning slightly to the side so that she couldn't see what he was doing, he pulled up his trouser leg and started to tug loose his artificial leg. He felt someone next to him. He stopped, one hand on his stump, the other on his wooden leg, and looked up.

She was standing above him. There was warmth in the red-rimmed eyes that gazed at him – warmth, but not pity.

'Here, let me,' she said. And she knelt beside him and finished removing the leg. She put it on the floor next to his chair, and stood up.

'Friends accept each other just as they are, Thomas,' she said, smiling down at him. 'And as you say, they must be honest with each other. What I was going to say a moment ago was that I hope that we can meet on other occasions, too, and not just when you've something to tell me about James. When I look at you, I don't see a man with a missing leg and a damaged hand – I see someone I want as a friend. I hope we can share meals together when there's no reason to do so other than friendship.'

He looked up at her. 'New York was good for you as a person, Lily. It's brought out what was always there, but apart from Robert, the family was too blind to see it.'

She leaned forward, kissed his forehead and then returned to her chair.

36

KENTISH TOWN

The following Tuesday morning

As she sat on the bed in her room upstairs, Lily listened to the sound of Joseph talking to Thomas in the office below, intensely frustrated that she couldn't hear what they were saying.

It wasn't that she didn't trust Thomas, because she did – Thomas had promised he wouldn't say anything to Joseph until the following Saturday, when they would all see that she'd come back, and she believed him. But she was curious to hear Joseph's voice again. Once, it would have been enough to fill her with fear. Would it still have that effect, she wondered. She couldn't hear him clearly enough to know.

She was just going to have to be patient.

And it wasn't for long. In less than a week she'd be confronting him and would have the satisfaction of listening to him bluster in the face of his family's anger and disgust.

And in less than a week, she'd see Robert again. Her heart pounded with trepidation at the very thought. But with excitement, too.

What would he say when he saw her, she wondered. Would he feel anything towards her?

And how would she feel when she saw him in real life, not just in her head?

And how would Marian react?

And the other Linfords, what would they say?

From what Thomas had said about Nellie, she'd be very angry with Walter, and Sarah would be furious with Charles. Sarah wouldn't hesitate to tell Charles what she thought of him – she'd always been ready to put him down, and there was no reason to think she'd changed.

And she knew that like Sarah, Maud would be furious at her husband being responsible for such a deceit.

Maud had never made any attempt that she'd seen to soften Joseph's behaviour towards her, but she'd always sensed that Maud wasn't completely comfortable with her husband's hostile behaviour. This suspicion had been borne out by Maud suggesting on occasions that Lily join her for lunch. She'd been too scared to do so, though, not knowing what she and Maud could talk about, and she'd declined.

But from the way Maud used to look at Robert when he wasn't aware of it, she knew that Maud loved him deeply, and she was bound to be horrified when she learned that it was her husband who'd caused her son years of anguish.

She couldn't wait to see Joseph suffer!

Thomas had told her at breakfast that morning that he'd telephoned Robert the night before about them all getting together at Robert's house on the following Saturday afternoon. Robert had agreed. He'd clearly been curious about what Thomas wanted to tell them, but had been too polite to ask.

As soon as Thomas had got up that morning, he'd contacted

each of the family members who were being invited to attend, and they'd all said they would come.

Their conversation had broken off at the sight of Joseph's car pulling up in front of the window, and a few minutes later, by the time that Joseph reached the front door, Lily had been upstairs.

* * *

She heard the front door close. Glancing through her window, she saw Joseph go back to his car, some papers in his hand. The moment his car had pulled away from the kerb, she ran downstairs and into Thomas's office.

Thomas grinned at her. 'I thought it wouldn't be long before you were down. And before you ask, I didn't say a word about you. He was on the way to meet Charles for a late breakfast and he wanted some papers relating to the proposed designs for the bungalows. He was going to check that the comments on them were the points that he himself would've made. And that's from a man who's meant to be retired!'

'It's not easy being idle after you've worked for so long.'

'I'm sure that's true. But it was partly to warn me, too, I suspect, that Charles is thinking of asking if Louisa can join my team.' He pulled a face. 'He's given me the chance to prepare an answer. But I can work out something another time. Why don't we take your mind off the forthcoming weekend, and go to what used to be Charles's house? We could have a look round and discuss any changes you'd need for it to work as a dressmaking business, and also as a home for you.'

'I'd like that very much,' she said in delight. 'After working so hard in New York, and for so many years, I don't find it easy now to sit and do nothing, and ever since I got back from Chorton, I've been thinking about my business. It'll help a lot to know what the house is like. And after that, perhaps we can go into some quality shops. I'd like to look at their windows and see what they think will attract buyers. And how they set the clothes out inside. We could pretend I was thinking of buying something, but I'd really be watching the sort of things that other people are buying. Or would that be boring for you?' she asked, excitement yielding to sudden anxiety. 'I could always go on my own another day.'

'It would be different, and doing something different is very welcome. We'll go together today, but after that, I'll probably let you go by yourself. Or you could go with Louisa, if I end up being lumbered with her. It would give me some peace from her ministrations, if nothing else.'

'I also want to look closely at the stitchwork to see the standards the customers expect, although I wouldn't sell anything that wasn't perfectly stitched and finished. And I need to see how they take in the money. In the tenements, I'd tell them the cost in advance, and they'd give me the money when it was done. I kept records in ledgers, but nothing more complicated than that. I'm sure it'll be very different here.'

'We've got cash registers.'

'That must go on my shopping list, then. Thanks to you, I'll have a house, and not have to worry about rent. All I'll have to do is buy the fixtures and fittings for the shop, and anything I need for my displays. And my savings will cover that. I shall also buy some lengths of material.'

'I'm impressed, Lily.'

She shrugged. 'I ran my own business in New York until the Crash, and after that, I joined a class at the Settlement House about managing shops and businesses, so that I'd know what I was doing. And I'll do what I did in New York – buy directly from warehouses. It's cheaper to do that. Ruth's father said you should always go straight to the source and never buy from travellers.'

He smiled at her. 'You're going to make a real success of this, Lily.'

'If I do, it's entirely thanks to you. You've made it so much easier to get a business going than I'd expected. It means that when I've seen Robert and the family, I'll feel more settled, and knowing that James isn't far away, I can put my business plans into action.'

'I'm picking up that you don't think that seeing Robert again will have any effect on you. I just hope you're right, Lily.'

37

HAMPSTEAD

The following Saturday afternoon

Thomas's driver, George, drew up alongside the pavement in front of Robert's house.

Thomas manoeuvred himself out of the car, told Lily to stay in the car, and closed the door behind him. His crutch at his side to take some of the weight from his prosthetic leg, he walked up the path to the steps leading to the front door, and up the steps with difficulty. Then he rapped at the door with the heavy brass door knocker.

A moment later, Mrs Bailey opened the door.

'Good afternoon, Mr Thomas,' she said, and she stood aside to let him in.

Pausing in the doorway, Thomas asked the whereabouts of Robert. 'I told him we'd get here early.'

'He and Mrs Linford are in the garden. If you wait in the front reception room, I'll let Mr Robert know you're here.'

'Thank you. There's something private I need to talk to him

about before the others arrive. I'm right that James isn't here, aren't I?' he added.

'He's with Mr and Mrs Ames. I'll tell Mr Robert you've arrived.' She turned and went back along the passageway to the door that opened from the kitchen into the garden.

Thomas beckoned to Lily to join him. He waited for her, and then led the way into the reception room.

'I just hope the shock isn't too much for him,' Thomas told Lily, whose back was to the door.

The door swung wider open, and Robert came into the room.

'The shock about what?' he asked, a smile in his voice.

Lily spun round and faced him.

Robert gasped audibly.

Motionless, he stood staring at her, his face frozen in disbelief. He put his hand on the chair next to him to steady himself.

For a moment or two, he stood looking at her – just looking at her, uncomprehending, as if he thought he was dreaming.

'Lily?' he breathed, her name a question. 'Lily,' he repeated, the word gaining strength and filling with wonder. 'You're alive.'

Her heart racing, she nodded, unable to speak.

'Oh, Lily.' He let out a long low sigh of joy. 'You're not dead.'

'No,' she said, her voice trembling.

'You're not dead,' he repeated, and he caught her in his arms, spun her around and then hugged her as if he'd never let her go. 'I can't believe it,' he cried. Burying his face in her hair, he kissed the top of her head. 'You're not dead.'

She pulled away, frightened at feeling a depth of emotion within her that she'd never expected to feel again. Each stood motionless, their arms at their sides, studying the face of the other, oblivious to anyone else, tears streaming down their cheeks.

Looking beyond them, Thomas saw Marian standing in the doorway, her face deathly white, her eyes on Robert.

Then Robert took a step back. 'But I don't understand,' he said, shaking his head. 'Your clothes were on the beach. That was thirteen years ago, and we haven't heard from you. Not a word. Not even once. And James. What about James?'

Thomas moved forward. 'Lily will explain everything when the others are here,' he said. 'It might be an idea if she went upstairs and washed her face. She could wait up there till everyone's arrived.'

'I want to see James's room,' she said, glancing over her shoulder at Thomas.

'Marian will take you,' Robert told her, wiping his cheeks with the back of his hands.

She looked back at Robert. 'I'd rather go on my own, if you don't mind. I've not forgotten the way.'

Robert nodded. 'If that's what you want.'

She stepped to the side as if to walk past Robert, looked up at his face and stopped. Their eyes met, and locked.

'I just can't believe it,' he said, his voice choking.

'Nor me,' she whispered. 'You're even better looking than you were,' she added with a slight smile.

'And you're simply beautiful.'

He took an involuntary step forward and enfolded her in his arms.

Marian audibly caught her breath, but it went unnoticed.

Leaning her head against Robert's chest, Lily stood there a moment or two, neither saying a word, and then she slipped from his hold and walked unsteadily towards the door.

Marian stood to one side to allow her to pass.

'I'll check that Mrs Bailey is preparing the tea,' Marian said to no one in particular, her voice shaking. And Thomas and Robert heard a sob escape her as she walked along the passage to the kitchen.

'I'll see if Lily's all right,' Thomas said, and he went up the stairs after her.

* * *

Those of the Linford family asked by Thomas to be at Robert's house by three o'clock that Saturday afternoon settled as soon as they arrived, taking the chairs they generally used when they gathered in Hampstead for a Sunday lunch, and they sat there, waiting for Thomas to come in and tell them his news.

Pretty sure what they were about to be told, and dreading the moment, Charles sat on the sofa, picked up a newspaper and made as if he was reading it.

The others said little to each other beyond remarking at the strangeness of Thomas to have summoned them there in such a way – for a summons, it had been.

When Thomas had telephoned each in turn, his voice had been quiet, but insistent that they be there at that time. Just them, and only them.

So unlike Thomas, they muttered among themselves, to have brought about a family get-together. Thomas – who'd gone out of his way to avoid all such gatherings since he'd returned from the war. And to have been so precise about who was to be there, and who wasn't. He'd invited only Joseph and Charles, their wives Maud and Sarah, and Walter. And naturally Robert and Marian. But no one else.

No Nellie or Emily. No Louisa or Christopher. And no James.

They'd all had the same thought when Thomas contacted them – that unlikely as it seemed, given Thomas's general surliness, and his physical disability, he might have been planning to tell them that he was about to marry again.

But that couldn't be it.

If he'd been planning to make an announcement of that nature, there'd have been no need to exclude anyone from the assembled group. On the contrary, celebratory occasions called for as many as possible to take part.

And Thomas hadn't even joined them yet, but they could hear him upstairs.

And Robert was also upstairs. He'd let Mrs Bailey show them in.

Marian, too, had yet to make an appearance, which was also very strange. She would normally have been there to greet them on their arrival.

Thomas and Lily must have changed their minds about telling the family that Lily was back, Charles thought in ice-cold panic. He'd put any amount of money on it that she was upstairs, too. And he sat there, his face pale, the newspaper propped up in front of him, knowing there was no escape from what was to follow.

As a degree of alarm built within the others, they glanced at the walls, at the parquet floor, at the vase of cornflowers on the mahogany table, each face a mask of studied unconcern, but within each one, a growing sense of foreboding for they knew not what.

At the sound of footsteps coming down the stairs, the assembled Linfords sat up sharply, and with a single movement, stared towards the door.

A few moments later, the door opened.

Thomas came into the room, and stopped, his hand on the door handle, his balance steady. His face impassive, his gaze moved from Joseph to Charles, from Maud to Sarah, and then to

Walter. Then he stood aside, and Lily walked slowly into the room, stopped and faced them.

A stunned silence fell.

The three men rose to their feet.

Every eye was on Lily.

She'd been very pretty in a youthful way when first they'd met her, but the woman standing quietly before them, her complexion perfect, her dark brown eyes rimmed with long dark lashes, her blonde hair parted down the middle and swept back from her face into a cluster soft waves, was beautiful.

Only her lips, a vivid dark red, trembled slightly, betraying her emotion at the enormity of the moment.

Joseph's face was ashen. A tinge of blue lined his mouth and the tendons stood out on his neck. His eyes unnaturally bright, his fear palpable, he opened his mouth, but no sound came out. He closed his lips on his unspoken words, sat down heavily and looked at Charles. Charles glanced down at him, and their eyes met. Joseph's eyes were filled with alarm, and Charles's with acceptance.

Both looked quickly at Walter, who gave a slight shrug.

I'm sorry, Joseph mouthed to Charles.

Quietly, Robert slipped into the room behind Lily, and went and sat in the chair next to Walter.

His head bowed, Charles sat down again. He threw a quick glance at Sarah, who was on the sofa beside him. Observing his tenseness, and assuming it was shock, Sarah took his hand and gave it a comforting squeeze.

Maud, her face pale, rose from the armchair where she was sitting, brushed past her husband and went up to Lily.

'I don't know what this means, my dear, nor what happened to make you leave us in such a way,' she said, a tremor in her voice, 'but I'm so pleased you're alive. We all are, I'm sure. But you'll understand, this is a tremendous shock, albeit a happy one.' She put out her arms to Lily, gave her a brief hug, and then turned, went across to Robert, and rested her hand against his cheek. 'Darling boy,' she said, looking into his face with compassion, and then she returned to her seat.

Walter gestured with his hands, his palms upturned. 'The floor is yours, I believe, Lily. I suggest you say what you've come to say. As you can see,' he indicated around him, 'we're all listening.' And he sat down.

'Here's a chair for you, Lily,' Thomas said, and then he sat down a little way to the side of her.

'We all want to understand what happened, Lily,' Maud said quietly. 'Why didn't you at least get in touch with us to tell us you were alive? You should've done that. Robert was in a terrible state. We all were.'

Lily hesitated. She glanced at Thomas, and then at Joseph. Her eyes lingered on Joseph for a long moment.

Then she folded her hands in front of her and took a deep breath. 'As you know, my clothes were found on the beach and it looked as if I'd drowned. I'd been feeling very low because I thought you didn't want me here, so I'd decided to run away,' she began. 'I thought that if I made it look like suicide, you wouldn't come after me.'

Thomas turned sharply, and stared at her in open surprise.

'I don't believe it!' Robert exclaimed. 'You'd never have willingly left James. In the end, I forced myself to believe that you'd killed yourself by mistake, not meaning to go that far, but I will never believe that you deliberately abandoned James. And that you stayed away from him for all those years. You were a wonderful mother. You truly loved James. And you loved me. I know you did. I felt your love every single day that we were together. You would never have left us like that.'

'I'm afraid you're wrong—' Lily began.

'No, he isn't,' Joseph cut in. 'You'd never have left either James or Robert if I hadn't forced you to do so.' He gave her a rueful smile. 'It seems that I can't let you take the blame, Lily.'

Maud caught her breath. She and Sarah looked quickly at Joseph. Charles and Walter kept their eyes on the floor. The silence seemed to stretch forever.

'Whatever Joseph's about to say, it wasn't all his fault. In the end, it was your choice to go, Lily,' Walter said, looking up. 'You could've stayed and fought for your husband and son, but you didn't.'

'You knew I couldn't.' Scorn hardened her voice. 'You counted on it. Charles would've backed Joseph's claim that I'd stolen the emeralds. With both of them against me, who would've believed me? I was blind with terror, and couldn't think straight. So I did what Joseph knew I'd do – I gave in.'

'Charles?' Sarah exclaimed. She dropped Charles's hand and stared at him, horrified.

Maud glanced at her husband's face. 'I think you should tell us what happened, Joseph, don't you? Right from the beginning. And make sure it's the truth.'

And Joseph told them the broad outlines, playing down Charles and Walter's involvement as far as it was possible.

* * *

When Joseph finished talking, there was a moment's silence.

Robert broke it. He turned to Lily. 'I thought you were dead,' he said quietly. 'I grieved for you. Why didn't you write in all that time? I would've known you were alive.'

'I didn't know they'd fake a suicide, did I? If I'd known that, I would've written. They were going to say I'd just disappeared. I always knew I'd come back for James as soon as I'd saved enough money to support him and me. But I thought you didn't want me back, that you regretted our marriage. I thought you'd have hired a detective to find me, and if you had, he would've found me, and you'd have come for me. But you didn't. Thinking you didn't want me, I was worried that if you knew I was going to come back, you might've done something to stop me from having James.'

Robert shook his head. 'I'd never have done that – I knew how much you loved him. But thirteen years. To have stayed away for so long. Couldn't you have come back sooner?'

'I was going to. But we worked very hard, for very little – you've no idea what it was like. I got a dressmaking business going, though, and started making much better money. But just as I was about to return, the Crash happened. Looking back, I should've left then, but I didn't realise how bad things would get – I thought my business would carry on as before. It didn't, though. My orders dried up. When I started dipping into my savings to live, that's when I decided to come back while I could still do so.'

Robert changed his position. 'You said *we* worked very hard. Did you get married over there?'

Their eyes met. She shook her head. 'I've always thought I was married to you. But Thomas explained that I'm not.'

Robert looked across at Walter. 'Lily's right, isn't she? I'm legally married to Marian now, aren't I?'

'That's right,' Walter said. He leaned back in his chair. 'You've long been at liberty to marry someone else, Lily.'

'I didn't want to. I never stopped loving Robert, even though I knew it was pointless.'

Joseph cleared his throat. 'You said that your business ultimately failed. Is your return after so long actually about money?'

Walter rose swiftly. 'With respect, sir, it might be premature to discuss such matters. Lily's return has been a shock. We need to let it sink in before we consider its implications.'

'Ever the lawyer, Walter,' Thomas said scornfully. He glanced at Lily. 'But he's right about allowing everyone time for this to sink in, Lily.' He faced his family. 'I think we've all had enough for today. You now know that Lily's very much alive, and is back. Maud will have something to say to Joseph, I'm sure, and Sarah to Charles. It's up to Walter how much he tells Nellie. I suggest that I now take Lily back to Kentish Town, and that we all get together again at some point next weekend. Lily can tell you then what she wants to do, and we'll see how we can help.'

'If no one objects, I'd like Nellie to join us next week,' Walter said. 'I intend to tell her what happened as soon as I get home today.'

Thomas glanced at Charles. 'What about Louisa and Christopher? How much do you want them to know?'

Charles bit his lip. 'I'm not sure they need—'

'Well, *I* am,' Sarah interrupted sharply. 'They're hardly children any longer. There've been enough secrets in this family to last us a lifetime. I suspect that Joseph has spared us some of the details of your involvement, Charles, and that of Walter, but by Sunday, you'll have acquainted us with everything there is to know. Isn't that so?'

His face drawn, he nodded.

'Is that all right with you, Lily, if the younger ones join us next week?' Thomas asked.

'Yes. But I definitely don't want James to be told that I'm back yet.' She hesitated, and glanced at Robert. 'Where's Marian?'

He shook his head. 'She couldn't face it. I left her upstairs, stretched out on the bed with her eyes closed.'

'It can't be easy for her, me being back.' Her voice caught, and she stood up. 'I want to go, Thomas.'

Maud got up instantly and came towards her. She put her hand lightly on Lily's arm.

'Before you leave, Lily, there's something I have to ask,' she said. 'When you began to tell us what happened all those years ago, you started with a lie. Joseph stopped you, and he told us the truth. You were going to keep Joseph's involvement from us, weren't you? After the truly terrible thing he did to you – to the three of you – why would you try to protect him?'

Lily stared at Maud, her brow furrowed. 'I don't really know,' she said slowly. 'When I came here today, I intended to tell you the truth. I wanted everyone to be really angry with him, and to despise him for what he did.'

'What made you change your mind?'

'Perhaps it's because of something James said to me last week,' Lily began. Robert gave a sudden start. 'He didn't know who I was, Robert,' she added quickly. 'I could tell he loves Joseph, and that he's a very happy boy. If I destroyed his family, I'd destroy his happiness. And Robert's, too.' She glanced at Robert, her eyes glistening. 'I've known since we married how much Robert loves his father and wants to be close to him. When it came to it, I found that I didn't want to break those ties.'

'Oh, Lily,' Robert said, rising to his feet.

'And also...' She turned to look at Thomas, and smiled at him with warmth and affection. 'Thomas loves you all, although, knowing Thomas, I don't think he'd ever put that into words. He's been the best of friends to me since I got back. It'd be a poor way of thanking him if I tried to destroy the family he loves.'

'Thank you, Lily,' Maud said, with tears in her eyes. 'I don't know that any of us could have been as magnanimous as you, had we been in your position. We're very grateful for what you tried to do.'

Lily turned to Joseph. 'And to answer the question you asked me earlier, Joseph, about if I want money from you, no, I don't. I've come back for my son, which I told you years ago I'd do. If you think of the strength of your feelings for Robert, you might understand.' She turned to Thomas. 'I'm ready to leave now, Thomas.'

With a quick glance at his family, Thomas followed her to the door, and a few minutes later, they heard the sound of a car driving away.

Joseph turned to Robert. 'I need to talk to you, son.' He put his hand on Robert's arm.

Robert pushed his hand away, and stepped back. 'It's time you left,' he said coldly. 'I need to go up to Marian.'

* * *

Robert stood at the window and watched the last of the cars drive away, his head in a turmoil.

When he'd got up that morning, he'd been a widower who'd married again, and who loved his second wife. And now, before night had even fallen, he was no longer a widower, but a divorced man – a divorced man with a second wife.

And both of his wives were now back in his life.

And he didn't know what he felt.

The moment he'd seen Lily, it had hit him with force how much he still loved her. At the sight of her face, her beautiful, beautiful face, it was as if something inside him erupted. His whole body had been on fire, and he'd just had to hold her, had to feel her in his arms again.

But he loved Marian, too.

Marian was the perfect wife for him. The seven-year wait between Lily's disappearance and the declaration of her death had been rendered bearable by Marian's presence, and his marriage was a truly happy one. They came from the same worlds, and they wanted the same things. He loved her deeply, and James did, too.

He'd always known, though, that his love for Marian was different from his love for Lily. He'd never felt the same toe-curling thrill when he looked at her that he'd felt when he looked at Lily. But it hadn't mattered. He hadn't expected ever again in his life to feel the heart-stopping love that he'd had for Lily.

He, Marian and James had a wonderful life together, and that was all that mattered.

Marian must be truly distressed by Lily's return, and feel as lost as he in a situation that neither of them had thought they'd ever have to face. She was bound to be worried about his feelings for Lily, for they must have been visible to her. He'd been so caught up in the moment that he hadn't attempted to hide the absolute joy he'd felt at Lily's return.

But Lily had returned for James, not for him, and he should take note of that.

And James? Would James accept Lily as his mother, when all his life he'd known only Marian, who'd been a wonderful mother to him, and whom he loved? And if he did accept Lily, would that affect his feelings for Marian?

He didn't know, but he fervently hoped it wouldn't.

What he did know was that he must go up to Marian, and put her mind at ease. He must tell her... But tell her what?

How could he work out what to tell her when all he could think about was Lily?

38

PRIMROSE HILL

Later that afternoon

The afternoon light was failing.

Lengthening shadows slid through the windows into the drawing-room, their dusk-grey arms reaching out across the parquet floor to Joseph and Maud, who sat facing each other in the wing chairs that flanked the large marble fireplace.

The housekeeper, Mrs Morley, came in to turn on the lamps, but Maud indicated that she should leave, and she and Joseph continued to sit in the darkening room, Maud's silent reproach lying heavily in the air between them.

'And you've told me absolutely everything, Joseph?' she asked finally. 'I should be greatly displeased if there were to be any more surprises.'

He hadn't left out a single thing, he assured her.

Had he known that a few days before Nellie's birthday celebration, he'd stressed, Lily had seen Robert talking to Marian, seeming relaxed and at ease with her in a way that suggested mutual affection, and had then accused Robert of regretting their marriage, he would have thought again about what he'd been planning to do. He probably wouldn't have gone ahead, he told Maud, owing to the risk that Robert might assume all of the blame for what happened.

Everything he'd done had been done for the best of motives, he told her. But he'd long recognised that he'd been very wrong to interfere in someone else's life, whatever the motives, and he just hoped that Maud could find it in her heart to forgive him.

He'd stopped talking, sat back and waited.

She crossed one elegant leg over the other, leaned back against the plush velvet upholstery and considered him. 'Well, at least I now know why you wanted me to wear my emeralds for what was just an eighteenth birthday party,' she said at last. 'I did wonder. You're stubborn, Joseph, hot-headed and unwilling to listen. And you're always convinced you're right. Therefore, mistakenly, you ignored our warnings that your hostility would push Robert even more firmly into Lily's arms. But knowing you as I do, I can see how you would seek to rectify the situation you created.'

Gesturing agreement with his hands, he nodded. 'That's what I was trying to do. I couldn't bear to think of Robert being unhappy for the rest of his life.'

'And that doesn't make you a bad man. You love your family and want what's best for them. Yes, you were wrong in how you went about it – very wrong – but you acted for what you thought was a very good reason.'

He stared at her in gratitude. 'Thank you, Maud, for believing that I genuinely thought I was doing the right thing.'

She inclined her head. 'And I think the children will eventually see that, too. It'll take Robert longer – after all, he suffered for years. But on the other hand, you introduced Marian into his life, and they've been very happy together. I'm sure he'll recognise the part you played in that.'

'From what he's said in the past, he does.'

'But at the same time,' she added. 'The effect of Lily's return on both Robert and Marian can't be over-estimated.'

'I realise that.'

'As for Lily, her kindness today in abandoning a desire for revenge, which would have been quite understandable in the circumstances, does her real credit. That she wanted to protect the family shows how much she's grown as a person over the years, and we should respect her for this. You must be supportive of whatever she decides to do.'

'We'll do whatever we can to help. If she needs a house, we'll get her one. It's the least we can do.'

'I agree. And I'm sure that Nellie will forgive both you and Walter. She's very close to Robert, and she's bound to be extremely upset at what you did, and angry that Walter got caught up in it. But I'm confident that she, too, will see that you thought you were doing it for the best. Don't expect too much too soon, though. At least you don't have to worry about telling Dorothy. She won't have known anything about this – she'd moved to Germany long before Lily took root in our lives.'

He gave her a wry smile. 'Surely, you don't expect me to believe that you're unaware that Nellie's been secretly writing to her sister for years?'

Maud smiled. 'You don't miss much, do you, Joseph?'

'Not if I can help it. But I'm sure Dorothy's got more than enough to worry about at the moment, now that Hitler's in power. The newspapers are full of the violence inflicted by his Brownshirts. He's a nasty piece of work. But to go back to Lily. I should have told Walter before we left Robert's that he must make it clear to Nellie that he wasn't involved in framing Lily, and I should have told Charles to stress to Sarah that it was *my* plan, not his. I rather forced him into supporting me.'

'You're worrying needlessly. I doubt that any of us would believe that Charles could have thought up such a devious scheme, nor have been motivated to do so.' She smoothed her skirt over her knees. 'Of course, of real concern is what's going to happen to Robert and Marian in the future, not to mention James.'

'Why should anything happen?'

'You clearly didn't see the expression on Robert's face every time he looked at Lily,' she said drily. 'But I did.'

* * *

Knightsbridge

Charles sat upright in the carver chair at the end of the large mahogany dinner table. He never once raised his eyes from the silver place setting in front of him as he recounted what had happened those many years ago. Sarah sat on one side of the table, at the end closest to him, and Louisa and Christopher sat opposite her.

'Well, that's it,' Charles finished. 'Lily's now back, and who knows what's going to happen. I've told you everything. Whatever you want to throw at me, I deserve it for being party to such a despicable action.' He sat back in his chair and waited for their response.

'Despicable. That's a good word,' Louisa said, her tone cutting. 'I can't believe you'd go along with such a thing. Pretending someone's dead when they're not.'

'All I can say in my defence is that I tried to talk your uncle out of it, but I failed. He was certain that this was the best thing to do for Robert and James, and even for Lily. He honestly thought he was giving Lily the chance of a happier life than she would've had with us.'

Her eyes flashing, Louisa opened her mouth to speak again.

Sarah raised her hand. 'Stop right there, young lady!' she said, firmly. 'You'll notice that your father didn't counter your criticism of his behaviour by referring to your own many transgressions over the years. He could've reminded you of the damage you caused by your disobedience, but he's basically a kind man, and he didn't.'

Louisa slumped back in her chair. 'You're right. I'm sorry, Father; I shouldn't have said what I did. We all make mistakes.'

Sarah nodded. 'That's the right way to look at it, Louisa. What about you, Christopher? Do you have anything to say about your father's misguided action and its tragic consequences?'

'Not really. Uncle Joseph absolutely terrifies me. He always gets his own way as no one dares to say no to him. I know I wouldn't stand a prayer of a chance against him, so I'm not surprised that Father gave in.'

'Thank you, everyone,' Charles said. Suddenly feeling very emotional, he wiped his eyes. Sarah took his hand, and smiled reassuringly at him. 'What a wonderful family I've got,' he said when he felt able to continue. 'You've given me a degree of support that I don't deserve, and I'm deeply grateful. I only hope that Walter gets the same level of support from Nellie. He came upon something that hadn't been his idea, and he did what he could to help us through it.'

'And I hope that Mrs Garner brings our dinner in soon,' Christopher said.

'I asked her to delay the meal until I'd finished talking to you. As you're so hungry, Christopher, you can ring the bell and tell her we're now ready to eat.'

Sarah glanced at Charles. 'Forgiving the perpetrators of this appalling deed is only the start, you know. The ramifications of what's happened could be enormous. I feel tremendously sorry for Robert and Marian. Indeed, I wonder how Marian's taking this. Lily is still a very attractive woman. I'm just glad that Marian wasn't there to see him all but drooling at the sight of her.'

* * *

Camden Town

Walter and Nellie remained at the walnut dining table. Emily had left the table and gone up to bed, and the housekeeper had cleared away their plates. At their request, she'd left a glass of port next to each of them. Nellie raised her glass to her lips and took a sip of her drink. Walter's glass remained untouched.

'You've been very preoccupied since you got back from Robert's, Walter. Not even Emily could get a word out of you.' She put her glass back on to the table, and looked at Walter in growing concern. 'What *is* it, Walter? Is anything wrong? It's not like you to be silent throughout a meal, especially as you knew we were dying to know what Thomas said.'

'I've something to tell you, Nellie, and I've not been looking forward to doing so. I've waited till now as I didn't want to ruin your dinner by telling you before you'd eaten, and I didn't think it anything that Emily needed to hear. Or at least, not this evening. It's about what happened this afternoon.'

She paled. 'You sound very serious. You're frightening me, Walter. What is it? Tell me.'

In a low voice, he told her how he'd come to be involved in the disappearance of Lily.

It had been his idea, he confessed, to go one stage further

than Joseph had intended and make it look as if Lily had drowned herself, and he'd told Joseph how they could fake her death, and had helped them to do so. He'd wanted to make sure that the finger of blame was never pointed at Joseph, which would have happened if Robert had hired an investigator.

She stared at him, aghast. 'But you let Robert marry Marian,' she said, 'knowing Lily was alive. How could you?'

The Court Order meant that Robert was no longer married to Lily, Walter assured her. But also, they'd never expected Lily to come back.

'I don't know how you and Father could have done such a terrible thing! And Uncle Charles, too. Poor Robert. Do you remember what he went through?'

'Of course, I do. We were devastated by his anguish. I'm truly sorry that we caused him so much suffering. We all are.'

She stared at him, her eyes accusing. 'That's lawyers' talk! You're sorry he was sad, but you're not sorry for what you did.'

'You're right. I'm not sorry that we enabled Robert to marry Marian, who's an excellent wife to Robert and mother to James. And I'm not sorry that we haven't had to endure Lily's tedious presence at every family gathering for the past thirteen years. I'm not sorry, either, that I ensured that your father would never be blamed for making Lily leave. When you encouraged me to ambush your father so that he'd get to know me, it worked both ways. I got to know him, and I genuinely liked him. He did what he thought was right, and I'm glad that I was able to prevent him from being punished for it. So, you're correct, Nellie. I'm not sorry for what I did. Just for the misery it caused Robert.'

She fingered the stem of her glass.

'Lily *was* boring, wasn't she?' she said thoughtfully. 'She was always going on about James. It was the only thing she could talk about. Can you imagine it if we'd had to listen to all the details of

James's ailments over the years?' She gave a theatrical shudder. 'Uncle Thomas was the only one who seemed able to find things to say to her.'

'Which would explain why she went straight to Kentish Town when she got back to London. It's pretty obvious that that's what she did.'

She stilled her finger and looked at him, her face serious. 'It was a very bad thing to do, Walter, but I understand why Father did it, and why you chose to help him, and I'm actually grateful to you for caring so much about Father. And as you said, everything that's happened since then has shown that it was the right thing to do. Robert and James are really happy, and that's the most important thing.'

'Thank you, Nellie. It's kind of you to look at the *mens rea* rather than the *actus reus* – the intention rather than the deed.'

She leaned across to him, and ran her fingers down his arm. 'I know you, Walter, and I know you'd never do anything you didn't believe was for the best. And that's true of Father, too.' Then she sat back and took another sip of her port. 'What d'you think's going to happen next? I know Robert hasn't really got two wives, but in fact, he has. And one of them used to be very beautiful.'

'And still is, unfortunately.'

Nellie pulled a face. 'Poor Robert. I wonder what he'll do. And poor Marian. Whatever happens, it won't be easy for her.'

'I sense you've forgiven me, Nellie, for which I'm very grateful. And from what you've said, your forgiveness has stretched to Joseph, too. And also to Charles, I hope. Joseph will have forced him to be involved, so Charles shouldn't be blamed. I know how close you and Sarah are, and I wouldn't want anything to come in the way of your friendship.'

'Does Sarah know?'

'She was there today. And so was Maud. And Marian is sure to know. My guess is that Marian was downstairs when Lily arrived with Thomas. It would explain why she didn't join us this afternoon. It's now only James who's unaware that Lily is alive and back, and Lily's adamant that he mustn't be told; at least not yet.'

'It could be risky to try to keep it from him for long.'

He shrugged. 'I agree, but the timing's up to Lily. When we get together next weekend, which I believe is the plan, that's sure to be one of the things we'll talk about. But Lily's reappearance will have a number of repercussions, and Robert and Marian will have to work through those themselves.'

39

KENTISH TOWN

Monday

'This way, Mrs Linford,' Mrs Carmichael said, indicating that Marian should go through into Thomas's sitting-room. 'I'll tell Miss Lily you're here.'

'Thank you, Mrs Carmichael,' Marian said, and full of dread, she went into the room.

The morning sun was pouring through the windows in columns of hazy light, and she stood for a few minutes in a stream of sunlight, looking around the room. Then she crossed to the window and stared out at the meandering row of plane trees that lined the far pavement.

How strange that a place so much closer to the centre of London than Hampstead should be so quiet, she mused.

A horse-drawn float laden with bottles of milk passed slowly on the opposite side of the road, and her gaze followed the milkman as he placed a bottle in the doorway of each of the run-down shops that she glimpsed between the trees. He's late in the day, she thought, and she turned back to the room.

She couldn't wait for the visit to be over.

Above her, she heard a floorboard creak, followed by the sound of footsteps on the stairs.

Her breathing quickened.

A moment later, Lily opened the door and stood hovering on the threshold. She looked equally uncomfortable and nervous, Marian thought.

'Mrs Carmichael told me you were here,' Lily said. 'Thomas is working. Shall I get him, or would you prefer to speak to him in the office?'

'Neither. It's you I wanted to see, Lily,' Marian said, and she attempted a smile.

'I see.' Flushing in discomfort, Lily came further into the room and closed the door behind her. She indicated the fireside chairs, and went and sat on one of them. Marian took the chair opposite her.

Marian cleared her throat. 'This isn't easy. And to be honest, I don't really know how to begin.'

'Then I'll start.' Lily clasped her hands in her lap. 'When I came back,' she said, a trace of defiance in her tone, 'I didn't realise that Robert wasn't married to me any longer, and that you were now his wife. But if I'd known, I would've still come back. James is my son. Nothing can change that. And I want to be with my son, like any mother would.'

'It's about James that I've come,' Marian said quickly. 'I know you love him, Lily – of course, you do, you're his real mother – but Robert and I have been close to each other since James was two years old, and I've been like a mother to James since then. That's a long time, and I, too, love him. Very much.'

Lily frowned and stared down at her hands. 'So what're you saying?'

'That as we both love James, it's up to both of us to make sure that we do what's best for James, not for us.' Marian paused. 'This is so hard to say.' She gave a slight sob, and put her hand to her lips. 'Yesterday evening, after Robert had seen you,' she went on after a moment or two, 'he tried hard to reassure me of my importance to him, and of his love for me. And this morning, too. I know he loves me, Lily, and I know he very much wants to do the right thing. But poor Robert, he doesn't really know what that is. I do, though.' She choked back another sob. 'I saw his face when he looked at you...' Her eyes filled with tears. 'I saw what he was feeling... What he couldn't help feeling...'

'I've come back for James, not Robert. You're Robert's wife now.'

Marian swallowed hard. She blew her nose. Clutching her handkerchief tightly, she continued. 'Anyway, as I said, I'm here about James. Robert told me that you don't yet want him to know you're alive. While I understand that you're trying to protect him until he's a little older, when he might find the whole thing easier to understand, I have to say that I think you're mistaken—'

Lily shook her head. 'No, I'm not. That's what I want – it's best for James.'

'—and what's more, I don't think it's possible,' Marian continued, ignoring Lily's interruption. 'Too many people now know. Everyone in the immediate family knows – if they didn't before Saturday, they do now. One day, someone will inadvertently say something that tells James you're back, and that would be the worst possible way he could find out.'

'So what're you suggesting?' Lily asked sharply. 'That I go to your house tonight and tell him? Without him or me being prepared in any way? And without me having had time to work out how to explain what happened? I don't want him to hate his grandfather, but I don't want him to think badly of me, either.'

Marian leaned forward. 'Of course, you don't. I'm suggesting that we speak to James together, and as soon as possible. This afternoon, perhaps. I can ask Robert to come home early. The three of us could be there when James gets back from school, and we could tell him then. But we need to do this together. James must see that there's no hostility between you and me.' Tears rolled down her cheeks. 'James loves me, Lily, just as I love him, and he's going to love you, too. Everything will be so much easier for him if he knows from the outset that he won't be forced to choose between us. Seeing us together will tell him that.'

A lump in her throat, Lily nodded. 'All right, then. But what do I tell him about why I left?'

'Well, the only thing I can think of, that uses some of the truth, is that you say you went swimming and must have hit your head. Perhaps you could say a large wave threw you. Later you learned that you'd been pulled from the water, unconscious. When you recovered, you'd no idea who you were. You could describe it as a sort of shell shock. Because of Thomas, he'd understand that. You could say you were transferred to a place in Southampton, where you got better. But you still didn't know who you were, and in the end, you had to leave as there was nothing more they could do for you. You needed money so you got a cleaning job on a ship to New York, and you stayed there till your memory returned. When it did, you came back to England. You won't need more details than that.'

Lily thought for a few minutes. 'I think that'll work well. Thank you. And you're probably right about telling James today, both for him and for me. It's better I don't have time to get into even more of a panic about what he might say and whether he's going to hate me.'

Marian wiped her face with her handkerchief. 'He won't,' she said.

'He might think I'm trying to take him away from you, and he won't like that. Thomas has told me how good you are with him.'

'It'll be strange at first, I grant you, but children can cope with more than adults realise.' She hesitated. 'I hope you'll let him visit me at times, Lily. And my parents will want to see him, too. They, too, love him.'

Lily eyes flew wide open, and she stared at Marian in alarm. 'You're talking as if he'll be living with me at once, and not with you and Robert. I obviously want him with me, but I'm not yet ready. I will be, but not right now. When he comes to live with me, I want him to see me as successful. I will be when I've got my dressmaking business running – I'm good at that – but I've not got it started yet. I'm only just back.'

'He'll see his real mother, Lily, if we find the right words this afternoon, and that's all that matters. Everything else can follow. Let's the three of us tell James together, and then let's give him time to absorb it.'

Lily nodded slowly. 'All right.' She hesitated. 'Will you tell me a little about him, Marian? What's he like? What's his favourite food? Has he got lots of friends?'

Marian rose to her feet. 'It's for you to get to know your son, Lily.' She gave her a weak smile. 'You'll enjoy doing that, and he'll enjoy getting to know you. I suggest you come at four o'clock this afternoon. He'll have had his after-school tea by then.'

Forcing herself to walk steadily, she crossed the room to the door, opened it and went out into the hall.

Her eyes blinded by tears, she reached the front door and almost fell against the wood as her knees threatened to give way. With difficulty, she straightened herself, opened the door and half-stumbled along the street to her car.

* * *

The distant church clock sounded four.

George got out of the car, went round the side of the car and opened Lily's door for her.

If only Thomas had agreed to accompany her that afternoon, she thought getting out, but he'd insisted that this was something she should do without him. If he'd been at her side, though, she wouldn't have been quite as scared.

Trembling, she walked up to the front door, and knocked.

Mrs Bailey opened the door, and gave her a wide smile of welcome. 'It's good to see you again, Miss Lily. Very good, if I may say so.'

'Thank you, Mrs Bailey. I hope you're well.'

'I am, thank you, Miss. Mr Robert and Mrs Marian have just been having tea in the garden with Master James,' she said, leading the way to the rear reception room. 'I'll tell them you're here.'

Moments later, James came up the steps from the garden, opened the garden door next to the window and came into the room, carrying what looked to be a school book in his hand. Marian followed close behind, and Robert came after her.

'As you couldn't do it, Daddy,' James said, grinning back at Robert, 'I don't feel so bad that I made a mess of it. But it's strange, I thought there was nothing you couldn't do. At least that's what you're always telling me. Don't tell me that's not true.' He faced Robert with an expression of mock reproach.

'Funnily enough, that sum was the one and only thing I can't do.'

'Ha!' James exclaimed in glee. 'The first of many such exceptions, I rather think!'

Laughing, he looked from Robert to Marian, and then, pushing his light brown hair out of his eyes, he turned and saw Lily.

He lowered his arm, and stared hard at her.

Frowning as if trying to remember something, he looked questioningly back at Robert.

Robert came up to his side and put his hand on James's shoulder. 'We've someone you'll want to meet,' Robert said quietly. 'Let's all sit down, shall we? You can have Mummy's chair by the fireplace, if you like, James. I'll sit opposite you. Mummy can sit on the sofa with our visitor.'

With a reassuring smile at James, Marian went and sat on the sofa, and Lily sat down next to her.

Still looking curiously at Lily, and clutching his school book tightly, James went to the fireside seat. Robert sat in the armchair opposite him.

Leaning forward, Robert rested his elbows on his knees. 'I've something to tell you, son, and I think it's going to be a tremendous shock. But I know you to be a sensible lad, and you can take this in your stride.'

James glanced at Lily, and then back at his father. 'What're you talking about?'

'The thing is... the thing is.' Robert shook his head. 'It's hard to know how to tell you, son.' He glanced across at Marian, his eyes appealing for help.

She got up swiftly, and went and knelt beside James and took his hand. 'What your father's trying to tell you, my darling, is that we thought we'd lost your mother a long time ago. But something wonderful has happened, and we've discovered we were mistaken.'

'But you're my mother. Isn't she, Daddy?'

Robert nodded. 'Yes, she is. She's the only mother you've ever known. But you were told that you had another mother, before this mummy, and that your first mummy drowned in the sea by mistake. But you were too little to remember her.'

'Louisa told me ages ago that she'd drowned herself.'

'That was very naughty of Louisa, and quite untrue. No one knew what had happened. But, as it turns out, your first mother didn't die, and now she's come back. She's had something similar to shell shock for many years – Uncle Thomas has told you all about shell shock – it happened to a lot of the people he fought with. But she's better now, and she's come back to us. This is your first mummy, James.' He indicated Lily.

She sat very still.

James stared at Lily.

'I've seen you before,' he said, his tone accusing.

'That's right. We met outside Chorton House. You knocked me over with your bicycle.'

'You didn't tell me you'd had an accident, James!' Robert exclaimed.

Lily gave a wave of dismissal. 'It wasn't serious. I grazed my hand, that's all.' She smiled hesitantly at James. 'Seeing you that day was a shock, James. In my head you were still a tiny baby. But there you were, all grown up. I hadn't expected that. It threw me, and I didn't feel able to tell you who I was.'

Her voice trailed off, and she glanced at Robert.

James slipped down from the chair, ran across to Marian and hugged her tightly. 'This is my mummy, and I don't want another one.'

'We both love you, James,' Mariam said, her voice shaking. 'Your first mummy and I have become friends. You're not being asked to choose between us. It's just that you've now got one more person to love you, a very special person – your real mother.'

He stepped back, white-faced, and looked at Marian. 'You're my real mother, and no one else. I'm going upstairs now.'

'Please, James,' Lily begged, rising to her feet. 'Please, stay longer. I'd love us to talk for a while. I want to get to know you.'

'Yes, why don't you stay and tell your mother some of the things you like doing at school?' Robert hastily suggested.

'No!' He threw the school book with ferocity on to the sofa where Lily had been sitting, and ran from the room. A moment later, they heard him running up the stairs, crying loudly.

Lily sat down again with a thud. For a moment, no one spoke.

'That didn't go well,' Lily said at last, and to her horror, she broke down in tears.

Robert got up, took a step towards her, and stopped. 'It was never going to be easy, Lily – you knew that.'

'He just needs a bit of time,' Marian said, standing up and brushing imaginary dust from her skirt. 'But probably not as much time as you might think. He's almost fourteen, and has a healthy curiosity. When it's sunk in that his real mother is back, he's going to want to know more about her.'

Lily picked up her bag, pulled out a handkerchief and blew her nose. 'I do hope you're right,' she said, putting the handkerchief back in her bag. 'But I think I'll go back to Kentish Town now.' And she started moving towards the door.

'Why don't you stay a little longer, Lily?' Marian said. 'I'll ask Mrs Bailey to make us some tea. You could be surprised by how quickly James thinks of some things he wants to ask, and you should be here in case that happens.'

She frowned anxiously. 'Well, I suppose I could, if you think that might happen. All right, then.' And she sat back down.

Marian went into the hall, and along the corridor to the kitchen. Having given instructions to Mrs Bailey, she went back into the hall, walked past the door to the rear reception room and went upstairs.

'I wonder what's happened to Marian,' Robert remarked about ten minutes later. He glanced at the clock on the mantelpiece. 'Arranging afternoon tea for three people shouldn't be taking as long as this.'

Just as he finished speaking, Mrs Bailey opened the door, and came into the room with a tray. On the tray, there were two cups and saucers, a teapot, sugar bowl, milk jug and a plate of small cakes. She put the tray on a side table at the end of the sofa.

At that same moment, they heard the front door open.

Robert moved fast.

As he reached the hall, he saw Marian at the front door, her hand on the door handle, the door ajar. At her feet, there were two leather bags.

'What're you doing?' he exclaimed, stopping abruptly. His gaze went from her face to the bags, and back again to her face. 'What's going on, Marian?'

'I'm leaving,' Marian said, deathly pale. 'I'm going back to my parents. I telephoned them this morning, and they're expecting me. Father will be outside now.'

The blood drained from his face. 'But you can't go. I love you.'

She released the door handle and took a step towards him. 'Dearest Robert, I love you, too, and I probably always will. And I do believe you truly love me. But there are different kinds of love. In all the years of our marriage, I've known there was someone else walking alongside us, someone very special to you, whom you loved in a different way, who was lodged in your heart, in a place that I'd never be able to reach.'

He gave a low groan. 'Oh, Marian.'

'But it didn't stop us from being very happy. I've loved every single minute that I've spent with you.'

'And me with you.'

'But that special person is now back in your life, and I couldn't bear to stay and watch the politeness with which you'd come to treat me each day, the earnest determination with which you'd regularly let me know that you still loved me, while knowing all the time that you were wishing I was someone else. Dear Robert, I saw the way you looked at Lily.'

Her words hung in the air.

'I do love you, Marian,' he said quietly.

'I know you do. And we both love James. And that's another reason why I should leave. It would be very hard on James if when his desire to get to know Lily emerges, as it will certainly do, he feels he's being disloyal to me. I'd hate him to feel guilty about his interest in her, and possibly even angry towards me for the misery I was causing him. If I were still in the house with you both, that could happen.'

'I never deserved you, Marian.'

'Of course, you did. None of this situation is of your making,' she said, her eyes glittering with unshed tears. 'I like to think we'll always be friends, for James's sake and for mine. And I do hope that once James has settled down, you'll bring him to see me, and perhaps let him stay for the occasional weekend. I'd very much like to remain a part of his life, but as his friend, not as his mother. And my parents love him, too. They'll want to carry on seeing him.'

'Of course, I will. And you must come here, too, and also to Chorton. All of you must. You know how much my family loves you.'

Tears fell down her cheeks.

He raised her hands to his lips, and kissed the back of each hand. 'Thank you, Marian,' he said with feeling, and he released her hands, picked up her bags and walked with her to her father's car, which was waiting on the road at the end of the path.

40

When he'd closed the front door behind him, Robert walked slowly back to the reception room.

As he went through the open doorway, Lily was standing in the middle of the room, looking anxiously towards him. 'Did I hear Marian leave?' she asked as soon as he came in.

He nodded. 'Yes. She's gone back to her parents.'

She took a step towards him. 'Believe me, I didn't mean this to happen, Robert,' she said. 'Can't you go after her and ask her to come back?'

He paused where he was. 'I could, but it would be wrong of me to do so. You see, everything she said was right.'

She looked at him in bewilderment. 'I don't understand.'

'She accused me of having loved you all these years. She said that while I loved her – and she knew that I genuinely *did* love her – it was different from the love I felt for you, the love I never stopped feeling, even though I thought I'd never see you again. And now you're back.'

She took a step forward. 'But I'm a different person. I'm not the Lily you fell in love with all those years ago.'

He went up to her, took hold of her hands and looked down into her face.

'We've both changed over the years, Lily – it would have been impossible not to. But at heart, we're still the same. The very first moment I saw you in that field all those years ago, you took my breath away, and you still do. It didn't matter that I believed you were dead, and that I loved Marian, you were deep in my heart and I couldn't stop loving you. And when you returned... when I saw you again... I can't describe how I felt. It was as if my insides had been ripped apart.'

'And I never stopped loving you, Robert,' she said, gazing up at him. 'I've felt hurt, disappointed, angry with you – all those and more, but still I've loved you, even though I didn't dare let myself dream that I might one day be with you again.'

Slowly, he ran his fingers down the curve of her neck.

'My beautiful Lily,' he breathed.

She made an involuntary movement towards him, and he wrapped his arms around her.

'I adore you,' he said, and he pulled her closer to him. 'Just as I've always done. That's what Marian saw, and that's why she left.'

She stared up at his face, hope swelling within her, a hope she hadn't even known had lived on in her heart throughout her absent years.

'I want you here with me, Lily,' he went on tremulously, 'so that I can show you what you mean to me. Not in my bed, if you don't want that, though I hope very much that one day you will, but at my side. I couldn't bear it if you left me again. So please, dearest Lily, say you'll stay.'

She gazed up at him in growing wonder. 'How could I not stay, Robert? I was never able to stop myself loving you, even though I actually managed to kid myself that I no longer had any feelings for you. But I've always loved you. And yes, I will stay, if you really want me to.'

'Thank God for that!' he cried, and he brought his lips down hard on the lips that were raised to his.

There was a soft knock at the door, and they sprang apart.

Robert glanced at Lily and frowned slightly. Releasing her, he went to the door and opened it.

'Oh, it's you, James,' he said in surprise. 'Why did you knock?'

James shrugged. He glanced up at his father, and then peered round Robert to look at Lily.

'Where were you all that time, then?' he asked, and he stepped into the room.

* * *

MORE FROM LIZ HARRIS

A Wife's Betrayal, the next gripping instalment in the Linford Family Sagas, is available to order now here:

https://mybook.to/WifesBetrayalBackAd

ACKNOWLEDGEMENTS

The first thing a reader notices about a book is its cover, and I owe a huge thank you to the talented Jane Dixon-Smith for a truly striking cover.

Heartfelt thanks are due also to my Friend in the North, Stella, who is always the first person to see my completed manuscript, and who never fails to offer constructive comments, and to the amazing team at Boldwood Books.

Thank you also to author friends Charlotte Betts, Carol McGrath, Deborah Swift, Jenny Barden and Henriette Gyland for the helpful advice and discussion on our writing retreats. Our writing retreat is always a highlight of my year.

A thank you, too, to the members of the Romantic Novelists' Association and the Historical Novel Society, whose friendship over the years has helped to make the writing process such an enjoyable one.

Researching the background to the novel was a pleasure. I was lucky enough to spend a few weeks in New York for research purposes, and I can't recommend highly enough a visit to the Tenement Museum in Orchard Street, Manhattan. I had originally intended to take only two of their many tours, but I ended up taking them all!

I drew on far too many research books to list them all. I'll mention only *Factory Girl*, by Barbara Greenwood, and *Immigrant Kids*, by Russell Freedman, both of which gave insight into tenement life in NY in the 1920s. *A Social History of Housing, 1815–1970*, by John Burnett, helped greatly with the background to the Linford & Sons' building business, and I learned much about society between the wars from *The Thirties*, by Juliet Gardiner, and *A Century of Women*, by Sheila Rowbotham.

Last, but not least, a huge thank you to my husband, Richard, who kept our home ticking over while I was lost in my fictional world.

ABOUT THE AUTHOR

Liz Harris was born in London and studied law, before moving to California and working a variety of professions. Six years later she returned to London, completed a degree in English and became a secondary school teacher. Liz now lives in Windsor, and has written a great number of historical novels and short stories.

Download your exclusive bonus content from Liz Harris here:

Visit Liz Harris' website: www.lizharrisauthor.com

Follow Liz Harris on social media here:

facebook.com/lizharrisauthor
x.com/lizharrisauthor
instagram.com/liz.harris.52206
bookbub.com/authors/liz-harris

ALSO BY LIZ HARRIS

Linford Saga Series

A Daughter's Courage

A Wife's Betrayal

A Sister's Hope

Printed in Dunstable, United Kingdom

78528080R00188